A
FATAL
GROOVE

ST. MARTIN'S PAPERBACKS TITLES BY OLIVIA BLACKE

A
FATAL
GROOVE

OLIVIA BLACKE

St. Martin's Paperbacks

First published in the United States by St. Martin's Paperbacks, an imprint of St. Martin's Publishing Group.

A FATAL GROOVE

For information, address St. Martin's Publishing Group, 120 Broadway, New York, NY 10271.

www.stmartins.com

ISBN: 978-1-250-86010-1

Our books may be purchased in bulk for promotional, educational, or business use. Please contact your local bookseller or the Macmillan Corporate and Premium Sales Department at 1-800-221-7945, ext. 5442, or by email at MacmillanSpecialMarkets@macmillan.com.

Printed in the United States of America

St. Martin's Paperbacks edition / August 2023

10 9 8 7 6 5 4 3 2 1

I Will Always Love Brew

CHAPTER 1

"If I don't get some coffee ASAP, I'm gonna murder someone," Mayor Bob declared.

Bob Bobbert, aka Mayor Bob, was currently serving his sixth-straight two-year term as mayor of my hometown of Cedar River, Texas. He'd run the last four times unopposed. Everyone voted for him, mostly because he did his absolute best to never voice an opinion about anything. He literally could do no wrong, mostly because other than patching the potholes on Main Street quickly and making sure the school playground got a new coat of paint every year, he never actually *did* anything.

I'd heard stories about a town that elected a goat as their mayor. Mayor Bob was our version of that goat— blatantly inoffensive, mostly harmless, and completely useless. Today, he wore his bright blue mayoral sash that only came out on special occasions, like high school graduations, ribbon-cutting ceremonies, and of course, town festivals. Normally, he was affably pleasant, but he was grumpier than usual this morning. He must really need his caffeine fix.

"Don't worry, Mayor Bob. Coffee's almost ready," I assured him. As a part owner of Sip & Spin Records, a vinyl records/coffee shop, I'd become something of an expert in crafting delicious caffeinated beverages. But even I couldn't control how long it took to brew a carafe of coffee, especially when we were working with limited resources at a makeshift location in Cedar River Memorial Park. The fancy barista machine we had at Sip & Spin could foam, steam, froth, grind, and pressurize on demand. Our DJ booth at the festival only had room for an industrial-size coffee maker that didn't have any bells and whistles, but made drip coffee just fine.

"That's what I like to hear, Juni," Mayor Bob said.

Like all the women in my family, I was named after a flower. Juniper flowers to be exact. My full name's Juniper Jessup, but most folks around here call me Juni. I have two older sisters, Tansy, and Magnolia, who goes by Maggie. My mom's Begonia. Her mother was Grandma Rose. We named our cat Daffodil. He's a boy cat, but it seemed fitting to name him in the family tradition.

Most people thought that because of my name, my favorite flower must be juniper. They'd be wrong. I did have a tiny juniper flower tattoo on my hip, but don't tell my mom that. Sure, I was twenty-eight years old, old enough to get a tattoo without worrying about what my mother thought, but still—moms and tattoos. Anyway, I digress. My favorite flower wasn't juniper, it was bluebonnets.

A single bluebonnet wasn't all that impressive on its own, but that's the thing about bluebonnets. They're never alone. They grew in vast numbers, blanketing entire fields and transforming the rugged Texas landscape into brilliant blue and white flowers as far as the eye can see.

When the bluebonnets bloom, Texans drive for hours to find the best locations to photograph their babies or puppies or themselves posing in fields of flowers. Small towns all over the state compete to see who can draw in the most tourists for their bluebonnet-themed celebration.

Maybe I'm biased, but every year, Cedar River's Bluebonnet Festival was the clear winner.

Our festival was tiny compared to some, but we had the best music in the state. This year, my sisters and I were in charge of the musical entertainment, since Sip & Spin Records was the new go-to place for music in our little town. On top of that, we were only a few miles from Austin, the self-proclaimed Live Music Capital of the World.

Mayor Bob continued, clucking his tongue. "It's a shame. I really expected better from our vendors." As usual, it was hard to tell if he was teasing or not. It was a strategy that worked well for him by ensuring absolute neutrality.

"Then it's a good thing we're not vendors," Tansy, my eldest sister, said, matching his tone. Standing behind the DJ booth, she pulled a Willie Nelson album off the record player and slid it into its sleeve.

Tansy was tall and slender. She had short, straight hair, flawless teeth, and perfect eyesight. My sister wore lots of pastel coordinating twinsets. Today was a baby blue top paired with dark blue slacks. "Somehow you talked us into sponsoring the festival, running the DJ booth, and providing the coffee."

Compared to Tansy, I was a few inches shorter, a few pounds heavier, and seven years younger. My outfit, like the rest of my life, wasn't quite as carefully put together as hers, but I was wearing my blue glasses and a blue vintage Jimi Hendrix T-shirt over blue jean shorts, so we sort of matched.

"Speaking of DJ duties, what album should we play next?" I asked. The turntable was hooked up to the park-wide sound system. Local bands would rotate on and off the main stage throughout the weekend. Between sets, we would play a wide variety of music over the speakers.

I riffled through one of the crates of records we'd brought for the occasion and held up two. "I can't decide between Bad Bunny and Ace of Base."

"That's our Juni," Tansy said with a grin. "Decisive to a fault." She held out a hand. "Bad Bunny, please." I handed it to her, and she set it on the player.

"You're supposed to supply the coffee. You should have set up one of those single-cup machines like I suggested," Mayor Bob said, bringing the conversation back around to our earlier discussion.

"No way," I said. At the same time, Tansy said, "Not on my watch."

Neither of us were fans of single-cup coffee makers, and not just because our business depended on customers coming to us for their pick-me-ups instead of brewing it at home. Those plastic pods were a nightmare for the environment, for starters. They're great for some situations, but we were expecting hundreds of people to stop by for a cup of our own blend of coffee today, and if we took the time to brew each cup individually, our line would circle the entire park.

"It's just a suggestion," Mayor Bob said, holding his hands up in surrender.

"Good thing we didn't listen to you, because coffee's ready." Tansy gestured at the machine, which had stopped gurgling. The red light turned green, and we were officially open for business. "Juni, what kind of coffee is this again?"

"Today's special is Bluebonnet French Roast Forever, a dark, full-bodied bean blended with a blueberry coffee. It's deliciously sweet and strong at the same time, guaranteed to start your day off right," I said.

"Blueberry?" Mayor Bob sounded unconvinced. He shook his head. "I prefer a nuttier coffee. Amaretto.

Hazelnut. Even pecan will do in a pinch. How long before something like that's ready?"

My sister and I exchanged glances. "We only have the one option today," I said. "There's barely enough juice for one machine." Between running power for the sound system and the nearby music stage, we were already maxed out. "But I guarantee you'll like this blend if you give it a chance."

Tansy handed him a to-go cup and lid. Between working the till and providing the music, we were going to have our hands full this weekend. With our other sister, Maggie, busy with her festival committee duties, it would be a challenge to keep the booth staffed, so we'd opted for a self-serve model to speed things along.

Mayor Bob took the cup and filled it to the brim. He blew across the top before taking a sip. "It needs something."

Tansy gestured at the basket filled with sweetener packets and individual creamer cups. To reduce waste—and cost—we tried to avoid single-use anything when possible. But since we were going to be out here in the open all day, we bit the bullet. The condiments cut into our profit and filled up the trash cans, but it beat serving spoiled milk or sugar with ants in it.

An alert on Bob's phone chimed. He pulled the phone out of the holster he wore on his belt and checked the screen. "Never mind. I'm needed at the office."

"Opening ceremonies are in a few minutes," Tansy said. "You're the emcee."

"Don't worry yourself none. I'll be back." Coffee in hand, he strode away from the booth, leaving us alone.

"I thought Town Hall was closed today," I said. The annual Bluebonnet Festival was a big deal in Cedar River. We planned for it all year long, and when the festival finally came around, everything in town shut down so everyone could join in on the fun.

"It is," Tansy agreed. "He probably set that alarm himself to get out of doing any work."

Now *that* sounded like our beloved mayor. According to my mom, he'd made an entire career out of pretending to be busy while doing the absolute bare minimum needed to ensure his next reelection. "What can I do to help?" I asked.

"We're pretty much good to go," she said. "Have you seen the stickers?"

"Stickers?"

"For the shop? Maggie had a bunch of stickers made up with the Sip & Spin Records logo on them for us to hand out, but I can't find them anywhere. They're in a plain brown box."

I grimaced. "About yay big?" I asked, pantomiming a box with my hands.

"Yup." Tansy glanced under the table. She pushed aside a crate of records to look behind them. "Where are they?"

"I think I saw them back at the shop." I'd noticed a brown box sitting on the counter when I was blending coffee for the day, and meant to ask Tansy about it, but I got distracted and forgot.

"Well, shoot," Tansy said.

"Don't worry, I'll run back and grab them." I glanced around the park. The festival didn't officially start for another few minutes. Most of the people milling around were locals who had already set up their booths and were strolling the paths to get a sneak peek at the other wares. The weather report called for a perfect day—sunny and mild. The park would be packed soon.

"You sure you don't mind?" Tansy asked.

"It's not a problem. Maybe I'll even whip up a custom

drink and drop it by Town Hall for the mayor, so he's in tip-top shape to emcee the festivities."

"Generous offer, little sis," Tansy teased. "You're just afraid that if Mayor Bob's mood doesn't improve, you'll end up on the wrong end of the microphone."

The idea of announcing upcoming bands over the loudspeaker made my knees knock. Public speaking was my biggest nightmare. "You know me too well, Tansy." I picked up my bag. I tried to recall the last time I'd served the mayor at Sip & Spin, and came up blank. "What's his usual?" While most of our patrons were happy with the special of the day, some habitually ordered the same thing.

"Tall sugar-free vanilla frap blended with unsweetened almond non-dairy creamer, two pumps of amaretto, and a dash of nutmeg. Fat-free whip," she said without hesitation. Tansy had always been a genius when it came to music. She had a sixth sense when it came to suggesting something patrons would have never picked out themselves that they ended up loving. Apparently, she was pretty good at remembering coffee orders, too.

"And his favorite kind of music?" I asked, testing Tansy's recall abilities.

"Mayor Bob absolutely adores Bobby McFerrin."

"Really? I always thought of him as more of a Charlie Daniels Band kind of man."

"Juni, if you're going to recommend music to people, you have to stop judging people by their covers."

"True," I agreed. "I'll be right back."

I'd parked my ride—a lime green adult tricycle with a market basket mounted to the back—behind the booth. The paved paths were still empty enough to navigate my trike without much trouble. As I pedaled, I took time to look around and appreciate the expertly decorated vendor booths that transformed Cedar River Memorial Park into a festive fairground. I slowed when I saw a cart advertising cotton candy, but it wasn't open yet. I made a mental note to return later. Maybe I'd even share with my sisters.

What could I say? Food was my love language.

I topped a small rise and surveyed the park sprawled out below me as I rode. While Texas was flat in places, it's a big state and the landscape was as varied as the people. There were rivers, mountains, canyons, and the Gulf coastline. There were deserts, forests, and sandy beaches. Here in the hill country of Central Texas, it could range from long, low fields in the shadow of granite mounds perfect for grazing cattle to deep cave systems ideal for escaping the summer heat.

While I rode, I saw my sister Maggie and her husband J.T. heading in the other direction and rang my trike's bell to get her attention. Maggie waved before continuing on her way. I caught a glimpse of our mom walking with a man I didn't know, but they disappeared behind a booth before I could get a good look at him. I recognized several other locals—friends from childhood, neighbors, and fellow shopkeepers—and exchanged smiles with them all.

I'd left for Oregon right after college graduation, and had only recently moved back home to Cedar River. I hadn't realized until just now how much I'd missed all this while I was away. I was happy to be back home where I could celebrate bluebonnet season with my family.

CHAPTER 2

Sip & Spin Records was eerily quiet when I let myself in. I wasn't used to being in the shop without music playing, so I stopped at one of the listening stations. An early Depeche Mode album was already on the turntable. I dropped the needle, unplugged the headphones, and smiled as "World in My Eyes" began to play. My sisters and I had only opened Sip & Spin recently, but our grandparents had operated a record shop in this very location before CDs, MP3s and streaming services made vinyl obsolete.

Fortunately for us, records were enjoying a revival, and being so close to the world-famous Austin music scene gave us an extra boost. Growing up in a record shop had given me an eclectic taste in music. I was probably the only person I knew who loved the Beatles as much as I loved Ariana Grande. Some of my favorite albums, like the one currently on the record player, were recorded before I was born. There were definite perks of being raised in a family that appreciated good music.

The shop was two stories. The main floor hosted new releases and albums from local bands, with expensive collector albums framed on the walls. The back wall behind the counters that held the barista station and the cash register was exposed brick, but the rest of the walls were painted a shimmery gray. The second floor was a wide balcony that ringed the store. Along the walls and railing were bins that held older music, from the golden age of jazz to the early rock 'n' roll my grandparents were so fond of. On any given day, the music we played for customers ranged from old-school country western to rap, and everything in between.

A fluffy orange and white cat appeared seemingly out of nowhere and greeted me with a pitiful meow. "Daffy, did no one feed you this morning?" I asked, scooping him up. Daffodil had shown up when we were setting up the shop and made himself at home. After verifying he was a stray, we officially adopted him as one of the family. "Poor baby. We were so busy with the festival that we forgot all about you."

The cat came and went as he pleased. Locked doors did not seem to deter him in the least. It was still early-ish, but as Daffy was loudly telling me, he must be starving to death. I went behind the counter to where his food dish sat. Inside it was a bright orange Post-it note that read "Daffy's been fed" in Maggie's handwriting, with today's date scribbled under it. "Liar," I accused him. He meowed at me.

In the corner, behind several café tables and high stools was our shiny, complicated barista station. I headed there next. It felt like a waste to dirty the whole machine for a single frappé, so I started a small pot of drip instead. I could make Mayor Bob a drink he would love without the fancy machine.

As I set the ingredients I needed on the counter, the front door opened with a jingle of bells. "Sorry, we're not open today," I said, turning around to greet our customer.

But instead of a customer, it was Teddy Garza, Cedar

River's favorite mail carrier and a friend from as far back as I could remember. We'd recently gone on a few dates, and were having a great time, despite several complicating factors.

"Thought I might find you here," he said.

Teddy was a Hispanic man with the tan of someone who spent most of his time outdoors. His black hair—cut short on the sides but long on top—was unfairly lush and shiny for someone who rarely put any effort into his appearance. When we were in chess club together in high school, he'd buttoned his shirts up to the very top and wore a pocket protector to class. He still had a serious air about him, but was more confident and a little less buttoned-up these days.

"And hello to you, little dude," he said as Daffy wove around his cowboy-boot shod, denim-clad legs. He glanced up at me. "Does this mean I'm one of the cool kids now?"

Daffy was skittish around strangers. Most of our customers didn't even realize we had a shop cat. That he'd finally accepted Teddy as one of his people was progress.

"Looks like it," I told him. "Can I get you something? A nice café au lait or macchiato maybe?" I offered. I knew Teddy wouldn't take me up on it, but I'd gladly clean the barista station again for an opportunity to get him to try something new.

"Do you have anything a little less . . . fancy?" he asked. Teddy liked his coffee plain and black.

"One No More I Love Brews coming right up," I said, glancing at the pot of coffee I'd started to judge its progress. Technically the plain coffee didn't need a special name of the day, but I didn't want it to feel left out.

"Much appreciated," Teddy said, leaning against the counter as the smell of the coffee brewing filled the shop. "You stuck in here all day?" he asked.

I shook my head. I hated losing revenue this week-end, but with everyone at the festival, Main Street would be a ghost town. Besides, my sisters and I would be busy enough at the DJ booth that if we also tried to keep Sip & Spin open, we'd never find time to enjoy ourselves. Blue-bonnets only bloomed once a year, and I didn't want to miss out. "Nope. Just had to pick up something for Tansy."

I poured coffee into a reusable mug, knowing he'd bring it back for refills. Teddy stopped by Sip & Spin every day, even when the post office was closed. I think he had a caffeine addiction.

"You know me so well, Juni," he said, taking the offered coffee. "What do I owe you?"

"It's on the house, like always." Truth be told, we probably gave away as much coffee as we sold, but the real purpose of our little coffee café was to drive traffic to the record shop, and a mug of black coffee cost us virtually nothing.

"Much obliged," he said, nodding. "I'll see you at the festival?"

"You will," I agreed, following him out so I could lock the door behind him before mixing up the mayor's drink. Instead of a frappé, I made an iced coffee in a clear to-go cup. Then I added the unsweetened almond creamer and amaretto syrup the way he liked it. I topped the drink off with a healthy serving of fat-free whipped cream and a sprinkle of nutmeg.

I turned off the coffee maker. There was a little left, so I made a small iced coffee with a drizzle of caramel for myself before rinsing out the pot. "Now where are those stickers?" I asked out loud as I sipped my drink.

Daffy meowed, getting my attention before knocking something off the counter. I heard my keys clatter on the floor. "Really?" I asked him, as I scurried over. "Is this because I didn't fall for a second breakfast?" I bent over to retrieve my keys, and when I straightened, noticed that the cat was perched on top of a plain brown box.

"Good kitty," I said, scooping him up with one arm and opening the package with my free hand. Inside were the missing stickers. "Fine, I'll give you a treat, but just because you found the stickers." I put him back on the counter before grabbing the bag of his favorite treats out of the supply closet. I knew I was being silly, but ever since finding a dead body in this closet, I was always nervous opening that door. Can't imagine why.

Pushing that unpleasant incident out of my mind, I tossed a few treats to Daffy and watched him catch them out of the air. I felt guilty leaving him alone all day, even though he'd hate being in a crowd of strangers a lot more than being here by himself. "Be good now, hear?" I told him before letting myself out and locking Sip & Spin behind me.

The box of stickers fit neatly into my basket, but the coffees were more difficult. It was times like this that I missed having a car, or at least I missed cup holders. I finished my coffee and put the empty cup in the basket to wash and reuse later. As awkward as it was, I held Mayor Bob's coffee in one hand and the handlebar in the other.

I headed downtown. The lot near the park must have been full, because people were starting to park in the municipal lot. We should really have a shuttle bus, I realized. It was too late to do anything now, but I'd suggest it for next year's festivities.

Cedar River Town Hall sat on the far side of the parking lot. Cedar River was small enough that our town hall doubled as the community center. It was a modest single-story, redbrick building with large-paned windows under green awnings. Matching brick planters that held a variety of blooming bushes and young pecan trees adorned the sidewalk outside. The Texas and U.S. flags snapped proudly from their tall flagpoles on either side of the stately entrance.

I pedaled my trike up one of the ramps leading up to the arched front door. There weren't any lights on inside. I tugged on the door handle with my free hand, and the heavy front door opened.

"Hello?" I called as I stepped into the lobby. Overhead lights flickered on. "Anyone here?" I walked toward the front desk, but stopped dead in my tracks when I noticed a pool of red liquid spreading across the tile floor.

"Can I help you?" a gruff man's voice asked. I spun to face him. Pete Digby, the security guard, had come up behind me. He was holding a wad of brown paper towels, the cheap kind that dissolved before the job was done.

He shuffled around me. He dropped the wad of paper towels on the floor and pushed them around with his shoe. Pete had graduated with my sister Maggie, so he was only five years older than me, but with his 1970's-era mustache, he looked older.

"What happened?" I asked, watching his ineffective mopping technique.

"Spilled my Slurpee." He looked down at the mess with a scowl as if trying to wish it away before returning his attention to me. "And what are you doing here, Juni? We're closed. Everyone's at the Bluebonnet Festival."

"Is Mayor Bob still here?" I asked instead of answering his question.

He hooked his thumbs in his belt loops before pushing the wet paper towels around a bit more with his shoe. All he managed to accomplish was to spread out the mess. "Haven't seen him."

"Really? He told me and Tansy that he had to take care

of some business. Mind if I poke my head into his office real quick?"

He shrugged. "Don't see why not."

Pete Digby wasn't the best security guard in the world. I could think of a dozen reasons why a random citizen shouldn't be allowed to roam a supposedly unoccupied government building unescorted, but what did I know?

Town Hall was laid out with government offices down the hall to the left, community rooms that could host anything from bingo to sewing circles to the right, and a multipurpose banquet hall in the back. I'd never had a reason to spend much time in the office part of the building, but I had a vivid memory of the first time I'd ever been on stage in the banquet hall.

It was the town spelling bee. I knew how to spell my word, but stage fright got the worst of me. I stepped up to the mic and froze. I don't know what had been more embarrassing—getting knocked out in the first round or almost fainting on stage.

Pushing that humiliating memory back into the recesses of the past where it belonged, I turned toward the government offices. I walked past the county clerk's room, vital records, and several council members' offices. The doors were all clearly labeled and closed. Finally, at the end of the hall, was a door with "Mayor Bob" written on a gilded plaque.

I knocked. There was no answer. I tried the door knob. It opened.

The office was dark. The air conditioning was on full blast. When I stepped inside, the automatic lights flipped on. Mayor Bob's office was a lot like his politics—inoffensive and bland enough to not leave a lasting impression. Except for a framed portrait of Bob and his wife Faye hanging across from a large bookshelf filled with official-looking legal books, the walls were bare. His office could use the services of an interior decorator.

At the far end of the room was a cheap desk made of wood-grained particle board on metal legs. In front of the desk was a pair of matched guest chairs. Behind it was a large executive chair, turned to face the closed shades over the window. I could see the top of his head over the back of the chair and his arm draped over the armrest.

"Mayor Bob?" I asked, knocking again on the door frame. I shivered as another blast of air conditioning hit me and wished I'd worn something warmer than an old concert T-shirt.

"Bob?" I repeated, striding toward him. Either he was deep in thought or, more likely, had nodded off at his desk. "I brought you a coffee that you might like better," I said, rounding his desk, prepared to shake his chair to wake him up. But then I noticed that his eyes were already open. He was clutching the Sip & Spin Records to-go coffee cup from earlier. He was staring into space, his lips slightly open and tinged the same color blue as his mayoral sash.

"Mayor Bob?" I asked one more time, unable to help myself, even though I knew he was beyond answering. Mayor Bob was dead.

CHAPTER 3

Most people spend their entire lives without ever stumbling across a dead body, but I'd found two corpses in about as many months. It would be nice to go a decade or two between gruesome discoveries. Was that too much to ask? Apparently so.

I waited in the hallway for the police after I'd called them. I'd shouted to Pete, but he didn't respond. I wondered where he had gone—the building wasn't large. He should have been able to hear me, and I didn't want to leave Mayor Bob alone long enough to go looking for him. I knew the mayor was beyond caring about such things, but I wasn't, so I parked myself on a bench opposite the open door and tried to distract myself from thinking about the dead man in the office chair.

Still clutching the iced coffee I'd made for the mayor, my gaze roamed the strangely bare walls. They were dingy and in desperate need of a fresh coat of paint. The portrait of Bob and his wife smiled mockingly at me. It was a large photo in an even larger frame. Rather than being hung in the middle of the otherwise empty wall, it was offset, closer to the door than the center of the room where visitors couldn't miss it, but Bob himself would hardly see it from behind his desk.

Thinking of his desk drew my thoughts back to the dead body. There was no sign of violence. Mayor Bob was getting up there in years, but he'd acted fine this morning at the DJ booth. It all seemed so sudden. I was hit with a wave of sorrow for a man I barely knew, and rather than dwell on it, I focused on the bookshelf to distract myself. The books were all a uniform size. The only difference was a slight variation in the colors on the spine from reddish-brown to brownish-red, as if Bob had bought the lot of them as a set.

Granted, I wasn't the neatest person in the world. If you asked my sisters, they'd claim I was a slob. Whatever. Either way, compared to the mayor's, my bookshelves were pure chaos. Books were stacked wherever they fit with no consideration for size, color, genre, or author. Mysteries were shelved with sci-fi, cozies, and romance all willy-nilly. And any space between, in front of, or above the books was filled with knickknacks, from old Beanie Babies to a lopsided bowl I'd made at a pottery and wine place I'd gone to with Tansy.

There were no knickknacks in Mayor Bob's office. Not on the bookshelf. Not on top of the cabinets. Not on the desk.

Trying to ignore the body of the dead mayor just a few feet away, I turned my attention to the filing cabinets, wondering what they held. Plain manila folders, I presumed, if the rest of the office was any clue. Who even kept paper files anymore? Everything was digitized now.

My curiosity almost got the best of me. I was one breath away from going back into the office to open one of the drawers—just to take a quick peek, I wouldn't have taken anything—when I heard my name.

"Juniper Jessup," a familiar male voice drawled. "We've got to stop meeting like this."

The man walking toward me, leading a small procession of emergency personnel including a uniformed officer and two people wheeling a stretcher between them, wore a large cowboy hat tilted back on his head. His cowboy boots echoed as they clacked against the hard floor.

The automatic lights turned on as the EMTs headed inside the office to check on Mayor Bob. I could have told them it was a waste of time. I was no expert, but even I could tell he was beyond help. While we waited for them to do their job, I turned my attention to the man in charge.

"Detective Beauregard Russell," I replied. "Thanks for responding so fast."

Beau was Cedar River's only official detective. He pulled double duty as a uniform cop when crime was slow, and could usually be found lying in wait in speed traps coming into town or helping little old ladies cross the street. He was polite. Cocky. Whip-smart. Funny. He always had just the right amount of stubble and a wicked smile that could disarm a rock.

We dated back in high school and all throughout college. Then he dumped me—over text. He later claimed it was to keep me from turning down a dream job out of state, which I guess was chivalrous according to his logic, but at the time it had hurt. Bad. Since my return to Cedar River, he'd tried his hardest to pick back up where we'd left off, but until I knew what *I* wanted, I was keeping him at arm's length. Which was a challenge, since Beau Russell was my kryptonite.

He stopped a foot away from me, which was unfortunate because after finding Mayor Bob's body, I really could have used a hug. "What are you doing here? Shouldn't you be at the Bluebonnet Festival with everyone else?" he asked.

I held out the coffee. "I came by to drop off a drink and found him like that."

The paramedics joined us at the door. "He's gone," the woman said. "It's hard to tell with the air conditioner blasting cold like that, but he's been dead a while."

"Thanks," Beau said with a curt nod.

"Poor Bob," I said. "I swear it's not my fault."

"Uh-huh," the Black woman next to Beau said. She was my height, but looked petite next to Beau. Officer Jayden Holt held herself like she was in charge, even when everyone else in the room outranked her. She liked classic R&B music, ate salads with the dressing on the side, and was the first person Beau called whenever there was a problem.

"Miss Jayden," I said, nodding at her. Anywhere outside of Cedar River, it would be disrespectful to call a police officer by their first name, but that's just the way things were done around here. If I'd addressed her as "Officer Holt," she would have given me her signature glare, the one rumored to make grown men cry.

She returned my nod. "Was the light on when you got here?" I guess she'd noticed the automatic lights switch on when the paramedics entered the office.

I shook my head. "Nope. Not until I walked in." I was having a hard time concentrating on her question with a dead body just a few feet away from us.

Jayden pulled out a notepad. "How long have you been waiting out here?"

I pulled out my phone and looked at my outgoing call log. "About five minutes."

"How long before we got here did the lights go off?"

I had to think about that. Up until I saw Beau and company coming down the hall, the lights were on. I remember that because I was staring at the spines of his books and contemplating the contents of the filing cabinets. I was relieved I hadn't acted on my impulse to snoop. Getting caught riffling through a dead man's files wouldn't have looked good for me, not even if I was the lead detective's ex-girlfriend.

Although, I wasn't a hundred percent sure that was the best label for Beau and me. Beau certainly didn't think so. He seemed to believe us getting back together was inevitable. And then there was Teddy. Why did everything have to be so complicated? And to make matters worse, now I had that Avril Lavigne song stuck in my head.

"Juni?" Jayden prompted.

"Yeah, um, just trying to remember." I shrugged. "The lights must have gone off about the time y'all arrived."

"Did you touch anything?" she asked.

"Not much. The door handle, from the outside." I thought hard, trying to recall the seconds between opening the office door and realizing that Mayor Bob was dead. "Honestly, it's all a blur. I don't think so, no."

"Holt," Beau said, drawing her attention. "Give me a hand."

The paramedic who had pronounced Mayor Bob dead stood in the doorway, blocking my view of the proceedings. I was okay with that, to be honest. I'd already seen enough. "You need us?" she asked Beau.

"Not yet," Beau replied. "Take five. Grab a coffee or something." He paused. "Then again, maybe you'd be better sticking with water."

The tone in his voice sent a jolt up my spine. I strained to see around the paramedic. Beau crouched in front of the dead mayor, hands gloved as he directed Jayden to take pictures of the to-go coffee cup in Bob's hand. The Sip & Spin Records coffee cup. "Why don't you find a quiet place for Miss Jessup to sit," he continued. And I thought it was bad when he called me Juniper. "I'll want to talk to her later."

In a daze, I let the paramedics guide me back to the main entrance. I sunk into one of the chairs in the lobby with a paramedic seated on either side of me as if they were worried I would pass out or make a run for it. My phone rang, startling me. I glanced down at it and saw it was Tansy, probably wondering where I was.

I started to answer my phone, but one of the paramedics put her hand over the screen and gently took it away from me. "They can leave a message," she said, placing my phone on the chair on the other side of her, where it continued to ring until it dumped Tansy into voicemail.

"That's my sister," I explained.

"I know," she said.

I studied her face. The paramedic didn't look familiar, but in a town like Cedar Creek, even if I didn't know someone, they probably knew who I was. I glanced at her name tag, which read "Kitty Harris." It rang a bell. "You're J.T.'s cousin," I said, my brain filling in the blanks. My sister Maggie's husband, J.T., had mentioned that his cousin Kitty was moving to Cedar River to work at the local hospital. "Why haven't you come to family dinner yet?"

"I'm the noob, so my schedule's all over the place," she said with a shrug. "Pulling a double today." She looked down the hallway to where I assumed Beau and Jayden were documenting the crime scene. "Lucky me."

"Tell me about it," I said, letting my head fall back to rest on the wall behind me. Then I realized that I was sitting in the same position as Mayor Bob had been in when I found him, so I jumped up and started pacing the lobby. At the far end, I studied the off-brand candy bars in the vending machine, but nothing grabbed my attention. Next to it was an automatic coffee dispenser with an Out of Order sign on it.

I shivered. The image of Mayor Bob sitting with his back to his desk and one of my coffee cups in his lifeless hand was going to haunt me for a long time. Since I poured coffee for a living, I'd be reminded of his death every day. "At least he didn't get decapitated by a record," I muttered to myself.

"Excuse me?" the other paramedic asked.

I recognized Rocco O'Brien. He'd been a couple of years behind me in high school. Our paths didn't cross socially, but he was one of the paramedics who had responded when I found a dead woman in the supply closet at Sip & Spin. If I wasn't careful, I was going to get myself a reputation.

Pretending I hadn't heard his question, I resumed my pacing.

"Maybe you should sit down," Kitty suggested. "You're probably in shock."

"I'm good," I assured her, even as Rocco said, "She's fine. It's not the first time she's found a dead body."

"What?" Kitty asked.

"It's getting to be a bad habit," he said with a chuckle.

I guess it was too late to worry about my reputation. "You were at both crime scenes, too, Rocco," I pointed out.

He glanced down at his uniform, as if confirming that he was a first responder. "Yup, I sure was, wasn't I?"

After a while, I heard the familiar clack of Beau's boots on the tile floor as he and Jayden returned. He jerked his chin at the paramedics. "He's all yours." They stood and headed back to the mayor's office. I reached for my phone, but Beau scooped it up before I could. "Not so quick. I need a word." He glanced over at Pete Digby, who was hovering nearby. "Bingo hall open?"

"I'll unlock it," the security guard said.

We followed Pete. He flipped through his key ring until he found the right key. He unlocked the door for us and held it open. "Knock yourselves out."

"Thanks," Beau told him. Then to me, he said, "Take a seat."

I sank down into one of the plastic chairs, the kind that always reminded me of elementary school. Beau took the chair next to me, spun it around, and sat down backward with his hands propped up on the back of it. "You okay, Junebug?" he asked.

A tiny part of me melted every time he called me by that old nickname. Junebug was the girl who used to sneak out of the house to make out with Beau in his truck, not someone who found dead people. "Is Jayden joining us?" I asked, looking at the empty doorway.

"She's got her hands full," he said. Unlike his officer counterpart, Beau didn't pull out a notepad or look at me like I was going to spontaneously confess to some heinous crime.

"I didn't do anything wrong," I said, shaking my head for emphasis.

He nodded and took off his cowboy hat, letting it dangle from his hand over the back of the chair. "I reckon I know that. Just walk me through what happened from the beginning."

"You ever notice how you sound just a wee more country when you want something?" I asked.

"I'm sure I have no idea what you're talking about," he said as the corners of his mouth twitched just a bit.

"I reckon you don't," I said, imitating him. Then I cut to the chase. "Tansy and I were setting up the DJ booth at the festival this morning with Mayor Bob. He was supposed to emcee the event, but he had to take care of some business. Before he left, he complained about our coffee selection, so I whipped him up something and was going to drop it off here." I held up the iced coffee. The ice had mostly melted and the whipped cream had dissolved. The result was less than appetizing.

"I'll take that," Beau said. He plucked the drink out of my hand and set it on the floor next to him. "I figured Sip & Spin would be closed today, with the festival and all."

"It is. But I went back to grab some stickers we'd forgotten. While I was at the shop, I made him a drink," I explained, feeling like we were talking in circles.

"And when you got here, how'd you get in?"

"Door was unlocked. Pete said it was okay." I gestured at the doorway, but Pete had already returned to his post.

"When you found Mayor Bob, why didn't you call Pete before calling me?"

"I tried to. I shouted for him. He didn't answer and I didn't want to . . ." My voice trailed off.

"You did right, not leaving the scene." With his free hand, Beau reached out and touched my knee. "But next time, you might want to call 911."

"Huh? I did," I insisted. "I told you. When Pete didn't respond, I called the police."

Beau chuckled. "You called me direct, Junebug."

"I did?" I guess I'd been more shaken than I realized. Then again, Beau was always the first person I thought of in an emergency.

He nodded. "You did."

"Sorry."

"Shucks, Juni, you can call me anytime," he assured me. Beau squeezed my knee before removing his hand. "Did you see or talk to anyone this morning other than Pete?"

"Tansy was at the DJ booth, of course. And Teddy

dropped by Sip & Spin while I was brewing coffee for the mayor."

"Of course he did," Beau said affably. I searched his face for any sign that he was bothered that Teddy and I were together this morning. Beau knew I'd gone out with Teddy, and vice versa. Both of them assured me that they were fine with me seeing anyone I wanted to, and seemed content to let me take things at my own pace. Frankly, they were both handling the whole situation a lot better than I was. It was low-key suspicious.

"I know you've had a rough morning. I have just one more question for you and then you can be on your way," Beau continued. "If your shop is closed, and you never had a chance to deliver this drink, how did Mayor Bob get the Sip & Spin coffee he was drinking when he died?"

CHAPTER 4

I liked to think that I was an intelligent person. I was in all the academic clubs and events in high school—chess club, spelling bee, AP English. I graduated from UT with honors and went on to become a moderately successful software developer before moving back home to open my own small business.

Of course, I made mistakes. Who doesn't? But I liked to think I learned from my mistakes, and this conversation was red flag city.

Letting Beau lull me into dropping my guard with a friendly grin and a few well-timed "Shucks" was, to be perfectly honest, par for the course. Truth be told, I had a soft spot for him big enough to drive a tractor trailer through. He knew it, and wouldn't hesitate to exploit it. But I wasn't mad at Beau for being Beau. I was mad at myself for letting him get away with it. Again.

"Before I answer that, I need to talk to my brother-in-law," I said.

"Shucks, Junebug, you don't gotta bring J.T. into this," he said, his drawl getting more pronounced as he laid it on thick. "Can't two old friends have a casual conversation with getting lawyers involved?"

I nodded. "No doubt. But this? This is no casual conversation."

True crime podcasts, murder mystery books, and even reruns of *Law and Order* had taught me well. Blue lips on a dead body meant one of two things. Mayor Bob either froze to death or he was poisoned. Intense air-conditioning or not, I could safely rule out hypothermia. Of course, the detective in charge was focusing on anything that the mayor ate or drank before his death, and while I was a part owner of Sip & Spin, I hadn't brewed that pot of coffee he'd drunk out of or handed him the cup. My oldest sister had. And anything I said could get her into trouble.

I held out my hand. "I'd like my phone now."

"You can have it back in a minute," he said. "But first . . ."

I stood up. The squeal of the chair sliding across the hard floor made my teeth ache. Rather than worrying over the return of my cell phone, I strode over to a phone mounted on the wall near the door. I lifted the handle, pressed nine, and got a dial tone. It took me a second to remember J.T.'s number, but he'd insisted that we all memorize it instead of relying on speed dial. I was glad he had.

Personally, I never answered my phone if I didn't recognize the number, but my brother-in-law didn't have that luxury. "J.T. Taggart speaking," came his familiar voice after two rings.

"It's Juni. I'm at Town Hall being questioned about a murder."

"Again?" he asked.

"Again," I confirmed.

"Hold on, I'm on my way. And Juni, it goes without saying but . . ."

"Yeah, yeah, I know," I told him. "Don't say anything

until you get here." I heard a sigh on the other end of the line before he hung up. J.T. had to assume I'd already said too much, but he was riding to my rescue anyway. Family. Am I right? I turned to Beau. "My lawyer'll be here in a minute."

Beau raked his hand through his hair before settling his cowboy hat back on his head. He stood in a smooth motion and spun his chair back into position, without making the annoying screech that I'd made. "Like I said, it's not necessary." He let out a sigh. "There's nothing more important to you than family, so if you're clamming up, that means that one of your sisters served him the coffee. Which one was it? Maggie or Tansy?"

"Neither," I said. "It was self-serve. Mayor Bob poured that cup himself."

He pulled out his phone and glanced at the screen before walking in my direction. "Jayden just had a chat with Tansy and confirmed that your sister made the coffee this morning. We're taking the coffee maker and any remaining cups and fixings as evidence to test, but since no one else has gotten sick, I don't reckon we'll find anything." He put a hand on my shoulder. "You know you can trust me, right?"

I swallowed the lump in my throat. While we were in here, his partner was questioning my sister. Seemed like a dirty trick from someone who wanted my trust. "I want to trust you," I said.

"Let me walk you out." He scooped up the formerly iced coffee.

I followed him, noticing that the hall leading to Mayor Bob's office was still bustling with activity. I didn't recognize most of the people wearing white paper gowns with matching masks. I presumed these were crime scene techs from Austin. Cedar River didn't have enough crime to need our own. I glanced over at Beau. Even our only detective was part-time.

Beau handed me my phone. "We needed to talk to Tansy before the word got out about what happened. I'm sure you understand."

We stepped outside. I blinked, adjusting as the sunlight beat down on me. The parking lot was now full of tourists' cars. Beau's police car and the crime scene van were blocking the driveway. J.T.'s BMW pulled up in front of the town hall. He stepped out of the car. Beau waved at him. J.T. scowled in return as he hurried toward us.

"I know we had a date tonight," Beau said, as if we weren't standing outside of a crime scene. We were supposed to go to dinner and a movie. "Obviously I'm going to be working. Rain check?" He bent down, adjusting his hat so he could kiss my cheek. "I'll call you later. And look, I know people talk and news travels like wildfire, but try not to say or do anything that might impede our investigation. At least let us notify the widow before you start spreading gossip. Please."

J.T. joined us. "Stop harassing my client," he told Beau.

Beau raised both his hands. "She's all yours," he said, before walking away.

"Juni?" J.T. asked.

"Mayor Bob is dead. I found him."

J.T. rubbed his eyebrows with one hand as if he had a headache. "Of course you did." He put an arm around my shoulders and steered me in the direction of his car. "Come on, let's talk in my office."

I waved my hand at my trike. "Let me get the stuff out of my basket first." We walked over to my tricycle and I lifted the stickers out. "I should get these to Tansy, and I have a feeling she might need your services more than I do today."

J.T. looked around at the stream of pedestrians heading toward Cedar River Memorial Park. "It's probably too much to hope for a parking spot closer to the festival?" he asked.

"Yeah. Those spots were taken a while ago," I agreed.

He looked down at his cowboy boots, then over at my feet. My tennis shoes might not be fashionable, but they were made for walking and standing all day. "I guess we ought to get started. You can fill me in while we walk."

I texted Tansy to let her know that we were on our way. While J.T. and I strolled through the park, past the lush patches of bluebonnets where people posed for selfies, I told him everything I knew. By the time we made it into the throngs of tourists, I'd worked up an appetite. The morning's events aside, the smells of food roasting, frying, smoking, and baking coming from the food trucks lining the park paths were calling my name.

"Hold up," I said, when I couldn't take it anymore.

"We don't have time for this," J.T. grumbled, but he knew better than to argue.

"In a feat of extraordinary willpower, I walked past the honey roasted brisket, the spicy taco in a bag, and the caramel apple booths, but the day that Juniper Jessup passes up a fried ice cream and churro sundae is the day I'm dead," I told him.

"Don't I know it," he replied.

The line was long but it moved quickly, and soon we were at the window. As I placed my order with the bored teenager behind the counter, Carole Akers deserted her post at the deep fryer to pay attention to us instead. I've known Carole since we were both in pigtails. We were in Girl Scouts together. Her parents owned a pool, so she was the most popular kid in school. Now she owned a successful chain of food trucks that had been featured on two different food shows.

"Juni! Is it true?" she asked, leaning her head out the window.

"Is what true?"

"Is the mayor dead?"

I looked over at J.T. He shook his head. "Don't. You're already in enough trouble."

The woman who had ordered before me picked up her ice cream. "I heard he was stabbed to death with a pencil," she said.

"Don't be silly," the man in line behind us said. "The elevator door crushed his head."

The first woman scoffed. "And you call me silly? There are no elevators in the police station where he was killed."

"Help," I mouthed to J.T. He made a zipping-the-lips motion in return.

I knew that the rumor mill was fast, but this was downright ridiculous. Mayor Bob hadn't been dead long and the stories were already flying. Although, to be fair, I wasn't exactly sure when he'd died. It had taken me a while to pedal to the shop, prepare three drinks, and then ride to Town Hall. He was still holding his coffee, but I had no way of knowing if he'd drunk it immediately or if he was one of those people who let their coffee get cold and then—shudder—heated it in the microwave.

I hadn't noticed a microwave at his office, but there had been a mini-fridge next to the filing cabinets. The refrigerator at Tansy's house was covered in magnets, notes we leave each other, and invitations to weddings or baby showers. The one in the mayor's office had been free from any decoration. Like his desk with its large green blotter, a simple stainless steel pencil cup filled with matching pens, and an empty outgoing mail basket, it was functional and generic. Even his laptop, which had been closed, was a plain black model. Elections were coming up in the fall, which meant that Bob had been mayor for nearly twelve years, and he had yet to personalize his office. How sad.

"Juni, you stay right there," Carole told me. "I'll bring your order around the side." She turned to the teenager. "Her ice cream is on the house. And tell your cousin his break's over, I need him back on the fryer."

While we waited for Carole, I turned to J.T. "Speaking of cousins, I met Kitty today. She seems nice."

"She's fantastic," he said. We stepped to the side to let the next customer order. "I keep meaning to introduce you two, but she's always working."

"That's no excuse. She's family." J.T. might be my brother-in-law, but he'd married Maggie while I was just a teenager, and I thought of him as a brother. "Give her my number and tell her to text me."

Before he could respond, Carole emerged with two large balls of fried ice cream on a bed of churro bites, topped with whipped cream, a sprinkle of cinnamon, and a bright red cherry. She handed it to me. I plucked a plastic spoon out of the condiment tray mounted to the side of the truck and took a bite. "Tell me everything," she demanded.

"This is delicious," I said around a mouthful of melty ice cream and warm, crunchy batter.

"I already know that," Carole said, losing patience with me. "What about the mayor? Is he really dead? Was he strangled with his own tie? Is it true that he was wearing only boxers?"

I shook my head. How did these rumors get started? I guess what the grapevine lacked in accuracy it made up for with speed and imagination. "I'm not supposed to talk about it, but that's not what happened."

Carole grabbed my elbow, arresting my spoon halfway to my mouth. A dab of ice cream spilled over the edge and dripped onto my shoe. "So Mayor Bob's alive?"

I sighed. Beau had asked me not to contribute to the local gossip, but everyone was going to talk about it whether or not I kept my lips shut. They might as well have their facts straight. "Unfortunately, he is deceased. But he wasn't strangled. And he was fully clothed. The cops haven't had a chance to notify Faye yet, so please keep this to yourself."

Carole waved her hand at me in a dismissive gesture. "Faye's on a cruise to Alaska with her sister. You know how cell phone reception is on those cruises."

"Actually, I don't. I've never been on a cruise."

"You should try it. You'd love it. But Faye won't get her messages until they pull into the next harbor, and by then everyone in town will already know everything, so you might as well spill it. Speaking of spills . . ." She turned, snagged a napkin, and dabbed at my chin. "You're making an absolute mess."

"Yeah, well, we should really get going," J.T. said before I could respond. "Great seeing you, Carole. Tell Hank I look forward to seeing him on the links so I can win some of my money back." Carole and Hank had been a couple since high school. He'd proposed to her at graduation, and they'd been happily married ever since.

J.T. took hold of my upper arm and propelled me away from Carole's food truck. "I let Hank win."

"Sure you did," I agreed, but I knew better. J.T.'s competitive streak was one of the things that made him such a good lawyer. I couldn't imagine him letting anyone win. I'd once watched him humiliate a circuit judge over a round of pool, which couldn't have been great for his career. "Want a bite?" I held out the spoon.

"I'm good," he said and kept walking. That was just

like J.T. to keep his eyes on the prize, even when fried ice cream was right there for the taking.

When we got to the DJ booth, we had to wade through a crowd four or five people deep to get to my sister, who was looking harried. Our mother was beside her in the booth, along with an older man I vaguely recognized but couldn't name.

"Juni!" Tansy said as soon as she spotted me, and the crowd turned to stare at me. "Took you long enough." She looked over at our brother-in-law. "And you. Where were you when I needed you?"

He shrugged and turned to my mom. "Bea, if you don't mind, I need a word with your daughters."

"Don't worry, I've got this," Mom assured him. Unlike Tansy, she looked like she was having the time of her life. Holding court in the middle of a town scandal was her happy place.

J.T. and I pushed our way around the side of the crowd and joined Tansy behind the booth. As soon as we were close, my oldest sister hissed, "Juniper, what on earth did you get us into this time?"

CHAPTER 5

"I can explain," I said, even though I wasn't sure I could. "I was in the wrong place at the wrong time. That's all."

"Juni, you're always in the wrong place at the wrong time," J.T. said.

"Hey! Don't talk to my sister in that tone of voice," Tansy said, jumping to my defense.

"How is that any worse than what you just said?" he asked.

"She's my sister. I can talk to her any way I want," Tansy replied. As far as sisterly logic went, that made sense.

"Come on, y'all, we need to focus." I turned to Tansy. "I'm sorry I didn't call you. Beau took my phone so I couldn't warn you."

She nodded. "I should have known. Juni, sweetie, when are you going to come to your senses about him? Beauregard Russell is bad news."

"I appreciate you standing up for me, but if I can forgive him for breaking my heart ages and ages ago, you can too," I told her.

Tansy put her hands on her hips. "Six years wasn't so long ago."

"We were just kids," I replied.

"You were both in your twenties. You were old enough to move halfway across the country by yourself. You weren't kids anymore," she argued.

"Ladies, can we get back on topic, pretty please?" J.T. interrupted. "Tansy, Officer Jayden Holt came to see you this morning, right? Tell me what happened."

"Yeah, Jayden came by the booth. She asked me if I'd seen the mayor today, and I told her he was here this morning, but he'd left in the middle of setting up the DJ booth to take a meeting. Then she confiscated the coffee maker and all our supplies."

"Yeah, Beau told me." I glanced around to make sure that none of the gossip mongers from the DJ booth had followed us. A few nearby locals threw curious stares in our direction, but no one was close enough to overhear. "When I found Mayor Bob, he was already dead. His lips were blue, you know, like when someone has been poisoned."

"You watch too many crime dramas," J.T. said. "There's lots of reasons why lips could turn blue after death."

I shrugged. I was just a software developer turned records salesperson-slash-barista. What did I know about causes of death? J.T. was a lawyer. He knew more about criminology than I ever wanted to. "Anyway, he was holding a Sip & Spin Records coffee cup."

"He was *what*?" Tansy asked, loudly enough to turn a few nearby heads.

"Shh," J.T. said, putting his hand on her back. "People are watching."

"That's why Jayden was so interested in our coffee. The cops think our coffee killed Mayor Bob?" Tansy looked like she was going to be sick. "If that gets out, Sip & Spin is ruined."

I hadn't considered that. We relied on the coffee café

to bring in new and repeat customers so we could sell them music. If everyone in Cedar River was afraid to drink our coffee, they'd go back to ordering their music online, or worse, streaming it. Our dreams of a vinyl resurrection in town would be dead.

"Oh, girls," my mother shouted. We turned and she was waving us over.

"Don't tell her anything," J.T. warned us.

"Too late," Tansy said. "Half a dozen people overheard me talking with Jayden Holt, and they all called Mom immediately." The biggest downside of being the daughters of the biggest gossip in the county was we never got away with anything. If we so much as talked too much in a movie theater, our mom knew about it before we even got home.

Reluctantly, we returned to the booth. Once we'd walked away, the crowd had mostly dispersed, leaving the immediate area around us relatively empty. With no coffee to sell and no juicy details to share, there was no reason for anyone to approach the DJ booth except to request a specific song or ask us to broadcast a message. My mother studied us carefully before zeroing in on J.T. "Is there anything you need to tell me?" she asked him.

"No, ma'am," he said, but he sounded nervous. I thought it was hilarious that J.T. could face the sternest judges and hardened criminals without blinking, but my mom scared him. Then again, he'd be a fool to not be at least a little intimidated by his mother-in-law.

He turned to us. "You two, don't repeat anything we've talked about to anyone"—he cut his eyes to Mom— "anyone. And if Officer Holt or Detective Russell come sniffing around again, even if all they want is to ask for directions, you call me. Understand?"

I nodded.

"Understood," Tansy agreed aloud for both of us.

J.T. sighed. He knew we meant well, but he had a sneaking suspicion we weren't going to follow his orders. In his defense, he was probably right. Though it wouldn't be for lack of trying—it just wasn't easy keeping secrets from our mother. "If you need anything . . ."

"We'll call," I promised.

"You better. Now if you'll excuse me, I'm going to go find my wife." J.T. melted into the crowd of tourists, their arms laden with food and shopping bags. I noticed a lot of them were wearing Cedar River's signature Blue Bonnet—a bright blue baseball cap with plastic bluebonnets mounted on springs to the bill. It was a perennial best seller, and all the proceeds went into next year's festival.

My mother looked me up and down before making a tsking sound. "Juni, you're such a pretty girl. Would it kill you to wear a little makeup?"

"Mom, it'll be a thousand degrees out here by the end of the day and all my makeup would have sweated off, so what's the point?"

"It wasn't a thousand degrees when you spent the morning with a certain Beau Russell, was it?" she asked.

"Not this again," I said with a sigh. My mother meant well, but she was eager for me to settle down. The problem was I wasn't sure if I even wanted to settle down, much less who I wanted to settle down with.

She flapped a hand at me. "Not this again?" she repeated, shaking her head. "Is that any way to talk to your mother? Besides, I'm starting to think that your sister's right."

"Which one?" I asked. Maggie had been fantasizing about a wedding between me and Beau since I was eighteen. Tansy, on the other hand, would prefer to drive him out to the desert, shoot his kneecaps. and leave him there for breaking my heart. I wasn't sure which option sounded better.

"That Russell boy is trouble. Stay away from him," Mom said.

"Finally," Tansy said. "What made you come around?"

"He had the gall to pull me over and write me a ticket for speeding last week! Can you imagine?"

"Were you speeding?" I asked.

"That's beside the point." Mom fluffed her hair. "Since you girls are back, Marcus and I have to get going or we're gonna miss the hole-digging contest," Mom said.

"Marcus? Who's Marcus?" I asked. I leaned around her to get a better look at the stranger next to her in the booth. I still couldn't place him.

"Marcus Best, at your service," he said, offering his hand to shake. "You must be Juniper. You mom tells me you don't have a car. Swing by the dealership anytime, and we'll see what we can do about that. You know what they say, 'If you need a car, you need the Best.'"

That's when I recognized him. He ran a bunch of smarmy used car commercials on the local television stations for Best Used Cars, and that was his tagline. "Thanks, but I'm good," I told him.

"She needs a car. Right now, she's riding a tricycle," my mom said derisively.

"An adult market tricycle," I corrected her. The way she said it, it sounded like I rode a kid's bike, instead of a perfectly practical, environmentally friendly method of transportation.

"I can see you in a truck. Something big. A dually maybe," he suggested. "What do you think, Bea?"

"I think I'm happy with my trike," I said before Mom could speak up.

"Suit yourself. Girls, nice to finally meet ya. Bea, don't you think we should get going?" She nodded in agreement, and they walked away.

"Who was that guy?" I asked my sister.

"Marcus Best," she said. "Surely you've seen his commercials."

"I have, but what's he doing with Mom?"

"That's her new boyfriend," Tansy said.

For a moment I worried that the fried ice cream I'd just eaten was causing hallucinations, because it sounded like my sister had just said that my mom was dating someone, and that couldn't be true. "Excuse me? Her what?"

"Her boyfriend. Trust me, Juni, I was as shocked as you are when she introduced him, but he seems nice enough." She shook her head. "Honestly, I was afraid she'd never find someone again."

"Dad's only been gone a year!" I said.

"Almost a year and a half," she corrected me. "Mom's lonely. And she doesn't do lonely well. I think it's sweet that she's met someone she likes."

I took a minute to think about that. Tansy had a point. Mom wasn't good at being alone or being idle. She needed to be needed, and as much as my sisters and I loved her, we didn't exactly need her anymore, not full-time at least. "But does it have to be him?" I asked.

"You'll like him if you give him a chance," she said.

"I'm sure you're right." Then again, how much time had she spent with him? An hour? Less? "I'm not calling him Dad."

"No one's asking you to, Juni. They're just dating."

I made a noncommittal noise in the back of my throat. Out of everyone in my family, I'd always felt closest to our dad. He'd died suddenly while I was in Oregon, and I'd never had a chance to say goodbye. I wanted my mother to be happy, I did, but I wasn't ready for her to be dating anyone, especially a used car salesperson.

"I'm gonna go watch the hole-digging competition," I announced. I wasn't being nosy, honest. I had no intention of spying on my mom and her new boyfriend. I just really liked watching people dig holes. That was my story, and I was sticking to it.

"Juni, don't leave me here alone. I've been in the booth all morning. We promised we'd all rotate."

"You'll be fine," I assured her. I noticed that a band was setting up on the main stage. "Looks like they're getting ready to start. Once they do, it will be too loud for anyone to bother you with questions about Mayor Bob."

"Juni . . ."

"Look, if I see Maggie, I'll ask her to come relieve you, okay?"

"Fine," Tansy said. "But come right back after the contest is over, and bring me a sweet tea."

"Deal," I agreed, and scurried off before she could change her mind.

To an outsider, a hole-digging competition didn't have much of a place at a Bluebonnet Festival. Digging up bluebonnets was the last thing that any native Texan wanted. They were the state flower and even if it wasn't technically a crime to disturb them anymore, most folks I knew felt bound to protect them so they'd be around every spring for generations to come.

They were pretty. And more important, they were quintessentially Texas, like longhorn cattle and Shiner Bock beer. A real Texan would sooner burn down a Buc-ee's travel stop than pick a bluebonnet. And for the record, Buc-ee's was the absolute best.

But the hole-digging contest had little to do with bluebonnets and everything to do with the festival itself. Way back in 1956, during the tenth annual Bluebonnet Festival, while everyone was busy enjoying the festivities, the First Bank of Cedar River was hit by four robbers. They got away with a million dollars in cash. An hour later, the police caught up to them at the town limits. There was a shootout. The four bank robbers and one of the cops were killed, but the money was nowhere to be found.

Almost seventy years have passed since that bank robbery, and the money still hasn't been recovered. There were all sorts of wild theories about where the money ended up, but since the bank robbers had mud on their shoes, even though it hadn't rained in a week, and two of them were carrying shovels along with their rifles, prevailing wisdom said they buried the money somewhere in Cedar River. No doubt they planned on coming back and retrieving it as soon as the heat died down, but with all four robbers dead, there was no one left to do so.

Over the years, there have been massive community efforts organized to find the loot. Cedar River has hired everyone from water witches to commercial companies with ground-penetrating radar to survey the town, to no avail. Every couple of years, someone hears the story or reads an article about the bank heist on the internet and comes down here looking for a quick buck. So far, every professional and amateur treasure hunter has left with empty pockets.

The mystery of where the money was buried remains elusive, but every year during the Bluebonnet Festival, the town hosts a hole-digging competition. I don't think anyone truly believes that they'll hit upon the exact spot where the money was hidden by hand-digging their assigned plot, but that doesn't stop anyone from trying. It's so popular, that people enter a lottery just to get their chance at a few square feet of ground and a shovel.

This year was no exception. The hole-digging site was several blocks away from where the main festival was being held, but the area was already swarming with spectators. This spot had been a grove of oak trees back in the fifties that were bulldozed in the seventies to build a roller rink. The rink had been closed longer than I'd been alive, and now it was finally being torn down. In a few months, they'd pour the foundation for a new condo building, but today it was prime digging ground. More importantly, it had never been surveyed by treasure hunters before.

The town had erected a chain-link fence around the approximately block-long area in preparation for the festivities. They'd staked out forty-eight individual plots to randomly assign to lotto winners. The rules were simple: No teams were allowed. Contestants used shovels generously provided by the local hardware store. They had one hour to dig—the precise time that the bank robbers were unaccounted for. At the end of the hour, the person who had moved the most amount of dirt, as determined by the judges, won. Unless, of course, someone managed to dig up the actual treasure, in which case, they would be crowned champion.

I was as invested as anyone else who'd grown up hearing the legend of the lost Cedar River fortune, but as much as I loved watching the contest, I always hoped that the diggers would come up empty-handed. Personally, I loved the mystery more than the idea of one person striking it rich.

CHAPTER 6

There was an empty spot against the chain-link that I claimed as my own. From there, I had a good view of the field and a direct line of sight to where Mom and Marcus were sitting in the grandstands set up for VIPs. Sure, they had bench seats, but most of the locals knew to spread out along the fence for a closer look at the action.

"Howdy, Juni," a nearby voice called.

I looked over to see Miss Edie and her little puggle dog, Buffy, on my right. Edie was an older Black woman who was the honorary aunt of just about every kid who grew up in Cedar River. She'd watched half of the town's children after school until their parents got off work. Even now that she was well into her seventies, she volunteered to babysit in a pinch, but mostly she spent her leisure time lavishing all that love on her cute, curly tailed dog.

"Miss Edie! Good to see you," I told her. My parents had worked at the record shop when I was young, and most days I would go straight there after school, but as often as I could manage it, I'd get off the bus at Edie's instead. Sure, the record shop had great music, but Miss Edie had grape Kool-Aid and sliced apples. "I see you came prepared."

"Of course I did, dear," she said with a chuckle. Edie

was relaxing in a lawn chair, with an umbrella anchored into the ground next to her, providing welcome shade. Her feet were propped up on a cooler that was no doubt filled with snacks and drinks, and she had a paperback novel in her lap. "I have a feeling in my bones that this is the year."

I nodded. I secretly hoped that she was wrong, but who was I to begrudge a sweet old lady a little fun? "Maybe so."

"I still remember that day, you know," she said.

"What? You were there?" I asked. I knew Edie was born and raised in Cedar River, but I'd never stopped to consider that she might have been around during the festival heist. It seemed so long ago to me that I could barely fathom 1956, but in a generation or two, people would feel that way about Y2K.

"Of course I was, silly. I was almost ten years old. My daddy was working for the oil company back then. The payroll was stolen along with everything else. That was some dark times. We lost all our savings. I even lost my Christmas money."

"I guess I always assumed that everyone's money was insured."

"Not back then, it wasn't, not the Cedar River Bank at least." She smiled. "You better believe that when they finally find that money, someone is gonna be paying me back."

I nodded. I hadn't thought about it that way. All these years I'd been rooting against the treasure hunters, maybe I should have been rooting for them instead.

There was a loud electronic squeal as someone picked up a bullhorn and began to speak. Numbers associated with individual plots were handed out randomly, and the contestants already had their shovels. A bell sounded and everyone dashed to their assigned spots to begin digging.

My spot along the fence was between plots 17 and 25, according to the markers on the ground. A young Black man, barely out of his teens, claimed plot 17. A broad-shouldered white man twice his age double-checked his number against plot 25 and started to dig. But I wasn't paying attention to either of them as soon as I recognized Teddy on plot 18.

"Teddy!" I yelled out before I thought twice about whether or not I would be distracting him. He looked up at the sound of his name, grinned and waved at me, and then got to work.

"Now that's what I'm talking about," Edie hooted as the man on plot 25 stripped off his shirt.

"Miss Edie!" I said, in my most scandalized voice.

"I'm old, child, not dead. You just wait until that pretty mailman of yours takes *his* shirt off. See who'll be hollering then," she replied.

For the record, I didn't blush. Not at all. I mean, I had a bit of sun on my cheeks, I'm sure, but that was all. Who wouldn't after being out in the sun? The worst part was, even over the sounds of digging and grunting and earth being tossed about, Teddy must have heard her, because he tossed his head back and cackled. Then he took his shirt off, revealing a black undershirt. I had to admit it was a nice look on him. Teddy whipped his shirt over his head once before letting it fall.

"You're welcome," Edie told me.

Esméralda Martín-Brown, the town's best—and only—mechanic, joined us at the fence. Esméralda's thick, curly hair was loose around her shoulders, and she'd traded in her usual grease-stained coveralls for a long white sundress. "Whoo, Miss Edie, you were right. You always pick the best spots." She sat down in the shade of the umbrella.

"What have you got there?" I asked her as she opened a hard-sided case and pulled out a tablet.

"Thought I'd get a bird's-eye view this year," she said as she unpacked a small drone. A few minutes later, the drone was in the air, filming the competition from the sky as Edie and I huddled around her tablet.

Half an hour passed as the contestants—locals and out-of-towners, men and women—dug. The diggers became harder to see as their holes grew deeper and the piles of dirt around them rose. It was a good thing Esméralda brought her drone. Otherwise we wouldn't have been able to see anything when someone in the middle of the field yelled, "I found something!"

The other contestants paused for a moment, as if trying to decide if this was a hoax or not, before abandoning their plots and converging on the one in the middle. Judges rushed in from the gates. I alternated from trying to see what was happening on the tablet screen and pressing myself against the chain-link, hoping to catch a glimpse of the action.

A few minutes later, the weary contestants returned to their own holes and resumed digging, but their hearts didn't seem into it anymore. Then again, I was exhausted just trying to watch the competition. "What happened?" I asked the nearest digger.

"False alarm," he said between jagged breaths.

Esméralda landed her drone. She'd already replaced the battery pack once. "I'll give it a rest unless something interesting happens."

"You're pretty good with that thing," I told her. I'd watched her fly it, and it took a steady hand. "Thanks. I won it in a raffle and I've been practicing at the garage."

"Is that safe?" I asked her. Esméralda's garage, George's

Auto Body—named after her retired father—was right next to the Cedar River Municipal Airport. I wasn't sure about the legality of operating a drone so close to air traffic.

She shrugged. "I got a permit."

As the sun beat down on the back of my neck, my mind began to wander. I tried not to think about what I'd seen at Town Hall this morning, but I couldn't help it. I'd never been too concerned about local politics before. Mayor Bob had been in office since before I was old enough to vote, so he was pretty popular, but obviously not *everyone* loved him. Someone had disliked him enough to kill him.

Or, maybe not. I thought about what J.T. had said about poisoning not being the only cause of blue lips after death. I had some time to kill while the contestants dug their holes, so I pulled out my phone and launched my internet app.

R.I.P. my browser history.

Wow, there were a lot more possibilities than I had imagined. Blue lips could be a sign of anything from heart failure to a lack of oxygen. And there were a variety of possible reasons, from anemia to high blood pressure. Here I'd been assuming that Mayor Bob had been poisoned, but it was just as likely that he dropped dead of natural causes. All this worry could be for nothing.

I closed my browser and dialed Beau before I could talk myself out of it. The phone rang so many times I thought I was going to end up in his voicemail, but then he picked up. "This is a pleasant surprise," he said in lieu of a greeting. "Does this mean you're not mad at me?"

"I was never mad at you," I admitted. "But I don't like being manipulated."

"There are going to be times that I can't tell you everything. It's not personal."

"It feels personal," I said. "Especially when it involves my family."

"Junebug . . ."

I cut him off. "How did he die?"

"This is one of those times that I'm talking about," he said with a heavy sigh. "I can't divulge that information."

"Figured as much," I said and disconnected without giving him a chance to respond. Of course Beau wasn't going to tell me what killed Mayor Bob. That would be too easy.

Next, I texted my brother-in-law. "What's Kitty's #?" A few minutes later, he replied with his cousin's number. I could always count on J.T. to come through in a pinch.

I dialed the number. No one picked up. Instead of leaving a message, I called back again and this time Kitty answered. "What?" She sounded annoyed.

"Hey, it's Juni Jessup. Maggie's sister? We met this morning?"

"Oh, hey." She sounded friendlier now, not that I could blame her. I was always suspicious when unknown numbers came across the screen. I knew some scammers have gotten in the habit of calling numbers two or three times in rapid succession if no one picked up on the first try, but for the most part, if someone called multiple times it's because it's important. "What's up?"

"When's your next day off? I'd like to take you to lunch."

"I don't know. They haven't posted next week's schedule yet."

"Okay, cool. Just text me when you're free. My treat."

"Yeah, okay," she agreed. "Sounds good. Anything else?"

"Actually, yes," I admitted. "Has the autopsy on Bob Bobbert come back yet?" Beside me, Esméralda's head turned in my direction. I met her gaze and tried to look innocent. Yup, I'm just over here innocently trying to get autopsy results from a paramedic. Nothing to see here, move it along.

"You've got to be kidding. Jayden told me to watch out for you."

"She did?" I asked.

"I think her exact words were, 'Don't go giving out any details to anyone, especially Juni Jessup or her nosy sisters.'"

"Oh," I said, disappointed.

"Except, you see, I only just met Jayden Holt. She seems cool, for a cop. But you're my favorite cousin's wife's sister, so we're practically family."

"I was just telling J.T. that this very morning!" I said, excitedly.

"Exactly. Officially, I don't know anything and of course, if I did, I couldn't pass it along to you."

"And unofficially?" I asked.

"The Cedar River Coroner is out on maternity leave, so we transported Mr. Bobbert to Austin General. It will take a few days before we get any results, but as soon as I know something, you'll know something."

"You are so my new best friend," I told her.

"Right? Hey, look, I gotta get back to work but I'll let you know when I have some free time next week."

"Good deal," I told her, disconnecting the call. I wasn't kidding about wanting to be her new bestie. I was starting to think that J.T.'s failure to introduce Kitty to the family had less to do with her schedule and more to do with knowing that his cousin and I would get along like a house on fire.

A loud horn sounded, announcing that the hour was up. The two men closest to me crawled out of the holes they'd dug, looking like they were ready to collapse. Miss Edie pulled two bottles of water out of her cooler and handed them to Esméralda. "Give these to those boys, will ya?" Esméralda tossed the bottles over the fence to the grateful competitors.

Teddy wound his way around the mounds of dirt on plots 17 and 25 and hooked his fingers through the chain-link fence. "Thanks for coming out to cheer me on."

"To be honest, I didn't even know you'd entered the contest," I admitted.

"I enter every year. This is just the first time my number got drawn."

"What exactly was all the excitement about?"

"Some tourist thought they'd struck gold, but it was just a rock."

"Wait a second, gold? I'd always assumed that the robbers had gotten away with paper money. I didn't know the First Cedar River Bank was filled with gold."

Teddy shook his head. Sweat was rolling down his face, and I think it was the first time I'd ever seen him with even a single hair out of place. If I was being honest, it was a good look on him. "Miss Edie, have any more water?" I asked.

She passed one to Esméralda, who handed it to me. I couldn't fit it through the links in the fence, so I followed Esméralda's example from earlier and tossed it up and over the chain-link.

"Thanks, Miss Edie, you're a lifesaver." He downed half the bottle before dumping the rest of it over his head.

"Bless your soul," Miss Edie said, clasping her hands to her heart. "You lock that one down, Juni, you hear?"

"If you don't, I will," Esméralda said, joining in on the fun.

"Oh shush," I told the other ladies.

Teddy was trying to pretend he'd missed the entire exchange, but was biting his bottom lip so hard to keep from laughing that it was turning white.

"Um, we were talking about gold," I said, trying to steer the conversation back to safer ground.

"It was mostly cash, I think," Teddy said with a grin. He had dimples that I hadn't noticed before. "There had just been a large deposit to cover the payroll for the oil workers. There was so much money in the vault, the robbers didn't even bother with the safety deposit boxes."

I remembered Edie mentioning that her dad was waiting for his paycheck when the bank got hit. "Don't you think that's a little suspicious? How did the robbers know about the payroll?"

"Just lucky?" he guessed. "They used the Bluebonnet Festival as a distraction, so they were going to hit the bank on that weekend no matter what."

"Yeah, that makes sense," I agreed. But I wasn't convinced. In 1956, no one had Facebook ads reminding them of upcoming events. Many families in rural Texas didn't own a television set back then. The Bluebonnet Festival had only been around for ten years at the time of the heist, which meant it wouldn't have been widely known.

Whoever planned the robbery knew about the festival. It stood to reason that they knew about the payday schedule, too.

"Whatcha thinking?" Teddy asked.

"Huh?" I asked. Juni Jessup, queen of the witty banter, in the flesh.

"You're thinking about something." Before I could answer him, he said, "Hey, the judges are coming. Gotta go, but I'll catch you later." He blew me an exaggerated kiss through the fence before heading back to his plot.

CHAPTER 7

Teddy didn't win the hole-digging contest. That honor went to a professional hole-digging champion from Sweden. I didn't even know that competitive hole-digging was an international sport. I was surprised how disappointed I was that no treasure was found. I guess after all the excitement over one contestant hitting a rock and Miss Edie sharing her story, I'd gotten my hopes up that today would be the day that the mystery would be solved, but that wasn't the case.

Esméralda and I helped Edie pack up. "That was fun," she said as she folded Edie's lawn chair.

"It was," I agreed, struggling to pry her umbrella out of the ground. Whoever had planted it was a lot stronger than I was. "I don't know why watching a bunch of people dig holes in the dirt is entertaining, but it is."

"Remember a few years ago when one of the contestants found that lunch box and everyone thought they'd found the treasure?"

I shook my head. "I must have missed that." I'd missed a lot of things while I'd been living in Oregon. It was hard enough getting time off to travel home once a year for Christmas that I'd had to skip things like the Bluebonnet Festival. At least I was home now. "It's a good thing that there are so few murders in Cedar River. Anyone trying to bury a body on the sly around here will eventually get caught when a treasure hunter accidentally digs it up."

"Right?" Esméralda agreed. "Speaking of which, rumor is you found *another* dead body this morning. You gonna catch the killer like you did last time?"

I shook my head. "First off, they haven't determined the cause of death yet. It could have been a normal, natural death."

"I don't know how a man having his head and feet cut off and wrapped up in an old map like butcher paper could be considered natural," Esméralda said.

"What? No! That's not at all what happened," I insisted.

"I did hear that the map that Mayor Bob kept framed in his office was missing," Edie added.

"What map?" I asked.

Esméralda elaborated. "Oh come on, you had to have noticed it. It's like the only decoration he has in his office besides a picture of Faye."

I'd noticed the portrait of him and his wife, but there was no map on the wall this morning. The wall had been a little discolored though. I remembered thinking it looked dingy and in need of a coat of paint. "What did the map look like?" I asked.

"It was an old map of Cedar River in an antique frame. I assume that's the map the killer wrapped him up in," Esméralda theorized.

"Seriously, I don't know how these stories get started." I knew I was supposed to keep the details to myself, but I had to set the record straight. Then again, with all these wild rumors flying around, no one seemed to have gotten wind of the theory that he might have been poisoned by a cup of Sip & Spin coffee, so I counted my blessings. "Mayor Bob was in his chair, fully clothed with his head and feet still firmly attached." I shrugged. "There were no signs of violence. It was probably a heart attack. He had to have been in his seventies."

"Pshaw. That's not old," Edie said. Then again, she was in her seventies, too.

Esméralda looked disappointed. "I heard he wasn't going to run in the next election. Faye's been on him for years to get out of politics. Guess she finally wore him down."

That was interesting. If the killer had a political motive, it didn't make much sense to murder a longtime mayor who was retiring in a few months. Then again, maybe that was just another unfounded rumor. "Where did you hear that?" I asked.

"My friend Leanna is the head of the town council. A few weeks ago, we were talking about the possibility of her running for mayor if Bob Bobbert finally retires. Personally, I think it's about time that Cedar River gets a female mayor, but she seemed reluctant to commit to politics full-time. Hey, I see some people over there I need to talk to. Catch you later?"

"Yup. Have fun," I told her. She headed off to meet them. "Miss Edie, where are you and Buffy headed? I can walk with you if you'd like, help you carry all this."

The little dog wagged her tail and jumped up on me at the mention of her name. I scratched her under her chin.

"Don't you worry about me," Miss Edie assured me. "Someone's coming to pick me up in a minute."

I gave her a quick hug. "Good seeing you today."

"Likewise," she told me. "Now you run along and enjoy the fair."

The sidewalks were jammed with pedestrians. People veered off the path to navigate around long lines queueing up at vendors. My stomach growled. The fried ice cream churro sundae I'd had this morning seemed like a long time ago. I was tempted to cut across the lawn toward the main stage, but it was roped off to protect the real star of the show—the bluebonnets.

While bluebonnets were technically wildflowers, many municipalities seed them to ensure the best possible fields. Cedar River didn't have to. We had them in abundance all over the town, but they grew the thickest here in Cedar River Memorial Park, where no one was allowed to mow until after they'd finished blooming for the year.

Every year between mid-March and mid-April, my hometown was awash in the lovely blue flowers, something I never took for granted. A child clambered over the low fence separating the bluebonnet field from the park paths, and started rolling around in the flowers, crushing them as he played. "Hey!" I yelled out to him. I carefully stepped over the barrier and picked the kid up by his shoulders. He couldn't have been more than a few years old and as soon as I grabbed him, he started to wail.

"Let go of my son!" a woman demanded. She was a white woman in her late thirties. She wore lilac capri pants with a pink-and-white checkered button-down shirt tied at her waist. She balanced a powdered sugar-topped funnel cake in one hand and an oversize novelty cup of lemonade in the other. No wonder the kid was tromping through the flowers and rolling around like a puppy. I'd be doing that too if I was loaded up on that much sugar.

I turned and deposited him on the sidewalk before gingerly stepping back over the fence, trying to not do any more damage than necessary.

"How dare you lay hands on my Davey," she said, glaring at me in full-on mama bear mode. The kid was still wailing.

"Sorry," I said.

"Sorry? Is that all you have to say for yourself? I should call the cops."

"Is there a problem here, ma'am?" Beau asked, materializing out of the crowd like a mirage. He was still dressed in plainclothes, but he wore his badge clipped to the belt of his jeans. He tapped it idly with one finger to draw her attention to it.

The blonde woman pulled herself up to her full height. Teetered on open-toe heeled sandals, she was still several inches shorter than me. "This *woman*," she spat, as if it was a curse word, "assaulted my son and I'd like to press charges."

"Her son—" I said, but Beau cut me off with a finger to his lips.

"Ma'am, I understand why you're upset. Of course, a stranger touching your child must be very disconcerting indeed."

She gave me a triumphant look. "It most certainly is."

"And if you want to press charges, I'd be happy to go to the station with you and take your statement. It's just a few miles walk that-a-way." He gestured back the way I'd come. "Probably won't take but an hour or two of your time. Three, tops."

The woman chewed her bottom lip, contemplating this turn of events. The last thing anyone wanted to do on a beautiful day like today was spend it in some stuffy police station, especially with an over-tired, over-stimulated child. "Well, I don't know about all that," she said, hesitantly.

"While you're making up your mind about that, I'd like to show you something." Beau leaned over the fence and plucked something out of the long grass. I cringed, thinking he was going to come up with a crushed bluebonnet. Contrary to the myth I'd been told growing up, it wasn't illegal to pick bluebonnets and hadn't been since the seventies, at least not outside of a state park or private property, but as a native Texan, the idea of hurting even a single bluebonnet was upsetting.

When Beau lifted his hand, there was a tiny snake wound around his fingers. The woman gasped. She dropped her funnel cake to wrap a protective arm around Davey as she took a step back. "These fields are beautiful, but you never know what might be hiding in them," Beau said, with a shake of his head. The snake flicked its tongue out. "Now this here's just a little ol' garter snake. Wouldn't hurt no one." He flinched as the annoyed snake struck at him and bit the meaty part of his thumb. "Okay, that stung."

He untangled the snake and gently returned it to where he'd found it. With the area roped off, both the snake and the festivalgoers should be safe. Beau shook his hand and flexed his fingers. "I'm sure you understand that these fences are here to protect y'all as much as they are to protect the bluebonnets. Garter snakes are just the tip of what you'll find around here. Could have been a rattler, or a copperhead. Wouldn't want anyone to get hurt, now would we?"

"Of course not," the woman said, still hugging her son to her legs.

"I'm so glad we see eye to eye," Beau drawled. I noticed he was putting it on extra-thick. The mother was eating it up. So was the crowd that was gathering around us. "Now the way I see it, we've got two choices. Y'all can follow me all the way back to the station and file that complaint we talked about, or, you can thank this nice lady for saving your son from a snake." He gave her that dazzling smile that turned my insides to butter, and asked, "What'll it be?"

She turned to me, looking a little off-balance. I felt sorry for her. I'd been on the receiving end of that smile a time or two and I knew what it could do to an unsuspecting victim. "Uh, I guess I owe you an apology."

"No worries," I said, using my friendliest customer-service voice. "Just happy Davey's safe."

"Yeah, um, okay. Well, thanks?" she said, but didn't sound sincere.

"Now that we got that all cleared up," Beau said, taking a half step between me and the unsettled mother, "I'd suggest you keep a closer eye on your son from here on out." He nudged her fallen funnel cake with the tip of his cowboy boot. "And you might want to pick that up. We don't appreciate litter in these parts. You know what they say; don't mess with Texas."

"Yeah, yeah, of course." She released her death grip on her son so she could bend over and clean up the mess. "Come on, Davey, let's get out of here," she said, nudging him forward as she hurried to the nearest trash can.

As soon as she was out of earshot and the small crowd we'd attracted dissipated, I nudged Beau with my shoulder. "Thanks."

"You know, keeping you out of trouble is getting to be a full-time job," he replied.

I nodded. "Not the first time I've heard that." My sisters had told me that a time or two when I was growing up.

"I'm on my way to Austin to chat with the coroner," he said. "You think you can behave for a few hours?"

"I could come with you if you want," I offered. "So you can keep an eye on me."

Beau bent over and gave me a peck on the top of my head. "Not a chance, Junebug."

"Whatever," I said. I knew he'd never agree to such a thing, but the fact that he was telling me that he was going to meet with the coroner was progress. He might not ever officially tell me anything about the investigation, but he was keeping me up to date. Baby steps. I smiled and let the slow-moving crowd propel me to my destination.

CHAPTER 8

When I reached the DJ booth, my sister Maggie saw me and threw herself around the table to catch me up in a bear hug. My middle sister was a few inches shorter than me, and her chestnut hair had enviable spiral curls that fell past her shoulders. As always, she wore a pretty, floral dress with a full skirt that would look equally suited for anything from running errands to attending a wedding. Keeping with the theme of the festival, all the flowers on her pale blue dress were darker variations of blue.

Out of the three of us, Maggie was the most reliable Jessup sister. I could always count on her to be there when I needed anything, just as I knew she'd be the first to tell me the hard truth when I needed to hear it. She was a math whiz, the perfect Texan hostess, and had a consistent swing that made her the anchor of the Cedar River softball team.

"I was so worried about you," she said once she'd stopped trying to crush the air out of my lungs. She stepped back to look at me. "Did you wear sunscreen today? You're looking a little pink."

"I knew I was forgetting something," I told her. I had to raise my voice to be heard over the live band on the stage.

Maggie dragged me behind the DJ table. Behind the enormous speakers, it was still loud, but no longer painfully so. "I heard you'd gotten arrested for killing the mayor."

I rolled my eyes. "That's not even close to true. Have you talked to your husband today? He was there."

"I haven't seen him since this morning. We keep missing each other. I texted him, but I don't think the message went through."

It was difficult to get a good cell phone signal in the park on a normal day, since it was right on the edge of the nearest cell tower's range. Days like this, when it was crowded, it would be easier to stand on the table and yell real loud than to call someone. "Have you started a suggestion list yet?" I asked her.

"Seriously? It's like you don't know me at all." My sister's lists were extraordinarily detailed. It was how she managed to keep the rest of the family organized.

"Can you add 'look into a cell phone booster,' and 'arrange shuttle service from the municipal parking lot,' please?" I asked.

She picked up a yellow legal pad. The first page was already half-full. Maggie jotted my suggestions down before coming back to her original question. "So you weren't arrested?"

"Of course I wasn't. I found the mayor's body and gave a statement to the police."

Maggie made a harrumphing noise. "Oh please. Let me guess, a certain Cedar River detective used a supposed interrogation to flirt with my baby sister."

"It wasn't like that," I said. "Beau was a perfect gentleman."

"Likely story. But if you're not on the hook for killing Mayor Bob, why did you call J.T. this morning?"

I clicked my tongue. "Does no one in this family talk to each other anymore? Mayor Bob died holding a cup of Sip & Spin coffee that he'd gotten from Tansy. But half the town dropped by the booth this morning to get a fix and no one else got ill, so I doubt there was anything wrong with the coffee. I can't believe Tansy didn't tell you any of this."

"By the time I came by to relieve her, she'd been working the booth by herself all morning without so much as a bathroom break. She waved at me and darted out of here like the devil was chasing her."

"Is that so?" I asked. That was odd. Not the running part. Our oldest sister ran marathons for fun. Sometimes I didn't think we were even related. But it wasn't like her to take off without catching Maggie up on the events of the morning. Like our mother, who practically lived for gossip, Tansy was almost always in the know. She didn't spread it around willy-nilly, and never exaggerated, but she was good at sharing information with us.

"I'm sure she'll be back," Maggie said. She looked around at the crowded park. "It's a great turnout this year."

"Y'all did a great job," I agreed. She was on the Bluebonnet Festival Committee, and deserved credit for all her hard work. "I'm so glad you suggested having Sip & Spin sponsor the music booth. That was a stroke of genius." Technically, marketing fell under my job description as the internet guru of the family, but we were all responsible for the success of our record shop.

"Thank you," she said proudly. The band onstage wrapped up their performance. After a hearty round of applause, they started packing up their instruments. Maggie selected a record from the stack, placed it on the turntable, and set the needle in the groove. As Bob Marley began playing over the loudspeakers, Maggie turned to me. "All jokes aside, I hear you're getting friendly with Beau Russell again. Joyce Whedon saw you two at a bar in Austin, and it looked cozy."

I didn't want to talk about Beau right now. Unlike Tansy, Maggie was rooting for us to get back together. I knew that no matter which way I went, I would be disappointing someone. Since I'd rather not worry about that at this moment, I changed the subject. "Speaking of dates, have you met Mom's new boyfriend yet?"

"Her *what*?" Maggie asked, her eyes wide.

"His name's Marcus Best, the guy from the car commercials."

"Mom's dating a used car salesperson?" Maggie looked like she was going to cry.

"I'm sorry, I didn't mean to upset you. I assumed you'd be happy for her. You're always such a romantic."

"There's nothing romantic about a married woman dating a used car salesperson," my sister said, crossing her arms over her chest.

"A widowed woman," I gently corrected her. "As much as I don't want to like it, Dad's gone. And Mom deserves to be happy."

"You think this Marcus Best joker can make Mom happy?" She snatched up her purse and dug through it until she came up with her phone. "Ugh. No bars. I'm gonna take a walk until I get a signal." She dropped her purse on the table and took off before I could stop her.

"Um, excuse me?"

I looked up and there was a white woman standing on the other side of the DJ booth. She wore a straw cowboy hat and a long sundress covered in yellow sunflowers. She was holding out a piece of paper. I took it automatically. "Here's the introduction for the band, and between the second and third songs, if you'd just read what's on the back, that'd be great. Thanks!" She turned and hurried toward the stage.

Without waiting for the song on the record player to come to an end—I didn't want to give myself a chance to chicken out—I lifted the needle and turned on the microphone. Stage fright or not, someone had to introduce the next band and I was the only person in the booth. Which, come to think of it, was all my fault. If I'd only answered her question about Beau honestly instead of bringing up Mom's love life, Maggie would be here to do the announcements. Served me right. With trembling hands, I stumbled through the intro and then the band launched into their set.

The rest of the afternoon passed uneventfully. Neither Tansy or Maggie returned, but I cycled the bands through without any major incident. I didn't like being behind the microphone, but I didn't embarrass myself too badly. Still, I was happy when the last band wrapped up their set.

Like pretty much everything in Cedar River, the Bluebonnet Festival wound down at sunset, when Cedar River Memorial Park officially closed for the night. The vendors around me were busy cleaning up their surrounding areas and securing their merchandise. I wasn't sure what the plan was for the DJ booth. I didn't want to leave the expensive equipment and records out overnight, exposed to the elements, but my bike was still parked at Town Hall and it would take me forever to carry all of this back to the shop one load at a time, just to have to set it up again in the morning.

"Can I give you a hand with that?" I looked up to see Marcus Best standing in front of the table. "Your mom suggested I swing by and see if you need anything."

The rumble of an approaching truck got my attention. I looked up and recognized my uncle Calvin's old Bronco. He must have circled the park on the far side and come up between the trees to end up behind the booth. Thank goodness for four-wheel drive. The truck rolled to a stop and Tansy got out of the driver's seat. "Sorry I'm late. I had to wait for the crowds to thin out to get back here." Leaving the headlights on to help illuminate the booth, she walked around to the bright orange and white rental tow-behind trailer that was hitched to the back of the truck and opened the door.

"I still can't believe Uncle Calvin loaned you his truck this weekend," I said. Calvin didn't let anyone drive his precious Bronco. I'd borrowed it recently—without his permission—and got a flat tire. I wasn't sure he was ever going to forgive me for that.

"He owes us," Tansy said. "Let's get started."

"What can I do?" Marcus asked.

Tansy shielded her eyes from the bright lights of the headlights, noticing him for the first time. "What are you doing here?"

He held out his hands. "Came by to lend a hand, and it looks like y'all can use it. So how can I help?"

Tansy said, "We need to get the soundboard and the record player into the trailer. I've got some tarps to cover the big speakers, but anything else that isn't nailed down needs to be secured."

Together, the three of us made short work of it. Once everything was locked up, I asked Tansy, "Mind giving me a ride back to town? My trike's in the municipal lot."

"Sure. Jump in." She hesitated a second, then added, "Marcus, need a lift?"

He smiled at her. "Thanks, but it's such a nice night, I think I'll walk back to the parking lot."

"You live nearby?" I asked. "I've never seen you around town before."

"I've got a place up north of Dallas, near my original

dealership, but I mostly stay at my condo in Austin these days, so I don't have far to drive," he replied.

"Have a safe trip home," I said. He waved and headed down the path. "That was nice of him to help out," I said as I climbed into the passenger seat.

"Yeah, he's not so bad," Tansy said, putting the Bronco into gear and carefully backing out. "Have you heard anything more from the police?"

I shook my head. "Nope." I pulled out my phone and checked the screen. There were no new notifications, but I still didn't have a signal. "Not yet."

"I can't believe they think that we had something to do with Mayor Bob's death." My sister concentrated on the windshield as she navigated our uncle's Bronco over the bumpy ground surrounding the park. "It's nonsense. I don't even know why he was drinking our coffee this morning, if he disliked it so much."

"I don't want to think about it," I admitted.

Most of the tourists had left, but there was a minor traffic jam as the vendors filed out of the parking lot. "Your trike is in the municipal lot?" she asked as we waited our turn.

"Yeah. Mind dropping me there?"

"No problem." Tansy pulled into the lot and stopped in front of Town Hall. I looked up at the dark windows and felt a tugging sensation in my gut. "You alright?" she asked.

"Yeah." I unbuckled my seat belt and opened the passenger door. "I would just be a lot better if I'd stop finding dead bodies."

Tansy laughed. "Trust me, Juni, we'd all be happier."

I had to chuckle along with her. "Thanks for the ride. See you at home." I hopped out of the Bronco and closed the door behind me.

My tricycle was just where I'd left it. Normally I didn't worry about it. Cedar River was a close-knit community. If anyone took my lime green adult tricycle for a joy ride, someone would turn them in before they got more than a few blocks away. But with all the strangers in town for the Bluebonnet Festival, I should probably get into the habit of locking it to a bike stand.

As I rode back to the house I shared with my oldest sister, the stresses of the day faded away. I knew Marcus meant well by offering to help me find an affordable used car, but I truly enjoyed riding through the streets of Cedar River on my trike, especially on a quiet, mild spring night like this one. It was relaxing. By the time I got home, I felt like a new person.

CHAPTER 9

The second day of the Bluebonnet Festival started with Tansy flinging open my bedroom door and announcing, "Wakey, wakey, eggs and bakey."

I groaned. Unlike my sister, I was *not* a morning person. I burrowed under the covers and pretended I didn't hear her.

"Come on, Juni, we've got to get set up."

"Five more minutes," I pleaded.

She flung my covers off. "Come on. You're not a teenager anymore."

"Fine," I said. I sat up and rubbed my eyes. The world was a blur. I reached for my tortoiseshell glasses and put them on. "That's better," I said, stumbling toward the bathroom.

"We're late. You don't have time for a long shower this morning."

"Oof," I said.

"Hurry up and get dressed."

I loved my sister with my whole heart, but she could be so bossy sometimes. I showered quickly before dressing in shorts and a blue Taylor Swift concert tee. Feeling slightly more like myself, I wandered into the kitchen.

"You haven't started coffee yet?" I asked, making a bee-line for the empty pot.

"No time for that," Tansy said, propelling me toward the front door.

"This is cruel and unusual," I muttered, as I trudged to our uncle's Bronco.

"Stop complaining," Tansy said with a sunny grin. "I've already been up for an hour. I got a three-mile run in this morning while you slept in."

"Slept in?" I glanced at the clock on the dashboard. "It's not even seven o'clock yet." I must have dozed off, because before I knew it, Tansy was pulling the Bronco around to the back of the DJ booth. I stumbled out of the truck and blinked at the sight of Beau leaning against the table, grinning at me. He straightened and met me half-way, holding a deli bag in one hand and a reusable coffee mug in the other. He handed me the mug.

"I'm dreaming, right?" I asked.

"Aww, I'm the man of your dreams," Beau joked.

I took a sip of the coffee. It was the Goldilocks of coffee—not too hot, not too bitter, and not too sweet. I couldn't have made it better myself. I pointed at the white deli bag. "That for me, too?"

He opened it and held it out. "Orange cranberry scones, baked fresh this morning."

Before I could take one, Tansy reached around me and snatched the one on top. She pushed half of it into her mouth, and then asked with her mouth full, "Where's my coffee?"

"For you, I have something better." He gestured at the table, where our coffeepot had returned. "The lab assures me that there's nothing wrong with it. And yes, I cleaned it before I brought it back."

"You better have," Tansy said, checking it out to make

sure it was no worse for the wear. "Thanks for bringing it back so quickly."

"Anytime," he said, nodding at her. I don't think that Beau Russell would ever be my biggest sister's favorite person, but he'd earned massive brownie points this morning. Not only did he rush to bring the coffee maker back, but orange cranberry scones weren't my favorite breakfast treat. They were hers.

"Oh no," I said. "In all the excitement, I forgot to grind fresh beans this morning."

"No big deal. After we set up, you can go get some from the shop," Tansy suggested.

"Put me to work," Beau offered.

Tansy might never like him, but he had shown up early, with a delicious peace offering, and was now volunteering to help us haul the heavy sound equipment back out of the trailer. If that didn't make him just about perfect, I didn't know what did.

"Thanks," Tansy said, grudgingly.

A few minutes later, the trailer was empty. Tansy was running wires. We offered to help, but she waved us off, saying that we would just get in her way. Then she tossed me Uncle Calvin's keys with a stern warning to not get so much a scratch on his almost forty-year-old truck and told me to hurry up with the coffee.

Beau got into the passenger seat.

"You're coming with me?" I asked.

"Well, it's either that or you leave me alone with Tansy and hope that she doesn't murder me."

"She wouldn't murder you," I assured him.

"I'd rather not take my chances." He rested a hand on my knee, which was a distraction as I maneuvered the unwieldy Bronco over the rough terrain.

I noticed he had a bandage on his thumb. "That from the snake bite?" I asked.

He nodded.

"Sorry about that."

"Don't apologize. I'd rather get nipped than some kid get hurt." He frowned. "That woman should have given you a medal."

"To be honest, I was more worried about the bluebonnets," I admitted. "I never saw the snake until you picked it up. I'm glad you came along when you did."

"You know I always look out for you, Junebug," he said.

"And, thanks for bringing the coffee maker back. That was awful fast. Did you get the rest of the test results back yet?"

Beau barked out a laugh. "Good try, but unlike that snake, I'm not going to bite."

"Fair enough," I agreed affably. I hadn't expected him to give me a real answer. I didn't even need him to. I had Kitty for that. I'd call her later and see if she knew the cause of death by now.

"That was too easy," Beau said, grabbing the handle over the door as we bumped over the curb. "I've never known you to give up that quick. What are you planning?"

"Me?" I asked, trying to sound innocent. I shook my head. "Nothing."

"If you're going to try to charm the coroner into releasing information to you, I'm telling you, you're wasting your time. The Austin morgue is a lot more secure than the Cedar River one."

"Nice to know," I said. He knew me well enough to guess that I was up to something, but couldn't figure out what. Good. I liked making him squirm.

I navigated downtown and pulled up in front of Sip & Spin Records. Normally I despised parallel parking and would never have attempted it in the Bronco, especially with a trailer hitched to the back. But with no one around, I was able to pull up against the curb with no difficulty. In a few hours, every parking spot in town would be taken, but I guess there were some bonuses to being the early bird. "Want to come in for coffee?" I offered.

"Some other time," he said. We got out of the truck and he stood next to me as I fished the shop keys out of my bag. "Juni?"

"Yeah?"

"I was serious yesterday. Please, don't go sticking your nose into this."

"I heard you the first time," I told him.

It wasn't the promise he wanted, so he kept pressing. "Promise me you'll let me do my job. I can't focus on my investigation if I'm worrying about you."

I turned to him. "There's nothing to worry about, Beau. This is nothing like last time. I don't have a stake in the matter," I said, honestly.

He gave me a wry laugh. "That's rich. See, this is why I have a hard time believing you. Your coffee is the probable murder weapon and you claim you don't have a stake in this?"

"What?" I asked, pausing with the key in the lock. "So it's true? Mayor Bob *was* murdered? And Sip & Spin is involved?"

Beau groaned. "I didn't say that."

"Yes, you did." I let that sink in. For the second time in as many months, my family was implicated in a murder. Ridiculous! And Beau thought I'd just sit around doing nothing while we were being investigated? Not hardly. "This changes everything."

"This changes nothing," he insisted.

I'd known Beau since we were both teenagers, but

sometimes I wondered if he knew me at all. This was one of those times. I opened the door. "Then find out who really killed him without dragging me, my sisters, or Sip & Spin through the mud."

"I can't promise anything," Beau said.

"In that case, neither can I," I replied. I stepped inside my shop, closed the door, and locked it behind me. Beau rapped on the glass. I ignored him, my brain preoccupied with this new information.

Running on autopilot as I tried to process Beau's revelation, I flipped on the lights before heading to the back of the shop. "Daffy? Sweet Daffodil, where are you, buddy?" I called out, and was immediately answered by a plaintive meow. "Hey, sweetie," I said, scooping him up. "You miss me?" I felt his purr through his soft fur. "I missed you too." I gave him fresh food and water, and cleaned the litter pan. Then I scrubbed my hands thoroughly.

The barista station was silent, as were the overhead speakers. It felt like Sip & Spin was holding its breath, or maybe that was just me. I knew that opening a small business was risky, but I had no idea just how risky it would be until our very existence had been threatened twice in as many months. All I wanted to do was provide good music and fun coffee flavors to my neighbors. Was that really asking so much?

Why did Mayor Bob have to die while drinking one of our coffees? It just didn't seem fair. I stopped myself. In the grand scheme of things, I shouldn't complain. Bob had paid a much higher price. Even if we did lose the shop over a fatal cup of coffee, at least I still had my family, and my friends, and a roof over my head.

I surveyed the record shop. It was so similar to the shop my grandparents and parents had run before us. I couldn't lose this. I just couldn't.

As if reading my mind, Daffy jumped up on the counter and meowed. "Don't worry, Daffy. Even if we close the shop, you'll always have a place with us," I assured him, but I wondered how true that was. This was Daffodil's home. If we lost Sip & Spin, would he choose to stay with the new shop owners or would he come home with Tansy and me? Hopefully, we would never have to find out.

One thing was certain. Clearing our name wouldn't matter if we couldn't pay our bills. Closing the shop for the weekend was hard on the bottom line. We would only make up a tiny amount of lost potential sales by selling coffee at the festival, but every little drop helped. Besides, it could drum up future business.

Buoyed by that thought, I opened the coffee cabinets and looked inside. We needed something special today to make up for the fact that we were working with a limited coffee maker with no foam or steamed options to offer.

Normally, I would never serve similar coffee specials back-to-back, but hardly anyone had the opportunity to try the blueberry coffee we'd ordered for this occasion. It was a mild coffee on its own, which is why yesterday, I'd blended it with a French roast. Today, I decided to lean into the natural smoothness and go for a lighter coffee, one that didn't need fancy foam art to make it special.

We had a mellow Ethiopian bean that was always popular with coffee connoisseurs. I mixed it carefully with the remaining blueberry coffee beans and ran enough through the grinder to hopefully last us through the day. Once it was packaged, I said goodbye to Daffy and let myself out, being sure to lock the door.

It would have been nice to have my trike, but since I'd left it at home, I walked to the park. It was early and festivalgoers hadn't started arriving yet. That gave me the chance to scope out the other vendors as I made my way back to the main stage, making mental notes of every place I wanted to visit once I had a break today.

"So? What did you come up with?" Tansy asked as soon as I got within earshot. She and Maggie were setting out cups and stir sticks in anticipation for my return.

I patted my reusable market bag. "It's a surprise." Tansy had already filled the reservoir with water and set up the filter. All I had to do was measure out the freshly ground beans and turn it on.

By the time the first pot was ready, we already had a line in front of the DJ booth. There was nothing like the smell of brewing coffee to draw a crowd. I poured cups for my sisters and myself. We toasted each other and then took our first sips.

"Oh my gosh, this is delicious," Tansy said.

Maggie took another sip. "She's right. This is amazing."

"It really is, if I say so myself. I'm calling it Bluebonnet Suede Brews."

I heard a few grumbles in the line, and turned to address them. "Hold your horses, there's enough for everyone." But then I realized they weren't complaining that my sisters and I were the first ones to sample my new creation, but rather were upset because a woman was weaving her way to the front of the line without so much as a "Pardon me."

When she got to the front of the line, she gave my sisters and me a pleasant smile. "Morning, Tansy, Maggie, Juni."

"Morning, Leanna," Tansy said through gritted teeth.

Leanna Lydell-Waite and Tansy had been rivals their entire lives. Both were in the beauty pageant circuit until their teens, and for years they competed against each other, always swapping out who came in first and who came in second. If Leanna won Homecoming Queen, Tansy would win Prom Queen. They were both on the regional track team and county swim team. Tansy would bring home first place for the 500-meter race, then Leanna would win the hurdles. If Leanna won the butterfly, Tansy would come in first for the freestyle.

When Leanna had announced that she was running for a seat on the town council, I'd asked Tansy why she didn't oppose her. "There are two open spots," she'd told me. "With my luck we'd both win and then I'd have to sit in the same room with her at every council meeting." It was probably for the best that Tansy hadn't run. If they were both on the council and one of them proposed an action to replace the streetlights on Main Street, the other would vote against it just to be contrary.

"Excuse me, but can I borrow the mic real quick?" Leanna asked, pulling me back to the here and now.

I switched off the record—we'd been playing The Smashing Pumpkins—and handed her the microphone.

She turned to face the line. "Morning, everyone. As I'm sure you've heard by now, we lost our beloved mayor, Bob Bobbert, yesterday. I know y'all feel just sick about that. I do too. Everyone knows the Bluebonnet Festival was his absolute favorite time of the year, and after calling an emergency town council meeting last night, we decided unanimously that the festival should go on as scheduled."

I glanced over at my sisters. I hadn't even considered that the festival might get cancelled. They looked as surprised as I felt.

Leanna continued, "It's okay to be sad. We'll all miss Mayor Bob very much. But he would want us to celebrate his life the way he lived—to the very fullest. Please join me in a moment of silence while we all reflect on the life and legacy of Bob Bobbert." She lowered the mic and bowed her head. After a moment of hesitation, everyone followed her example.

After what felt like only a few seconds, she lifted her head and the microphone, and continued. "Now let's all get out there and have the best Bluebonnet Festival Cedar River has ever seen. For Mayor Bob!" she said.

"For Mayor Bob!" the crowd echoed.

She handed the mic back to me. "Thanks. I just felt like someone should say something, you know? As acting mayor . . ."

"Wait a second, you're the acting mayor?" Tansy asked.

"Of course. I'm chair of the town council. Who else would step up in such a time of tragedy? As I was saying, as acting mayor, if you need anything, anything at all, don't hesitate to come to me." She gave us a toothy grin before walking away.

"I told you that you should have run for town council when you had the chance," I whispered to my sister. Then I turned to the waiting line. "Okay folks, who wants coffee?"

CHAPTER 10

Bluebonnet Suede Brews was a hit. Several of my favorite Cedar River citizens came back for seconds before the out-of-towners even started filtering into the park. Granted, almost everyone was more interested in details about Mayor Bob's death than coffee, but apparently the connection between his death and our coffee had yet to make the rounds, because everyone was drinking up.

"It's a crying shame," Sally Mae said as she poured her coffee. Sally Mae worked at the diner on Main Street. A short, curvy white woman a few years younger than me, she always had a sunny smile and a friendly word for everyone. "Mayor Bob was always so good at his job."

I nodded in agreement, even though I was still a little fuzzy about what he'd ever done that was so special. "What exactly do you feel he did that was so great?"

"Oh." She looked startled at the question. "I mean, look around. The Bluebonnet Festival is the best it's ever been, thanks to Mayor Bob."

"Uh-huh, yeah, sure," I said to appease her. I'd never been much into local politics, but even I knew that the Festival Committee was made up by citizen volunteers like my sister Maggie, and that its budget was approved by the town council, not the mayor.

As Sally Mae took her coffee and left, our uncle stepped up. "Well, lookee here. It's my three favorite girls."

"Morning, Uncle Calvin," we said more or less in sync.

Mom's older brother was a large man with an even larger personality. His hair and mustache were mostly gray these days, and as usual he wore a checkered button-down shirt with a bolo tie around his neck. Today's bolo had a pair of enamel bluebonnets as its clasp.

"Love the tie. Where'd you get it?" I asked him.

He waved behind him. "One of the artisan booths. Y'all really outdid yourselves this year. I can't remember ever seeing so many people at the festival before. That first year, back in April of 'forty-six . . ."

I cut him off before he could finish that thought. My uncle was a walking encyclopedia and a natural talker. If I let him, he'd still be rambling on about obscure trivia long after the festival was over. "Coffee?" I asked. "And apparently, all the credit for the festival goes to Mayor Bob."

He'd brought me a travel mug. As long as they were clean, I loved it when people brought their own reusable containers. It kept paper cups out of the landfills and cut down on our costs. "Hard to believe Bob's gone. I've been voting for him since 2010," Uncle Calvin said.

"You and everyone else in Cedar River," I agreed. "Why did you vote for him?"

"Well . . ." He scratched his temple. "I mean, he's almost always the only name on the ballot. Sure that one time that New Yorker fellow tried to run against him, and we all know how *that* turned out."

I had to smile. Anything less than a third-generation Texan was an outsider in a town like Cedar River. A politician from out of state didn't stand a snowball's chance in July of winning public office.

Mickey, the person in line behind my uncle, wasn't so generous with their praise. "I don't see what all the fuss is about," they grumbled as Calvin wandered off with his coffee. Mickey worked at the car rental place out by the municipal airport. "All politicians are crooked. Every single one of them."

"Not Mayor Bob!" the woman behind them said, looking scandalized. Jen Rachet was a middle-aged white woman who always looked like her shoes were one size too small. She was a several times great-granddaughter of one of the founders of Cedar River, and considered herself local royalty. Like my mother, she had a hardline wired directly into the town grapevine. Unlike my mother, she didn't mind spreading malicious gossip just to get attention.

"Especially Mayor Bob," Mickey said. "Just last month, he approved the sale of Cedar River town property to a commercial developer without so much as bringing it up for public debate. The last thing we need is one of those big box stores coming in and running the rest of us out of business."

I glanced over at Tansy and Maggie. "Did you know about this?"

They shook her heads. "This is the first I'm hearing about it," Tansy said.

Jen addressed Mickey. "Even if he did sell excess property, the mayor doesn't have the authority to rezone rural land without the council's approval, so it's useless for developers."

"Well, he did. Rawlings Hollow no longer belongs to the town of Cedar River. It's a commercial lot now," they said with an air of authority.

Rawlings Hollow was on the far outskirts of town. Back when I was in the Girl Scouts, we used to camp out there.

I could still recall the taste of campfire-roasted s'mores from those days. A few years later, someone tried to organize a Woodstock-like festival out there that flopped when all the musical acts got lost and ended up spending the weekend playing Austin bars instead. The original Bluebonnet Festival used to be held out there, until it was moved to Cedar River Memorial Park downtown, closer to paved roads and running water.

"Well, Cedar River can buy or sell property as it sees fit," Jen Rachet argued. "It's all aboveboard and legal. When we voted for him, we gave Mayor Bob authority, and I'd rather get rid of an overgrown plot that no one's worked for generations than raise taxes."

"Yeah, but selling public land to a developer? We should have a say in what happens in our town," Mickey said emphatically.

"You've got a point," I agreed. "And I'd love to hear more, but there's a line behind you, and I need to take care of them."

"See? That's what I'm talking about. Real service. Can't get that from a chain box store, can you?" Mickey paid for their coffee and left.

"I wonder what store is coming in?" I asked my sisters.

"No clue. This is the first I'm hearing about it. You should ask Leanna what she knows," Maggie suggested.

"Or," I suggested, "Tansy can. She's your friend, after all."

"I'd hardly call Leanna a friend," Tansy grumbled.

"Leanna? Leanna Lydell-Waite? Isn't she absolutely the best?" Jen said, leaning in to join the conversation. "I mean, sure, it's horrible under the circumstances, but I've been saying for ages that we need some new blood in the mayor's office, and a woman at that." She gestured to her cup. "Be a dear and top this off with steamed oat milk."

"I'm so sorry, but we're limited on what we can serve out here," Tansy said. She pointed at the basket with the cream and sweetener packets. "Help yourself."

"But you always have oat milk at Sip & Spin!" she insisted.

"True, but the steamer's back at the shop," I said. I fished a sticker out of the box and initialed the back. "Bring this in tomorrow for ten percent off your next cup of coffee."

Placated, Jen took her coffee and her sticker, and walked away.

"You're pretty good at that, Juni," said the next customer in line.

Happy to hear a familiar voice, I looked up to see Teddy waiting his turn. "And a good morning to you, too. Okay, I know you don't like fancy coffees but this is a drip brew with no added syrup. The blueberry coffee is naturally sweet because blueberries were packed with the beans, so no artificial flavoring. And the Ethiopian bean I blended it with is a milder version of the Colombian beans you already like so much," I told him, hoping to convince him to try something new.

"Sounds great, but I'm not actually here for coffee." He turned to my sisters. "Can I borrow her for an hour or two?"

Tansy looked over the line. It was only a few people deep, not like it had been earlier in the morning. "Sure. I think Maggie and I can handle it. You kids go have fun."

Why did I have the feeling that if Beau had asked the same question, she wouldn't have been so accommodating? No matter. I grabbed my bag, told my sisters I'd be back later, and followed Teddy.

"Sorry you didn't win the hole-digging contest yesterday," I told him.

"It was fun just being able to participate," he said diplomatically. He stepped off to one side of the path so we could pause without blocking traffic. "Where do we start?"

"That depends. What do you have in mind?" I asked.

"I'm thinking it's a toss-up between the blackberry cobbler bites, sweet corn cakes, tacos on a stick, loaded stuffed potato pancakes, or the beer-battered cheese curds."

"You realize that the way to my heart is through my stomach, don't you?" I joked.

He nodded. "Why do you think I scouted out every booth yesterday? Oh, and whatever you pick, leave room for dessert." He pointed over his shoulder. "My mom's serving homemade ice cream, and she has a new peaches and mint ice cream that will make your toes curl."

"That," I decided. "I want that first, before she runs out."

Teddy led me toward his mother's booth.

As we waited in the long line, I started to worry that she might actually sell out, but when we got to the front of the queue, peaches and mint was still on the chalk menu board. Teddy's mom beamed when she saw us. "Señorita Juniper, it's been too long," she said, reaching out to grab my hands warmly. "Teo says you've been back in town a few months now, but you haven't come around."

"Señora Garza, I've missed you, too. How's the dairy business treating you?" Teddy's family owned a small farm near the edge of town. His mother, and her mother before her, and on back as long as anyone could remember, had made flavored cheese and unique ice cream combinations.

"Bueno, bueno," she replied. "I've been thinking about making a new coffee variety, but I can't get it quite right.

Maybe I can bribe the best barista in town to give me some pointers?"

"Happy to help." I took a bite of the peaches and mint ice cream, and my eyes rolled back into my head. "But only if you let us start buying your whole milk for Sip & Spin. Our supplier was late on the last two shipments and we need a reliable, local source of dairy."

"You have yourself a deal, señorita," she agreed.

"Fantastic. Maggie will call you to make arrangements for the milk, and I'll stop by soon to work on the ice cream with you."

I tried to pay for the scoop of peaches and mint, but she waved me away. "On the house. You two have fun at the festival," she said, before turning her attention to the next person in line.

"I love your mom," I told Teddy as we wandered to the next booth. My bowl was already empty and now I was sucking on the spoon.

"The feeling's mutual. Out of all the kids we grew up with, she liked you the best."

"Really? Because everyone else in town seems to think I'm a troublemaker."

Teddy laughed. "You? You're not a troublemaker."

"I found a dead body yesterday," I reminded him. "And another one just last month."

"That's not your fault."

"Are you sure about that? Beau seems to think that somehow it is."

"Well, Beauregard Russell's an idiot," Teddy said matter-of-factly. "Always has been. Always will be."

"He means well," I said. "All this talk of dead bodies and ex-boyfriends is threatening to ruin my appetite."

"We can't have that, now can we?" Teddy said, with a gleam in his eye. "You have a big decision to make, Juni."

Uh-oh. I knew I shouldn't have mentioned Beau. I couldn't keep stringing them both along, but how was I supposed to pick one over the other? Teddy was fantastic. Sweet. Handsome. Down to earth. A hard worker who loved his mama. Beau? He made me weak in the knees, but he'd broken my heart once and, given half the chance, I was afraid he'd do it again. Teddy was the kind of man I could bring home to supper. Beau was the kind of man who skipped supper and headed straight for dessert. "Umm . . ."

"Come on, Juni, it's not that hard. Just follow your heart. Sweet or savory?"

"Sweet or savory?" I asked, confused.

"Ding, ding. Time's up. I'm making the decision for you." He dragged me into the next line. "This is gonna knock your socks off," he promised. "It's the best of both worlds. Deep-fried peanut butter and grape jelly sandwiches."

True to his word, Teddy and I ate our way across the festival until I couldn't eat another bite. "We can try the sack races. Or how about the midway?" he suggested.

I glanced up at the rickety fair rides taking up half of the parking lot. "I'm not so sure I'd trust those even on an empty stomach." Then I saw the signs leading to the 4-H tents. "Wanna check out the animals?"

I know, I know. I grew up in rural Texas. Many of my friends had chickens or goats, and half the people I knew owned at least one horse. Teddy had a whole farm's worth of cows. There were jackrabbits, road runners, and coyotes all over the place. When I was little, I once had an armadillo for a pet for three whole weeks—until Maggie ratted me out to Dad, and he made me release it. I'm not proud of it, but I've been cow tipping. It was silly for someone who grew up in the country to get excited to see baby piglets and sheep, but it was what it was.

"4-H tents it is," Teddy agreed affably.

We took our time, petting the smaller animals and entering raffles to guess the weights of the giant cow and enormous draft horse on display in the big tent. We watched a calf being born and tossed corn kernels to some fancy ducks. We bet on the pig races, but our pig came in last.

Then my phone buzzed. I looked down at the screen, impressed that a message had managed to get through, before realizing it wasn't a text. It was a reminder alert on my calendar. "Looks like the Blue Bonnet Parade is about to begin," I said.

"Come on, Juni. Let's hang around for just one more pig race. Since when did you care about bonnets anyway?"

"Since my sister roped me into being one of the judges," I told him. "Thanks, Teddy. This was a lot of fun." Impulsively I gave him a peck on the cheek before I turned to leave.

"Sure was," he said as I hurried toward the Blue Bonnet Parade.

CHAPTER 11

The Blue Bonnet Parade started as a joke. Back when the Cedar River Bluebonnet Festival was just getting started, hosting any gathering was enough to draw in crowds from surrounding towns. Then, as other festivals started to spring up—no pun intended—Cedar River had to up our game to stay relevant. We added more food vendors and carnival rides, but could never compete with the enormous fairs that got tens of thousands of visitors. Our little festival was destined for obscurity when someone came up with the brilliant idea to add a parade.

Anyone could join in, as long as they wore a blue hat. The parade evolved over the years until the Blue Bonnet Parade became the Met Gala of hats. Not even the Kentucky Derby or Easter Sunday could hold a candle to our over-the-top headwear, at least not in my opinion.

The rules were simple. The hat had to be made and decorated by hand. Store-bought or reused hats could be worn in the parade, but were ineligible for a prize. The hat had to stand on its own—the wearer could support it with a hand as they walked, but must be able to balance it for at least thirty seconds during judging. And most importantly, the hat *must* be blue.

I took my seat at the judges' table as the Cedar River

High School Marching Band kicked off the festivities, in their signature blue and white uniforms led by our mascot, Arty the Armadillo. "I was afraid you'd be late," Maggie said as she handed me an official clipboard to record my scores.

"Of course not. Wouldn't miss this for the world," I assured her. Granted, I'd been having so much fun I'd almost forgotten about the Blue Bonnet Parade entirely. Thank goodness I'd set an alarm. The only way I would ever prove to my family that I was a responsible adult was by consistently acting like one.

Officer Jayden Holt, out of uniform for the occasion, was seated to my right. "How'd they rope you into this?" I asked her.

"Have you ever tried telling your sister 'No?'" she asked in return.

I grinned. "Maggie has a way with people. Runs in the family. That's how I know that Tansy would never need to hurt a fly. If either of my sisters had a problem with someone, they could take care of it without slipping anything into their coffee."

"Look, about yesterday, I was just doing my job, okay?"

"Yup." I nodded. "And taking care of my family is my job. For the record, I'm not concerned that you interrogated my sister, just that you and Beau tricked me so you could ambush her."

Jayden lifted a finger and pointed it at me. "I needed to judge your sister's initial reaction for myself, and I couldn't have done that if you'd warned her ahead of time. And for the record, it wasn't my idea." She narrowed her eyes at me. "It's not my fault that you—and apparently every other woman within a hundred miles—turns to putty when Beau ratchets up the charm."

Whether or not I wanted to admit it, she had a point. "And what? You're miraculously immune?"

"He's not my type," she replied.

"Ladies, if you're done gossiping, we have a job to do," the other judge said as she approached. Leanna Lydell-Waite took her seat on my left.

"Acting Mayor Lydell-Waite," Jayden said formally.

"Officer Holt," she replied with a polite but terse nod.

I looked back and forth between the two of them. There was bad blood there, I'd bet on it. Jayden was fairly new to town, but as a member of the local police force, she was afforded a pass on the "outsider until three generations" rule. Besides, even if she wasn't from Cedar River originally, she was a native Texan.

Jayden crossed her arms and leaned back in her chair. "I'm surprised to see that the town found the money to host the festival this year, seeing as how the budget is so tight that cuts are necessary. Isn't that how you put it?"

"Officer Holt, this isn't the time to rehash that," Leanna replied.

"Leanna, that was a very nice speech you made this morning," I told her, trying to steer the subject into more neutral territory.

"Why thank you for saying so, Juni. I know I'm not the most popular person in Cedar River right now." She turned and glared pointedly at Jayden. "Of course, filling Mayor Bob's shoes is an enormous responsibility. But someone has to step up, and as chair of the town council, that someone is me. Which means that until we elect a replacement, I'm in charge of the town budget."

Jayden opened her mouth, but before she could say anything, I jumped in, continuing to play peacemaker. "And I'm sure you'll do a fantastic job." The marching band passed and the sound system—presumably DJ'd by

Tansy—took over, effectively cutting off any more attempts at conversation. The loud, lively music had the parade participants and the crowd dancing.

Plenty of people joined that Blue Bonnet Parade for the fun of it, wearing everything from top hats covered in blue craft-store-bought silk flowers to the baseball caps with bluebonnets on springs that were sold at the official Cedar River booth, but the real stars of the parade were the contestants. The first one stopped in front of our table and struck a pose. Her hat was made entirely out of LEGO blocks in the shape of a bluebonnet. Maggie ran out, measured it, and made a note on her own clipboard.

The next hat was a wide sombrero shape made entirely of blue feathers. The contestant left a cloud of feathers behind her as she walked, and I wouldn't be surprised if by the end of the parade her hat was plucked bare.

There were hats that lit up and hats that blew soap bubbles. There was an enormous hat made of balloons that reminded me of the grape Fruit of the Loom guy. There were knitted caps, bonnets made of crepe paper, and several oversize blue cowboy hats constructed from Styrofoam. There was even a hat with lit sparklers on it.

A group of children trooped past with pipe-cleaner gardens glued to their hats, followed by an air-filled, whacky, wiggly-wavy-arm guy balanced on someone's head. One woman had constructed an enormous bluebonnet piñata hat, and was tossing candy to the eager crowd.

Just when I thought I'd seen everything, a stout woman pushed her way through the crowd on the other side of the street, flanked by angry people who had staked out their spots along the parade route far in advance. Despite protests all around her, she shoved the temporary barricades separating the parade from the spectators aside and marched into the street, knocking down a man wearing a towering hat made of what looked like blue whipped cream.

Without pausing to see if he was okay—he wasn't; his hat splattered all across the pavement—she marched forward, coming to a stop in front of the judging table. It was hard to tell her age, but I guessed she was in her late sixties. The white woman was wearing a bright yellow shirt with white capri pants. Her hair was steel gray and she had on thick makeup topped with garish red lipstick. She dragged a large wheeled suitcase behind her, which was causing a parade traffic jam. She was yelling, but I couldn't hear her over the music. Then there was brief moment of silence between albums, and I heard, "What in heaven's name were you thinking?"

"Mrs. Bobbert?" Leanna asked, standing and scurrying around the table. That was when I recognized Faye Bobbert, Mayor Bob's widow, as the woman with the suitcase.

"Here, let me take your bag," Leanna offered. "Let's go somewhere we can talk."

"You are the last person I want to talk to, young lady," she snapped. Her chin trembled. "What were you thinking? You could have at least tried to contact me!"

Leanna looked around for support, before seeming to realize that she was the one in charge now. "I left you several voicemails."

"I was on a cruise," Faye Bobbert said, like she was speaking down to a child. "I didn't exactly have phone service."

Unaware of the drama playing out, the music picked up again. This time, a jaunty version of "If You're Happy and You Know It" blasted out of the speakers. I didn't know if the text would go through or not, but I dashed off a message to Tansy telling her to kill the music. I saw Maggie reaching for her phone, too. Next year, we should include radios if we hadn't solved the poor cell-phone reception problem.

"Our office tried to contact the ship, too," Jayden said.

"Next time, maybe try a little harder, Officer." Faye let out a huff of frustration. "Do any of you have any idea what it's like to get off a nine-hour flight with two layovers and hear on the radio that your husband of fifty years is dead?" She seemed to collapse in slow motion, catching herself on her suitcase. The music died abruptly as she began to wail, "Oh Bob! My Bob!"

Leanna led her away. The remainder of the parade dispersed quietly, leaving the street littered with ribbons, feathers, and shed glitter. "What do we do now?" I asked Maggie.

"We carry on, of course." She referred to her clipboard. "It appears that all of the contestants have already come by and posed for the judges. Faye's timing was spot-on. If she'd waited five more minutes, the parade would have been over."

Jayden handed her clipboard to Maggie. "I should join them," she said, then hurried after Leanna and Faye, texting as she walked. I assumed she was alerting the rest of the police force that Faye Bobbert was back in town.

I gathered up Leanna's abandoned scoresheet and handed it, along with my own, to my sister. Each contestant could win points on size, complexity, and originality. Awards were given out to the tallest hat and the most creative headpiece. The hat with the highest total score would win the Best Bonnet. "Need me to help tally?"

"Nope," Maggie told me. "I've got this. Do you mind relieving Tansy? She's been alone in the booth most of the morning."

Even with Faye Bobbert cutting the parade short, I was

curious about which hats won. I knew my favorites, but it was possible that Jayden or Leanna didn't score them as highly as I had. But it wasn't fair for Tansy to work the booth by herself all day long. "Sure thing," I agreed.

Rather than dealing with the crowds, I skirted the edge of the park on the way back to the main stage. I passed the kid's pony rides, where the ponies were being led in circles in a pen. Beyond that was one of the many photo op stations.

One thing Texans loved was posing in the bluebonnets year after year. It was particularly popular with new couples or families with young children. I wondered if Daffy would pose with me and my sisters in the bluebonnet fields, but then I remember the garter snake biting Beau yesterday and decided I'd better not risk it.

Each time the Bluebonnet Festival came around, the festival committee picked an official place for photos to limit the number of bluebonnets that got needlessly trampled. This year, the backdrop was a grove of ancient oak trees. I stopped long enough to watch a family pose with their puppy and get their picture taken by a professional photographer. It would make a nice souvenir for them.

The photographer, a woman in her forties with an expensive-looking camera set up on a tripod, saw me watching and waved at me. "Hey Juni, how's it going?"

"Pretty good," I replied. "How are you doing on coupons?"

My sisters and I were willing to try anything to make Sip & Spin Records a success, including hosting Arts & Crafts Nights. Instead of selling old, damaged records for a few pennies to local artists to transform into strange and creative artwork, we held our own classes and charged people to help them turn records into unique works of art.

This month, to celebrate the festival, we were creating picture frames out of vinyl. I'd printed up a stack of flyers to leave with the photographer. Last I checked, we had a full house.

"People love the idea," the photographer said. Then she turned to help pose the next set of customers.

Past the photogenic field was the First Aid tent. It was fortunately empty of guests. However, I recognized Kitty in her paramedic's uniform chatting with someone wearing scrubs. I stepped inside. It wasn't hot today, not by Texas standards at least, but it was much more comfortable in the shade.

"You're looking a little pink there," Kitty said, grabbing a tube of sunscreen. "Looks like you might have forgotten the sunscreen this morning."

"Come to think of it, I did," I admitted. I held my hand out. She squirted some cream into it. I removed my glasses and rubbed the sunblock over my face. I'd been living in Oregon so long that I'd forgotten how important sunscreen was in Texas. My face was warm underneath my fingers. If I wasn't careful, I'd end up covered in freckles by the end of summer. "Got any rubber bands while I'm here?" I asked. I'd rushed out of the house this morning without so much as a ponytail holder, and I was regretting it now.

Kitty pulled a colorful hair band off her wrist and gave it to me. "I was a Girl Scout," she said. "Always prepared."

"Believe it or not, I was too," I admitted as I pulled my hair back into a ponytail. I loved having long hair, but it was a lot on a warm day. "Wait a second, that's not the Girl Scout motto."

Kitty laughed. "You caught me. I was never a Scout. How's it going out there? Find any dead bodies today?"

The other medic she'd been talking to looked startled.

"Not yet, but the day's still young," I told her. Then I lowered my voice so we couldn't be easily overheard. "Speaking of which, I was talking with Beau this morning and he confirmed that Mayor Bob didn't die of natural causes."

Kitty raised an eyebrow in surprise. "He told you that?"

I nodded. "Apparently he hasn't gotten the test results back, but it looked like murder."

"No way did he tell you that. I've seen him twice today, and both times, he practically forbade me from speaking to you about the M.E.'s findings."

"I don't think he meant to tell me anything," I admitted. "It just kinda came out."

"Uh-huh. Likely story."

I held out my hands as if to protest my innocence. "He said, and I quote, he was waiting to see if my coffee cup was the murder weapon."

Kitty nodded. "As far as I know, we're still waiting."

I felt a lump form in my throat. Fearing Mayor Bob might have been killed by our coffee was bad enough. Getting confirmation that the police believed it, too, was devastating. When this got out—and it would, considering how fast gossip spread around Cedar River—we were ruined.

"Don't look so glum," she told me. "It's just a theory."

"Oof," I said.

"Hey, look, if I hear anything, I'll tell you right away."

"I really appreciate that," I said. "I ought to be going. I promised I'd help my sister at the DJ booth. But call me when you know your schedule so we can go out next week?"

"You betcha," she said.

By the time I reached the main stage, I was in a better mood. Despite Kitty's confirmation that our coffee was under the microscope, the smell of greasy fair food, the good music, and the happy crowds lifted my spirits.

"How was the parade?" Tansy asked as soon as I was settled behind our table.

"It was great until Faye Bobbert showed up. Apparently, she'd come straight from the airport and wanted a pound of flesh from Leanna Lydell-Waite. She was in shock and grieving, and it's understandable that she would lash out, but why lash out at Leanna?"

"Juni, you can't possibly be that naïve," Tansy said.

"Why? What did I say?"

"Mayor Bob dies under strange circumstances. The next day Leanna declares herself the new mayor? Very sus."

"Oh please. Just because you don't like Leanna doesn't mean that she's a killer," I argued.

"It doesn't mean that she's not, either," Tansy said. "You don't know her like I do. Every time I turn around, there she is. At the market. At the gym. She was even in my photography class last week, and she 'accidentally' opened the darkroom door while I was winding my film into the developer tank. Ruined the whole roll. She's incredibly driven and will do anything it takes to get what she wants."

"Sounds like a certain older sister of mine," I said.

"I am nothing at all like Leanna Lydell-Waite," she insisted.

"Tansy, I love you with all my heart. But maybe the reason that you and Leanna don't get along is because you're so much alike? I mean, you are the most competitive person I know."

"I'm not nearly as competitive as Leanna," she insisted.

I pursed my lips. "Do you even hear yourself? All you're doing is proving my point."

"Fine," Tansy said. "I can prove she killed Mayor Bob. Tomorrow, we'll visit Leanna at Town Hall and get her to confess."

The last thing I wanted was to ever step foot in the town hall again, but if Tansy was going to confront Leanna, I couldn't let her do it alone. "Okay. I'll come. Just promise you won't do anything to get us in trouble."

Tansy grinned at me. "Don't worry, Juni. I'm not you."

CHAPTER 12

As the sun set on Sunday, families filed out of Cedar River Memorial Park, heading back to their homes. The Bluebonnet Festival had been a success despite the shadow of the mayor's death hanging over the weekend. "Do you think the festival is cursed?" I asked Tansy as we packed up the equipment. We loaded some of it, like the record player, the crates of albums, and the large coffee maker, into the back seat of Calvin's Bronco to take back to Sip & Spin. The rest was due back to the rental place in the morning.

"Don't be silly," Maggie replied as she returned from carrying another load to the trailer.

"The bank heist happened during the festival," I pointed out.

Maggie dismissed me. "Nearly sixty years ago."

"What about Mayor Bob?" I asked.

"That wasn't a curse. That was Leanna Lydell-Waite and her unchecked ambition," Tansy said as she wrapped up what felt like miles of cords.

"Seriously?" Maggie asked, looking at me to back her up.

"We had this conversation earlier," I said. "There's no talking sense into her."

"Obviously, Leanna killed Bob to become mayor," Tansy argued.

"It wasn't Leanna's coffee in his hand when he died," I pointed out. "It was ours."

"Coincidence," Maggie said quickly.

"Bad luck," Tansy said. "Or Leanna planted it to frame me."

"Really?" I asked. "Why would she need to plant anything if you're the one who brewed the coffee? I'm telling you, it's a curse."

"I think we're ignoring the most obvious suspect," Maggie said.

"More obvious than Leanna?" Tansy asked.

"Marcus Best," she said.

"Marcus Best, the used car salesperson?" I asked.

"I don't trust him," Maggie said.

"You don't trust him because he's a used car salesperson, or because he's dating Mom?" Tansy asked. She wheeled a dolly out of the truck. Even using the dolly, it took all three of us to load the enormous speakers.

"I did some digging. Did you know he was a donor on Mayor Bob's reelection campaign?" Maggie asked. "He's listed on the website and everything."

Tansy sighed. "That's doesn't mean anything. Lots of people donate to political campaigns. That doesn't make him a murderer."

"But Mayor Bob always runs unopposed. Why would he need campaign funds?" Maggie asked.

"Yeah, I totally see where you're going with this," I said sarcastically. "He contributed a couple of dollars to a mayoral campaign in a rinky-dink town, and that's why he killed Bob. Sorry, Maggie, but it's quite a stretch."

"Everything's a stretch until it's not," Maggie said.

"I seem to remember you jumping to some pretty wild conclusions the last time there was a murder in Cedar River."

She had a point.

"Besides, you haven't even heard the best part yet," Maggie continued.

"Enlighten us," Tansy said.

"Remember what Mickey was complaining about this morning? About Mayor Bob selling off a bunch of Cedar River land under the table? You'll never guess who he sold it to."

"Who?" Tansy asked.

"Marcus?" I guessed.

Maggie put her finger on her nose. "Ding ding ding, we have a winner! I bumped into the county clerk at the dunk tank earlier. I asked them about the sale, and they told me all about it. Marcus Best bought Rawlings Hollow."

"I bet he got a good deal on it, too," Tansy said. "That would explain his campaign contribution." This new revelation had apparently changed her mind about Mom's new boyfriend.

"Well, no, not really," Maggie admitted. "He paid fair market value for the land, and it's gonna cost a fortune to develop. It's all the way out in the boondocks, and the only road out there isn't paved."

"What's a used car salesperson want with a lot of land that doesn't have a paved road?" I asked. "It's not like he can ask people to test drive their gently used sedan on a dirt road."

"That's exactly what I want to know," Maggie said. We hefted the last speaker into the tow-behind and closed the door.

I nodded. "Okay, here's what we do. Tomorrow, after

you two return this sound equipment and the trailer, Maggie can take over at Sip & Spin so Tansy and I can stop by Town Hall and question Leanna. Then Tansy can watch the shop while Maggie and I go talk to Marcus. Deal?"

My sisters and I stared at one another in the glow of the Bronco's headlights. "Are we really going to do this again?" Tansy asked. "Are we going to get involved in another murder investigation?"

"We're already involved," I pointed out. "You brewed the murder weapon and I found the body. If it gets out that our coffee killed Mayor Bob, Sip & Spin's toast. Then again, we can always just trust that Beau and the Cedar River Police Department are gonna do their job, and . . ."

"Nope," Maggie said firmly. "No way," Tansy said at the same time. They exchanged a glance.

"We're doing this," Tansy said.

Maggie nodded. "We're doing this."

I looked at my sisters and grinned. "We're totally doing this."

♪ ♫ ♪

The next morning, my sisters returned the equipment while I opened the shop. As usual, Daffy greeted me with a plaintive yowl as if to say he thought he'd never be fed again. "I missed you too, Daffodil," I told him as I scooped food into his bowl and topped off his water. "Good news is that we're back to normal, so you don't have to be alone all day."

He didn't look up from eating to acknowledge me, but I liked to believe he understood.

I put a George Strait album on the turntable and cranked up the sound system. Once the music started, I began the tedious work of reshelving the albums we'd taken to the festival. It would have taken less time if I'd organized them before I tried to put them back, but since I hadn't, I ended up running upstairs and then back down several times before I was finished.

Dusting my hands off on my T-shirt—today was an Eminem kind of day—I returned the crates to the storage room. Then I washed my hands thoroughly before starting the drip pot and setting up the barista machine. When we'd first got it, I'll admit, I was a little intimidated. My latte foam art was still shaky and lopsided, but I'd figured out most of the functions thanks to a bunch of tutorials I'd found on YouTube, and now I could make a variety of drinks from Americano to Viennese Roast.

Teddy knocked on the front door and I rushed over to unlock it for him. It was early, but he was already in his mail carrier uniform. "Getting a jump on the day?" I asked.

"Most of downtown was closed all weekend, so I've got a lot to deliver today." He handed me a stack of envelopes all neatly held together with a rubber band, a small Express Mail box, and a larger soft-sided mailer. "That one's actually from me," he said.

"Oh yeah?" I sat the rest of the mail on the counter and ripped the mailer open. Out came a T-shirt. I unfolded it and held it up. "Gin Blossoms? I love them. Did you know that gin is made from juniper berries?"

"Yup. But I've never seen you wear any of their concert shirts."

"That's because I didn't have one before now," I said, hugging the soft T-shirt to my chest. "Thanks. I love it. Hey, can I get you a coffee? Today's special, in honor of reopening the shop after a weekend off, is Sweet Home Cappuccino. It starts with locally produced Texas agave syrup for a sweet kick, then evenly layered espresso, steamed milk, and thick foam. The milk and foam can be substituted with several dairy-free options if you prefer. The result is a sweet, rich flavor with a velvety texture."

Teddy laughed. "Come on, Juni, you know me better than that."

I nodded. "That I do. One I'll Bean There for Brew coming right up." I draped the newest vintage shirt in my collection over my shoulder to free up my hands before doing the requisite five claps. Then I poured Teddy a cup of plain black drip coffee. "If you ever change your mind about trying something new, you know where to find me."

He accepted the coffee. "Thanks, but I know what I like. Well, this mail isn't going to deliver itself."

"See ya," I told him. Instead of locking the door behind him, I flipped the sign to Open. As much as I'd enjoyed the Bluebonnet Festival, it was good to be back in the shop.

Technically, we didn't open until ten, but as soon as they saw the sign, customers started wandering into the store. Though clearly, they weren't there for our great selection of music or even our delicious coffee creations. Even though there were at least a dozen people milling around, I'd only poured a few Sweet Home Cappuccinos because, apparently, all anyone wanted this morning was gossip.

"No, it wasn't a mob hit," I told Lana Lincoln after she explained the wild story she'd heard. Lana, a tiny woman around my mother's age, was a bartender at United Stakes, so she heard all the wacky gossip first.

"Are you certain?" she asked. "Because I heard Mayor Bob owed money to the mob, so they shot up his office just like they do in the movies."

"No one shot up his office," I assured her. "The police aren't even calling his death suspicious." That might change once they got the results back from the coroner. I continued, "For all I know, Mayor Bob had a heart attack." Beau hadn't used the word "suspicious," and I didn't have any medical training. How would I know the signs of a heart attack?

"It wasn't a heart attack," Joyce Whedon said with an air of authority. She worked as a bank teller at First Bank of Cedar River, and got the juicy dirt from her customers. "It was aliens."

"Okay now, I am one hundred percent certain he wasn't beamed up by little green men," I told her, shaking my head. "Where do you come up with these things?"

"I didn't say they were green," Joyce said with a humph as she folded her arms across her chest. "But you mark my words. He was probed."

"He wasn't probed," I said. "He was sitting at his chair, normal as could be. Except, you know, dead. Seriously, Joyce, if you're gonna spread gossip you might as well get your facts straight." I pitched my voice lower so only she would hear me over the music and the chatter. "You told my sister that you saw me out on a date with Beau. Why'd you have to go and do that?"

She smiled and shrugged. "Because I saw you. And it was obviously a date. He had his arm around your back and was leaning in real close." She paused and fanned herself. "I don't know what your problem is. If I was all hot and heavy with Beauregard Russell, I'd be screaming about it from the hilltops."

"We're not hot or heavy," I insisted, even though letting Joyce know that I was bothered was just adding fuel to the flame.

"She's not dating Beau Russell." A new woman spoke up. So much for keeping this conversation between Joyce and me. Jen Rachet made her way up to the counter. "I'll take one of those specials, with oat milk," she ordered. As

I turned to make her drink, she told Joyce, "She's dating the mailman."

"Teddy?" Joyce said, slapping her hand over her heart. "Teddy Garza? Juni, is this true?"

"I don't see how any of this is any of y'all's business," I said through clenched teeth. It was bad enough when everyone wanted to talk about murder, but this was crossing a line.

"See how defensive she is?" Jen asked with a smirk. "I notice she didn't get defensive when she shot down your stupid alien theory or Lana's ridiculous mob story." She had a satisfied grin on her face. She surveyed the assembled customers who were now hanging on her every word.

I pretended that the gossip wasn't a big deal as I handed her a cup. "One Sweet Home Cappuccino with oat milk, just like you like it, Jen."

Jen straightened her shoulders and recoiled like I'd just pointed a gun at her. "Land's sakes, dear, I can't drink *that*," she said, leaving me hanging with the cup. "I just remembered. Mayor Bob was drinking Sip & Spin coffee when he died, wasn't he?" There was an audible gasp from the assembled customers. She shook her head and made a tsking sound. "I guess the real question is did you poison him accidentally, or on purpose?"

Jen turned and marched out of the shop. Everyone followed her, eager to get as many details as they could pry out of her before scattering to every corner of Cedar River to spread the news. I bent over until my forehead rested on the counter. "What did I ever do to her?" I asked myself aloud. Granted, when I was sixteen and just learning to parallel park, I tapped her brand-new car pulling into a particularly tight parking space, but I'd paid for the damages. There was no way she was still salty about that. I guess Jen was just a mean person.

"Well, can't let this go to waste," I said to myself, and took a sip of the coffee Jen had ordered and then abandoned. It was delicious, but it didn't make me feel any better.

When my sisters breezed through the front door an hour later, they looked around the empty shop.

"Where is everybody?" Tansy asked.

"I thought we'd be booming this morning," Maggie added.

"We were," I told them. "Then Jen Rachet came in and told everyone that we poisoned Mayor Bob. That put the kibosh on the morning rush."

"She said what?" Maggie exclaimed.

"Don't worry, no one listens to her," Tansy said, but the lack of customers who would normally be lining up to get their morning caffeine fix said otherwise. "Never mind. We knew that would get out eventually. The only way to get around it now is to prove who really killed Mayor Bob, which means it's time to go have a little conversation with Leanna Lydell-Waite."

CHAPTER 13

"You're wasting your time with Leanna," Maggie said. "I'm telling you, Marcus is a far better suspect."

"Maybe so, but everything was closed this weekend for the festival. As the head of the town council, Leanna would have had access to Town Hall. Marcus wouldn't," Tansy said. "Back me up, Juni."

"You both have a point," I said. I'd learned long ago to not pick sides where my sisters were concerned. "That's why I think we should talk to both of them." I turned to the barista station and started making a drink. "Might as well come bearing gifts," I said.

A few minutes later, we were ushered into Leanna's office. It was across the hall from where I'd found Mayor Bob. I didn't know if Leanna was trying to be sensitive by not moving into the mayor's larger office so soon or if it was still an active crime scene. Either way, I applauded her choice to stay put.

Leanna's office was warm and welcoming. The walls were covered in framed photos. There were pictures of Leanna crossing the finish line at a race, of her and her wife in a hot-air balloon, Leanna astride a lovely bay horse, and a big black Great Dane holding a stuffed animal in his enormous mouth. Her desk was neatly ordered with stacks of color-coded folders sorted into wire baskets.

"Ladies, what can I do for you this morning?" she greeted us, sounding chipper.

I held out the cup. "I thought you might could use a little pick-me-up. I noticed your coffee vending machine was out of service the other day."

Leanna smiled but didn't reach for the cup. "I'm trying to cut down on sugar."

An empty candy bar wrapper on her desk told a different story, but I didn't point that out. Instead, I sat the cup in front of her. "It's a good thing I brought tea instead of coffee, then. It's a hot, dark green tea sweetened with local organic honey. I call it My Heart Will Go Oolong."

"In that case, thanks." she reached for the tea but didn't take a sip. "Why don't y'all take a seat?"

"How's the mayor business treating you?" Tansy asked as we sat.

"To be completely honest, it's not nearly as hard as I thought it would be," Leanna admitted.

"Oh? How so?" I asked.

"Mayor Bob always acted like he was busy twenty-four seven. Any time I needed something, he was swamped, and if I tried to get time on his calendar, he couldn't squeeze me in." She spun her laptop around so it faced us. "I finally have access to his schedule. Does this look busy to you?"

I squinted at the screen. Large chunks of time were blocked off, but there were few notes to indicate why. He had a pedicure scheduled on Thursday mornings and a standing four-hour golf game on Monday afternoons. "If he wasn't taking meetings, and he wasn't working, what was he doing?" I asked.

Leanna shrugged. "I don't have the faintest. The man's been in office over a decade, and the biggest impact he's had on Cedar River is getting those generic candy machines in government buildings and school break rooms. Seriously, what's a 'Sneekers Bar?'" She shook her head, crumpled up the wrapper, and tossed it toward her trash can, which was close to overflowing. The candy wrapper bounced off and landed on the ground instead.

"I thought you were cutting down on sugar," Tansy said, gesturing at the wrapper.

"I said I was *trying*," she said as she bent over to pick it up. "I didn't have time for breakfast this morning. Plus, it has peanuts. Peanuts are healthy, and I was craving chocolate. So I decided to treat myself."

"Actually, I'm more interested in your trash can," I said, changing the focus. We weren't going to get any information out of her by judging her snacks. "When's the last time it was emptied?"

"Seriously, if Mayor Bob wasn't doing anything, and they don't even empty the trash cans at Town Hall, where are my taxes going?" Tansy asked.

"Normally the janitor comes through on Wednesdays and Saturdays, but with most everything closed on Saturday, and then, well, you know, his death and all, I guess they didn't get around to it," Leanna said.

Mayor Bob's trash can hadn't been full on Saturday morning. Did he not spend much time in his office? I tried to remember if there'd been anything in the can. A crumpled-up piece of white paper. A wadded up generic salt and vinegar chip bag. A few sugar-free amaretto-flavored coffee creamer cups. A single-use water bottle with the label peeled off. I probably wouldn't have noticed his trash can at all if not for that water bottle. I remember being annoyed that he hadn't recycled it.

It looked like Leanna was telling the truth. She worked harder than Mayor Bob had, or at least spent more time in the office than he did, if their trash cans were any indication. "It's got to sting," I blurted out without thinking.

"What?" Leanna asked, looking confused.

"You did all the hard work while the mayor didn't do much, but took all the credit."

Leanna smiled and shook her head. "Why do you think I ran for town council instead of for mayor? The town council is where the real power's at in Cedar River."

"Yeah, but the mayor was working on Saturday morning and you weren't," Tansy pointed out.

"Actually, I stopped by the office to check my email."

"So you were here?" I asked. Tansy nudged the side of my foot, and I could practically hear her thinking that she'd told me so. "Couldn't you have checked your email on your phone?"

"It was on the way."

"Did you see anyone else while you were here?" Tansy asked.

Leanna shook her head. "Nope. Bob's door was closed, but his light was on. I heard voices inside."

"Whose voices?" I asked.

Leanna tapped one finger on her lips as she thought. "You know what? I'm not sure. I heard Mayor Bob, but he could have been on the phone, or even talking to himself now that I think about it."

"Have you told the cops this?" Tansy asked.

"They're stopping by in a bit to get my statement. I'll make sure to mention it," Leanna said. "Tansy, now that there's an open seat, you should really think about running for the town council. You could make a positive impact on Cedar River. Unless, of course, you're not interested in public service."

Tansy bristled at that. "Of course I'm interested in public service."

Leanna nodded smugly. "I'm looking forward to seeing your name on the ballot for the special election."

"Oh, you'll see it all right," Tansy replied. Then she stood. "I'm sure we've taken up enough of your time this morning. Juni, let's go."

I followed her out into the hall, closing the door behind us. "We didn't get to ask her any hard questions."

"Yeah, but we learned plenty. She didn't think Mayor Bob was doing his job. She's only acting mayor, but she's planning to run for mayor in the special election. Why else would there be an open seat on the council? All that baloney about the town council having all the power . . ." Tansy scoffed. "I'll bet now that she's acting mayor, they'll have no power at all. That's why she wants me to run, so she could boss me around."

"Wow, you got a lot more out of that conversation than I did," I admitted.

Tansy shook her head. "Were you even in the same meeting as I was? She practically bragged that she's been chomping at the bit to sit in the mayor's chair, and now she's got everything she wants. Motive, anyone? Plus, she confessed to being in the office the morning he was murdered. Who goes into work on a Saturday morning just to check email? Sounds like opportunity to me."

"We've all stopped by Sip & Spin when it was closed for one reason or another," I pointed out. "She admitted that she was here at the same time as Bob. But she said his light was on and the door was closed. His lights are automatic. Which means he was still alive when she left."

"Unless she was lying," Tansy said. "She wouldn't be the first person to bump off a political rival."

I shook my head. "She said she had more power as chair of the town council than as the mayor."

"Again, we only have her word to go on for that," Tansy pointed out.

We weren't getting anywhere. My sister had already made up her mind that Leanna was guilty, which meant this was a waste of time. "We should . . ." I started to suggest, as we headed back through the lobby, but halted in mid-thought when I saw Beau and Jayden coming up the front steps. "Quick." I grabbed Tansy's arm and hauled her toward the back door. "Let's go out this way."

"What on earth?" she complained, but followed me anyway, not that I gave her much of a choice. We hurried out the back door, which was slightly ajar. There was a sign on it warning that an alarm would sound, but luckily it stayed silent. The door clanged shut behind us.

"Do you think they saw us?" I asked when we were clear.

"You let the door close!" called out a man's voice.

I turned to see Pete Digby, the security guard. He was standing near the dumpsters smoking a cigarette. I looked back at the closed door. It was a smooth exit-only door with no handle on the outside. At my feet was a brick that Pete had likely used to prop it open.

"Sorry," I told him.

"Guess I'll have to walk all the way back around," he grumbled. "Who are you running from, anyway?"

"Running from? Nobody," I fibbed.

"Liar. I distinctly heard you ask your sister if they saw you."

"Do you spend a lot of time back here?" I asked him, evading his question. Admitting I was running from the cops would have sounded suspicious when, honestly, I was just avoiding Beau. If he knew that Tansy and I were here to interrogate Leanna Lydell-Waite, he'd be upset with me.

"You have no idea how boring my job is," he said.

"I'll take that as a yes." I glanced at my sister. Something had been worrying me. Whoever had killed Mayor Bob had managed to slip into and out of Town Hall without anyone noticing. That was literally the only reason I'd been willing to consider Leanna a suspect in the first place—she had full access to the building. Then again, so did Pete. But if Pete was as lax of a guard as I thought he was, a herd of elephants could have marched in here and back out again without him noticing.

The front door hadn't been locked when I'd come by on Saturday morning, even though Cedar River Town Hall was officially closed because of the festival. And Pete had been off in the bathroom getting paper towels to clean up the Slurpee he'd spilled. I'd managed to walk right in without being challenged. How hard would it have been for someone else to do it, especially if they were trying to be sneaky?

"Did you see anyone else on Saturday morning? Other than me?" I asked him.

"Nope. If that's all, my break's almost up," he said, grounding out his cigarette.

"Wait a sec," Tansy said, taking a step toward the dumpster. "What's that?" She pointed to the edge of an oversize picture frame sticking out of the open top.

Pete shrugged. "Looks like a picture frame."

Tansy gave him an exasperated look. "Can you pull it out for me?"

"I'm security. You'll want to talk to janitorial about that." He turned and strode away.

"Real helpful," she said. I nodded in agreement. "Give me a boost?"

"What's so important about a picture frame?" I asked. "You've got better picture frames than that at home."

"I doubt it," she said, grabbing the edge of the dumpster to pull herself up. "Remember when I was into antiquing a while back?"

I nodded. Tansy dabbled in a lot of things. Last week, it was photography. Before that, it was glass blowing. She never stuck with anything for long. She couldn't find a hobby that held her interest for more than a few weeks. Frankly, it made me nervous. If my sister got bored and decided she no longer wanted to run a record shop, I wasn't sure what Maggie and I would do, especially since Tansy was the biggest musicophile of the three of us.

"Believe it or not, a lot of time when you see a painting in a garage sale or a thrift store, the frame is worth more than the art." She tugged on the frame. "Especially if it's a large one like this." She pulled it free and lifted it out of the dumpster, handing it to me so she could climb down.

"And you think this frame is worth something?" I asked. I was trying to take an interest in my sister's hobbies, I really was, but it smelled awful by the dumpsters, and the frame I was holding was gooey on one side. I leaned it against the dumpster so I could take a step back.

Tansy was right. It was a nice frame. It had a distinct antique look to it. Most frames that size would be around a canvas, but this one had a backing to it like it had held a photograph. I picked at a flake of torn yellowed paper around the edge. "Whatever was in here was old," I said.

"That's usually the case with these old frames," Tansy said.

I leaned in and adjusted my glasses to get a better look. I could make out 'Town of Cedar River, Texas. 1955.' "It's the missing map!" I exclaimed.

"Huh?"

"Esméralda Martín-Brown told me at the hole-digging contest she'd heard that Mayor Bob's map was missing."

"I don't see a map," my sister pointed out.

"Someone tore it out, but I think maybe it used to be in that frame."

"That's quite a stretch," she said.

"Maybe," I agreed. "But I have an odd feeling about this. Leanna works right across the hall, she might recognize the frame."

"I hate to say this, Juni—" my sister started.

"Yeah, I know," I said, not letting her finish her sentence. I pulled out my phone and called Beau. "You still at Town Hall?" I asked when he picked up.

"How do you . . . never mind. What's up?"

"Can you come around back, by the dumpster?"

"Be right there," he said.

A minute later, the back door popped open. Beau put on his broad-brimmed cowboy hat to shade his eyes before scooching the brick over to prop the door open. "Tansy. Junebug. What do y'all got there?"

"I think it might be the map that's missing from Mayor Bob's office," I said, gesturing toward it. "Well, not the map, exactly. The map's frame."

"Uh-huh," he said noncommittally. He came closer and squatted in front of the frame. He paid close attention to the torn corner, where the name of our town was legible, just like I had done. He took a close-up picture with his phone before standing and addressing us again. "You found it sitting here just like this?"

"It was in the dumpster," Tansy said.

"Uh-huh," he said again.

"It was right on top," she said.

"Oh. It was right on top," Beau repeated. "And what were you two doing back here?"

"Visiting with Leanna Lydell-Waite," Tansy said. "Wanted to drop by and congratulate her on being acting mayor."

"And bring her a hot tea," I added.

"Tansy Jessup, you and Leanna Lydell-Waite have been at each other's throats since you were six months old," he said with authority even though Tansy was several years older than him, and there was no way he could have possibly known that from first-hand experience.

"That was a long time ago," she said with a fake smile.

"Yup. Ancient history. Try again. We all know that you can hold a grudge," he said.

"He's got a point," I told her with a nod. She was still mad at Beau for breaking up with me six years ago. He was the last person in town to believe that she and Leanna had let bygones be bygones.

"Let me guess. Your baby sister dragged you out here so she could sniff around Mayor Bob's office, looking for any clues she might have missed the other day. Y'all saw me coming and thought you'd nip out the back, only to recognize the picture frame in the dumpster." He shook his head. "At least you called me after you found it."

"That's not what happened," I said.

"Not even close," Tansy added.

Beau held up one hand. "Honestly, I don't care. Which one of you touched it?"

Tansy said, "Both of us."

"Of course you did," he muttered.

"So this is the missing map?" I asked. "Or at least some of it? Does that mean it's a clue?"

Beau sighed. "Can you please get it through your head

that I can't divulge any details from an active murder investigation? Especially if your sister is a suspect?"

"I didn't kill anyone!" Tansy sputtered.

"I know that!" Beau said, matching her tone. "But you're making it awful hard to focus on finding the actual killer when you're tromping all over my crime scene. You get that, right?"

"You know I'm innocent?" Tansy asked in a quieter voice.

Beau rolled his eyes skyward. "If you had a single murderous bone in your entire body, I would not be alive today. You would have killed me the second I hurt your baby sister. And I would have let you. So yes, I know you're innocent. Now will you two please step out of the way so I can do my job?"

CHAPTER 14

I'm not sure how long Tansy and I waited for Beau and his partner to finish their work, but it was long enough that I no longer noticed the smell of the dumpster. At first, it was interesting to watch Jayden photograph the scene and dust for prints, but after a while, it just got old. Another cop showed up with a long roll of plastic wrap that they used to wrap up the picture frame we'd found.

Finally, Beau turned his attention back to us. "Okay, y'all can go."

"Seriously?" Tansy asked. "You made us stand around for nothing?"

"I'm sorry, would you prefer that I take you in for questioning?" he asked, frowning at her.

"Nope. We're all good here," I said, before my sister could say something she might regret later. "Oh, and Beau? When we were talking to Leanna earlier, she mentioned that the janitor usually takes out the trash on Wednesdays and Saturdays."

"So?"

"So, with the building closed on Saturday, no one took out the trash. The picture frame was on the very top."

"Which means whoever put it out here did so after trash

was taken out last Wednesday," Beau said, putting the pieces together.

I shrugged. "That's what I thought. Anything else missing from Mayor Bob's office?"

"There was a you-know-I-can't-tell-you-that and a nice-try-Juni. We also noted the absence of a valuable mind-your-own-business. Any more questions?"

I grinned. At least Beau had a sense of humor about me inserting myself into the investigation. "You're welcome. I'm sure you would have noticed that the missing frame was sitting out here, in plain sight, eventually." A distinctive beeping sound caught my attention and I turned to see a garbage truck heading toward us. I watched as it backed up past the dumpster before turning slightly to position the forks to lift it. Then, only now noticing the police activity, the driver got out and approached. "I mean, who knows. You might have even noticed it before the garbage was picked up."

Beau pursed his lips. He knew I had a point. "Fine. Thank you both. Now skedaddle and let me do my job."

Tansy and I slipped through the back door, still propped open with a brick. We cut through the lobby to get to the parking lot out front. We got in Tansy's car and hurried back to Sip & Spin Records.

"What's the rush?" I asked her as she pushed her car well over the speed limit.

"Nothing," she admitted. "But how often do we know exactly where every cop in town is? Might as well take advantage. We could probably rob the bank right now and not get caught."

She had a point. About the speeding, not the bank robbery. "I guess that's what the cameras are for," I said, but I couldn't help thinking about the 1956 bank robbery.

That had been long before security cameras. "Why do you think the bank was open that day?"

"Huh? What bank? What day?" my sister asked.

Sometimes I forgot that not everyone could hear my thoughts. "Back in the fifties, when the bank was robbed during the Bluebonnet Festival. Everyone was at the festival. By the time the cops showed up, the robbers were long gone, but why was the bank open in the first place?"

Tansy looked over at me like I'd just asked her what color the sky was. "You do realize there were no ATMs in the fifties, right?"

I shrugged. "I've never thought about it."

"Back then, there were no ATMs or even credit cards. There was no online banking or PayPal. If you needed cash for cotton candy, you had to go to the bank. And if the bank wasn't open, you couldn't buy anything at the festival."

"Makes sense." I didn't point out that even though my sister was seven years older than me, it wasn't as if she'd been around back in ye olden days before ATMs. I tried to imagine a world without the internet. I couldn't. "Must have been inconvenient."

"Yup," she agreed.

We found a parking spot on Main Street. Unlike me, my sister had no problem parallel parking. When we walked into the shop, Maggie asked us, "Where have you two been? I was expecting y'all back ages ago. Oh!" She covered her nose. "What is that smell?"

I tugged the collar of my shirt and sniffed. "I don't smell anything."

Maggie pointed a stiff arm at the door. "Well, whatever it is, I don't want it in my shop. Go home and take a shower. Both of you."

"Whatever," Tansy said, turning around and heading back out the door. "Maggie's such a stickler. It's not like we complain that she always smells like Lysol," she said. We walked past a man who stepped off the sidewalk to give us a wide berth. "Huh. Maybe she's not completely overreacting."

We got back to the house in time to see a man unload a cow from a stock trailer and head toward our front door with an enormous black and white dairy cow in tow. Tansy pulled up along the curb behind him since he was blocking the driveway. I jumped out of the passenger's side and hurried after him, dodging a fresh present that the cow had left us on the front lawn.

"Excuse me?" I asked in a panic. I lived in Texas. I was used to seeing cows. Just not on my doorstep.

The man turned and nodded. He was the kind of cowboy who could be an extra in a John Wayne movie. A dusty cowboy. A working man's cowboy. He wore thick jeans, a long-sleeve button-down shirt that was covered in unidentifiable stains, and a cowboy hat that was likely older than I was. "Howdy, ma'am. I'm looking for a Juniper Jessup."

"Yeah, you found her," I said, staring at the cow. She was a very pretty cow, as far as cows went. She was a healthy weight, with a wide white stripe running down the middle of an otherwise black face. She had little horn nubbins, and while most of her body was white, she had large black patches, a black tail, and a pink udder. If I were to draw a picture of a cow, this is the exact cow that I would draw. "Whose cow is that?" I asked.

"Yours."

"No, you're mistaken. I don't have a cow." I swept my hand toward my sister's modest ranch-style house in the middle of a block filled with more modest ranch-style houses. "I'm pretty sure this neighborhood isn't zoned for cows. It's not even zoned for chickens."

The Home Owner's Association here wasn't bad as far as HOAs went. As long as there was no garden visible from the street, no car up on blocks, and the trash cans were pulled up the driveway no later than nine p.m. on trash day, they didn't bother us much. However, livestock was strictly forbidden, which meant never having to hear roosters at unearthly hours of the morning.

"Not my problem," the man said. He handed me the rope attached to the cow's halter. "Enjoy your cow." He started walking away.

"You don't understand," I said, taking a step toward him. The cow didn't budge, so I couldn't go far. "This isn't my cow."

"Sure it is." He pulled a business card—my business card—out of his shirt pocket. "Juniper Jessup, Sip & Spin Records."

"Yes, that's me. I own a record shop. *Not* a cow."

"Begging your pardon ma'am, but you do now. You entered a contest at the Bluebonnet Festival this weekend, and lucky you, you won." He touched the brim of his hat. "Have a good day."

He left.

And I was left holding a cow. Well, holding a cow's rope.

"What was he talking about?" Tansy asked. She gave the cow a wide berth.

"Apparently, I won her? I entered a few raffles at the festival on a lark, but I never win anything."

"Looks like your luck took a turn."

"Looks like it," I agreed. "What am I supposed to do with a cow?"

Tansy shrugged. "Beats me." The cow decided that was

a good moment to get a snack, but instead of munching on the bright green lawn, she took a bite out of Tansy's flowerbeds. "Fix this," she said through clenched teeth. "Now." She marched in the house, presumably to shower.

The mail truck pulled up in front of the mailbox, and Teddy leaned out of the window. "Nice cow," he called.

I tugged on the cow's lead. This time, she followed me to the curb. "This is all your fault," I said.

"How so?"

"Remember when we were checking out the 4-H tent, and you encouraged me to enter the raffle? I won."

"You're welcome," Teddy said.

"Yeah, but now I have a cow!"

"I'll tell you what, I'm almost at the end of my route. If you can hold off for an hour, maybe two, I'll be back to help. Seeing as how this is all my fault."

"What am I supposed to do with a cow for an hour or two?" I asked.

"Take her for a long walk?" he suggested. Then he crinkled up his nose. "No offense, but your cow smells kinda funky."

"Yeah, I think that might be me," I admitted.

"Well then," he said, "I guess I'll see you in a bit."

"Hurry," I begged him. "Please."

I led the cow around to the backyard. We didn't have a fence. We'd never needed one before. I tied her rope to the trunk of a mature pecan tree, making sure she had enough room to move around and some shade. "What's your name?" I asked her. She blinked at me, her long lashes shooing off a few flies that had been crawling on her face. I should have asked the man who dropped her off, but I hadn't been thinking logically at the time. Then again, if I'd been thinking logically, I would have somehow convinced him to take her back.

She blinked at me again. She really was a very nice cow. It wasn't her fault that I didn't want a cow. At least I didn't live in an apartment building.

"Daisy?" I asked her. She didn't respond. "Bessie? Clover? Bella?" Nothing. "Buttercup?" She mooed. Okey dokey, Buttercup it was. "Stay right there, Buttercup. I'll be right back."

My sister's garden tools were neatly stacked by the back door. I emptied a plastic bucket and used the hose to fill it with water. I lugged the bucket over to Buttercup and made sure she could reach it. Then I dragged one of the chairs from the porch into the shade of the pecan tree and stretched out. The flies were too thick, this close to the cow, so I moved into the sun. That was better.

Our mom had moved into the guest cottage in Tansy's yard after our father had died, but there were entire days that we didn't see her because she was always busy with a community project or one of her many clubs. She was the type that kept busy. She was a member of every club, social organization, and group in town, which meant her calendar was always full. But the last few weeks, I'd hardly seen her at all. I wondered exactly how much time she'd been spending with Marcus Best recently, and thought it was odd that neither me nor my sisters had noticed.

I'd promised Maggie that I'd help her investigate Marcus today, but between the unexpected delay at Town Hall and now the accidental cow, she'd have to take a rain check. I felt guilty as I texted her to let her know I wasn't coming back to the shop immediately. But just because I couldn't interrogate him today with my sister didn't mean I couldn't take this time to learn more about him.

Marcus was annoyingly difficult to google. Every time I typed in his name, the first hundred results that popped up were all about his car lots. He had a bunch of good reviews online, so I was starting to think that he wasn't as shady as Maggie wanted him to be, but I trusted reviews about as much as I trusted a used car salesperson.

I found an article confirming that he'd recently bought the land in Cedar River, presumably to expand his used car empire. The article mentioned that Marcus would have to bring in a ton of concrete and lobby the town council to pave a long dirt road to make the lot accessible. It seemed like an awful lot of trouble to go to when there were already plenty of paved roads around here. Frankly, it sounded like a bad idea all around. Why would anyone want an overgrown plot of land like Rawlings Hollow?

As I surfed, looking for more articles, Buttercup seemed content in the shade. I had no idea how long it would be before Teddy returned, but the last thing I wanted was to smell like a dumpster when he got here. After begging the cow to behave for a few minutes, I ran inside and took what was quite possibly a record-breaking shower. I dressed and ran outside, my hair still dripping wet, to find that Buttercup was exactly where I'd left her. I heaved a sigh of relief.

"Juniper Jessup, what in land's sake is going on here?" my mom asked, and I jumped.

"Hey, Mom. Didn't see you there."

"Uh-huh. I mean, I do live here, so maybe you don't need to be quite so surprised. But imagine my shock when I looked out my window and saw a cow in my yard."

"Yeah, about the cow, I can explain."

"This is because I never let you have a cat growing up, isn't it?" she asked.

"No, of course not," I assured her. When I was younger, I'd always assumed that having a cat was somehow easier than having any other kind of pet, but now that I had Daffy, I knew that wasn't the case. Being a cat owner came with a whole heap of costs and responsibilities I hadn't known about when I was a kid. Then again, it was probably nothing compared to being a cow owner.

"Are we just going to stand around all day, or are you going to tell me why there's a cow in the yard?" she pressed.

"I entered one of those 4-H raffles at the Bluebonnet Festival, where you pay five dollars to drop your business card in a fishbowl. I thought it was all in good fun—and I never win anything—but, well, we won a cow."

"We?" Mom asked. "Unless it was my business card you dropped in that bowl, I don't think *we* won anything."

"Technically, it was a Sip & Spin business card," I said. Mom, like Uncle Calvin, was a silent partner. They both invested some start-up cash and offered occasional advice, but that was the extent of their involvement. "So, it's kinda like a one-for-all situation, isn't it?"

"Oh, honey, no," she said, shaking her head. When Tansy was a baby, my mother hovered around her like a helicopter. She once ate a handful of dirt, and my parents rushed her to the hospital to get her stomach pumped. When Maggie was born, she was allowed to walk to her first day of school with Mom following an entire block away. By the time I came along, if I got stuck up a tree—something I did more than once—I was expected to get myself out of the mess I'd caused. "This is *not* an 'us' problem."

"Just as well I've got it all figured out, then," I told her. I didn't, yet, but I would. Somehow. "Frankly, I'm surprised to see you here. You've been spending an awful lot of time with Marcus lately."

Mom flapped her hand in a dismissive gesture. "Don't you dare try to guilt-trip me, Juni. You've been so busy lately, I'll bet dollars to donuts you haven't even noticed that I haven't been home."

"To be fair, you've never been a homebody," I pointed out. "What was it today? Were you organizing a volleyball tournament at the civic center? Drumming up donations for the new school gym? Candy-striping at the hospital?"

"I was sitting with Faye," she said. "Poor woman. I know what it's like, to lose a husband. She's like me. Never had to do for herself. Bob kept the books and paid the bills. He took the cars for oil changes and reminded her when her favorite show was coming on." She shook her head sadly. "I don't think Faye would even remember to eat without some of us ladies coming around. Speaking of which, I didn't see anything in her fridge from you or your sisters. I thought I'd raised you better than that."

"Don't worry, Mom," I said. "I'll bring something over tomorrow. Do you think she'd like a casserole?"

"She's got more casseroles than one woman knows what to do with. If you don't have time to make something yourself, you can always pick something up from the bakery. With all these people dropping by, she feels like she should entertain them, but all she has is a freezer full of casserole dishes."

"Okay, that's a good point. I'll drop something by tomorrow."

My mother patted my cheek. "That's a good girl."

"Mom?"

"Yes?"

"I'm sorry. I know losing Dad was hard on you."

"It was hard on all of us, Juni."

"Yeah, but it's different for you. I guess what I'm trying to say is that I'm glad you've moved on."

She let out a barking laugh. "Moved on? Don't be ridiculous. Marcus is"—she paused—"well, he's a very nice gentleman and we enjoy spending time together. He won't ever replace your father, but he's a dear friend."

"So why haven't you brought him around before?" I asked. "You never talked about him or invited him to family dinner. I haven't seen him visit you here at all."

"I didn't want to upset you or your sisters until I knew we were serious. You know how sensitive Maggie can be."

My jaw dropped. It was weird enough that my mom was dating. "Wait a minute, what do you mean by 'serious'?"

From the front of the house, a horn gave three sharp beeps. A minute later, Teddy walked around the house into the backyard. He'd changed out of his postal uniform and was now dressed in jeans, boots, and a Henley shirt with the sleeves pushed up to his elbows. "Hey, I thought I might find you back here. Mrs. Jessup, good to see you."

She grinned at him. "Mr. Garza. Like your manners, your timing is impeccable. Now you two must excuse me. I've got places to be."

"We'll talk later?" I asked her, but she was already walking away.

CHAPTER 15

"You came back."

"I said I would, didn't I?" Teddy grinned at me. "I spoke to my mom, and she'll look over your cow. Assuming she's healthy, she'll buy her from you and add her to our herd."

I flinched at the idea. "I can't *sell* her. Not to your mom, not after how many times she's fed me over the years. That would be weird. I didn't pay but five bucks for her, and I can't give her a good home here. If anything, your mom's doing me a favor by taking Buttercup off my hands."

"Buttercup?" Teddy asked.

"That's what she likes to be called."

He bobbed his head affably. "Then Buttercup it is. Does Buttercup have any other preferences I should know about?"

"She likes eating flowers."

"Most cows do. Come on, let's get her loaded up." He untied the knot from the pecan tree and led her around the house. A truck I didn't recognize was hitched to a stock trailer that was backed into the driveway. He loaded her with the ease of someone who had done it hundreds of times.

"Thanks. I can barely get her to follow me on a lead," I admitted.

"That's because you're a soft touch, Juni." He closed the back door and secured it.

"Am not."

"Are too. But that's nothing to be ashamed of. I like that about you. It's just hard to get a cow to listen to you if they sense you're an easy mark. They take advantage."

I nodded. "Daffy does that too."

"Cats do that to everyone. It's when people try to use that against you that you need to worry," he said, opening my door for me before walking around to the driver's side.

I buckled my seat belt. Teddy got in, adjusted his mirrors, and started the car. "And when you say that, you're talking about someone in particular, I suppose?"

Teddy chuckled. "Juni, you moved all the way back here from Oregon because your sisters asked you to open a record shop with them. You're nice to just about everyone, even your jerk ex. I mean, some stranger drops off a cow you don't want in your front yard, and your first instinct is to give her a name and find her a good home. You've got a big heart."

"I do, don't I?" I agreed, at least partially as a joke.

"And with an ego like that, I'm surprised you fit in the cab," he said, shaking his head.

As we drove to Teddy's family farm, I took a moment to appreciate how peaceful it was out here. Just an hour or so away from Austin, it felt like we were in the middle of nowhere. We took a turn and I could see the river stretched out in front of us, dark blue and running fast this time of the year. Finally, we bumped over a cattle grate and pulled up in front of a barn.

"Want to help get her unloaded?" Teddy asked.

"I'll do my best."

He got in front of Buttercup and tossed her rope lead back to me. "I'm just going to encourage her nice and slow, but if she spooks, don't worry about it. Just let her go. She won't go far."

"I'm not afraid of a little old dairy cow," I assured him.

"This *little* old dairy cow weighs over a thousand pounds more than you do. I've seen grown men seriously injured when a little calf got too feisty," he warned me.

"I'll be fine."

"I know you will be," he said. True to his word, he coaxed her to back out of the trailer, and then we led her to a stall inside the barn. He scooped out some oats for her and made sure she had water. "Someone will come along and take a look at her shortly, but in the meantime, you need to wash up."

"Wash up?" I sniffed my shoulder. I smelled fine to me. "I just took a shower."

"I mean wash your hands for supper, silly." Teddy led me inside the old farmhouse. Delicious smells and the sound of something sizzling made my mouth water.

"Hola," his mother called.

"Hola, Mamá," Teddy replied. "Juni's here. The cow's in the barn."

"Her name is Buttercup," I told her as I entered the kitchen. The smell of grilling onions, peppers, and garlic was so strong, I could almost taste it.

"That's a good name for a cow. Sit, sit. Supper's almost ready."

"I need to wash my hands," I told her.

"You know where everything is," she said, never taking her eyes off the skillet.

I did. Growing up, I'd spent a lot of time here studying, or just goofing off. When I returned to the kitchen, Teddy was setting the table. "Smells amazing," I said.

"Veggie fajitas," Mrs. Garza said, balancing bowls of lettuce, tomatoes, beans, grilled veggies, and slices of limes. "Meatless Monday," she explained. "It's good for the cholesterol."

"Well, it looks absolutely delicious," I said, helping her spread out the bowls.

"I'm glad someone appreciates Mamá's home cooking," she said, casting an eye at Teddy.

"What? What did I do?" Teddy asked.

"Last time I made veggie fajitas, Teo accused me of forgetting the steak." She wagged her finger at Teddy. Then she took her apron off and hung it over the back of her chair. "Do I look like a woman who forgets things?"

"No ma'am," I said. I helped myself to a fresh tortilla and stuffed it so full of fixings, I could barely hold it together.

"Does your mother not feed you?" Teddy's mom asked, making a derisive clucking noise. "I need to call Bea and have a talk with her."

"She'd love to hear from you," I said. Teddy's mom didn't get off the farm much, but my mom adored her.

The screen door opened with a squeal of hinges, and half a dozen people filed inside. Some, like Jorge, Teddy's dad, and his younger sister, Silvie, I knew well. I vaguely recognized Shelton Weaver and Lola Hammond, both longtime Cedar River residents. The others, mostly farmhands and various visiting friends or family members, I'd never seen before. I said hello and was treated to a hug by Teddy's sister and a flurry of names as everyone grabbed for plates and started loading them up.

I hadn't realized how much I'd missed meals in the Garza kitchen. Even with a few unfamiliar faces, it felt like

the Jessup family dinners that I loved—noisy, a little chaotic, and utterly delightful. Between the great company
and the delicious food, I was in heaven.

"Teddy tells me the Holstein's yours," his dad said, before passing the pitcher of ice tea to the person sitting
next to him.

"She's yours now, if you'll take her," I told him. Someone handed me a bowl of grilled corn salsa that I'd missed
earlier. I didn't have room in my tortilla, but I took a scoop
anyway. "Can someone please pass me the chips?"

"Big girl, that Holstein," Teddy's dad continued, handing me a basket of warm tortilla chips. "What's her milk
like?"

I shrugged. "No idea. I've only had her for a few hours."

"How much you want for her?" he asked.

"I already told Teddy, nothing."

"Don't be ridiculous," his mother said. "Jorge, give Juni
a good price."

"Seriously, what would I do with a cow? I can't take
your money," I insisted.

"No." Jorge shook his head. "That's no good."

I looked to Teddy, but he was no help. I turned to
his mom. "Señora Garza, I'll make you a deal." While I
called almost everyone in town by their first name, it had
never felt right doing so with Teddy's mom. I wasn't even
sure I *knew* her first name. "I've been craving your pan
dulce ever since I moved to Oregon."

Austin might call itself the Live Music Capital of the
World, but as far as I was concerned, it was the pastry capital of the world. From Czech kolaches to Mexican sweet
bread, there were more pastries to choose from here than
anywhere else I'd ever lived. In my opinion, even the fin-
est French bakeries couldn't hold a candle to Mrs. Garza's
conchas. "Do you think you could teach me to bake them?

That would be payment enough. In between rises, we can work on your coffee ice cream idea."

"That is not enough," she insisted, "but if you want to learn how to bake, I will show you. Come by anytime."

"I will," I promised. "And please, consider Buttercup a gift."

"Then it is settled," Teddy's father declared. "Pass me the frijoles."

Silvie looked up at me with a sly grin. She'd always been a sweet kid. Whenever I'd come to the farm, she'd followed me like a little shadow, asking a million questions and never giving me a second's peace. If that was what it was like to have a little sister, I don't know how Tansy and Maggie didn't lock me in the basement until I turned eighteen. Good thing we didn't *have* a basement.

"What did Mayor Bob look like when you found him? I heard he was purple," she said.

"Silvie!" her mother yelled.

All chatter at the table ground to a halt as everyone turned their attention to her.

"What?" she asked, trying to appear innocent. She had plenty of practice pretending. "It's a legit question."

"Not at the dinner table it's not," Jorge said. "Pass the tortillas."

As someone handed him the basket of tortillas, Silvie turned her attention back to me. "Sorry. I didn't mean anything by it. But it's not like I ever get to see you. You never come around anymore."

That's when I realized that Silvie wasn't trying to be rude or intentionally shocking. She was just feeling left out. Seriously, did I ever do that to my older sisters? Silvie was only a few years younger than me, but she'd grown up on a farm. Seeing death up close was more matter-of-fact for her than for most people.

"For the record, he wasn't purple. And you're right," I told her. She sat back with a self-satisfied look on her face and crossed her arms over her chest triumphantly. "We should hang out more. Come by the record shop sometime. I'll treat you to the coffee special of the day and we can catch up."

Silvie rolled her eyes. "Records, really? Aren't those obsolete already?"

"They were headed that way for a while," I told her, pasting on my best customer-service smile instead of letting her know that her comment had stung. "But there's a retro resurgence. Vinyl might not be as popular as streaming, but it sure sounds better. Come by anytime and I'll prove it to you."

"Deal." She stood and picked up her plate. "Gracias, Mamá. Supper was delicious, but we have a few cows calving any day now and I'd like to check on them before it gets dark." She turned to me. "Good to see you, Juni, and remember, when you're picking out bridesmaids dresses, I look fantastic in anything in the mauve family."

Teddy draped his arm over the back of my chair. "Don't mind her."

"No worries," I said, taking one last bite of tortilla to hide my blush. "I think maybe Silvie is giving me a taste of my own medicine. Are all baby sisters so, um, well so much?"

This time, it was Teddy's turn to blush. It said something that he was more embarrassed from my question than his sister's cheekiness. "You'd have to ask your sisters about that."

"I'll take that as a yes," I replied with a grin to show him I had no hard feelings. All around us, people were finishing their meals. They took their plates to the kitchen sink before scattering. I carried my plate to the sink, turned on the water, and grabbed a scrubby sponge.

"What do you think you're doing?" Teddy's mom asked from over my shoulder.

"Helping clean up," I said, scrubbing a plate and setting it aside so I could grab the next one.

Teddy's mom reached over my shoulder and turned off the water. "You're a guest."

I'd once read a fantasy book that went into great details of the traps of faery guesting rules and how one wrong move could result in forfeiture of your soul. All I can say is that faery hosts and guesting rites had *nothing* on Southern Texas guest landmines. For example, I was a bad guest if I didn't clean up without being asked, and Señora Garza would be a bad host if she let me. It was a catch-22.

"It's my turn to do dishes," Jorge said, taking the scrubby sponge from me and effectively sorting the situation without breaking any rules of etiquette.

Teddy came in carrying the serving dishes. Despite the horde of diners at the table all eating their fill, there were still leftovers. As he started packing up the extra food, his mom shooed us out of the kitchen. "You two are underfoot," she declared. She squeezed my hand. "Come by soon and we'll bake and make ice cream."

"Yes, ma'am," I told her, and let myself be hurried out the back door by Teddy. "Your mom is the best," I said as we settled onto the back porch swing.

The sun was setting. The sky was awash with pastel colors blending seamlessly together. The Garza farm stretched out in front of us, lush green fields dotted with grazing cattle. In the distance, the foothills cast a purple shadow over the yard. "Beautiful," I sighed.

"Beats a sharp stick in the eye," Teddy agreed. "Can I get you anything? Sweet tea? Lemonade? Beer?"

"I'm stuffed," I admitted. "As nice as this is, I need to be getting home." Honestly, I'd rather sit on the back porch swing with Teddy for a few hours, watching the stars come out and listening to the crickets sing. It was a little early in the year for fireflies—they didn't come out until the heat was too oppressive to be outside long enough to enjoy them—but I remembered being young and chasing them in Teddy's backyard.

"Come on, I'll drive you home." Instead of heading back to the stock trailer we'd used to transport Buttercup, he led me toward his Jeep, the same one he'd driven way back in high school.

"Mind if we check on Buttercup before we leave?" I asked. I knew I was being silly. I hadn't owned the cow long enough to form an attachment to her, and the Garzas would give her a better home than I ever could, but I still wanted to say good night.

"Of course." We followed the long path to the barn. It was a delicate balance building a barn close enough to the main house that someone would notice if there was a commotion, but far enough that the flies and smell of manure didn't drift in through the windows. Teddy stepped on the electrified wires of the fence with a booted foot so I could step over it without either of us getting a shock.

Buttercup looked agitated. "She's probably not used to sleeping in a barn," Teddy said, stroking the wide white stripe on her forehead between her stubby horns. "Once the vet gives her a clean bill of health, we'll turn her out with the rest of the herd and she'll settle in fine," he assured me. "And I'll check on her again before I go to bed."

"Thanks," I said, leaning against the stall door. "I know you'll take good care of her."

"Of course."

I followed him to his Jeep. As we bounced along the unpaved road, I asked, "Isn't Rawlings Hollow nearby? I heard that it just got sold to a used car dealer."

"Yup." Teddy gestured out the window at a vast darkness shrouded by a thick growth of trees behind a row of Posted: No Hunting signs. The thought of clearing all those trees made me sad. "No one's worked that land for generations. About time someone put it to good use."

"But they're going to destroy it."

He nodded. "Progress. What can we do?"

I sat back in my seat and thought about it. It would be advantageous to the Garzas if the town paved this road. For all I knew, they would welcome getting new neighbors. But it still bugged me that the land would be used to park cars on instead of for grazing cattle or growing crops. "It seems like you'll be more affected than most folks. What do *you* think about the deal?"

He shrugged. There were no streetlights out this way, so he had to concentrate on the road. If anything crossed in front of us, he wouldn't have much time to react. "I love it out here, you know? It's quiet. Peaceful. But it's also a pain sometimes, like trying to get to work when the road's washed out or we get an ice storm. I've considered getting an apartment in town, but it seems like an unnecessary expense most of the time."

"I understand. I don't always love living sandwiched between my mother and my oldest sister, but it beats paying rent and bills. When the shop starts making money, I might move out, but it's a nice setup for now." *If* the shop starts making money, I mentally corrected myself. Until we cleared up the nasty rumor that our coffee killed Mayor Bob, the fate of Sip & Spin Records was in limbo.

And here I was, thinking that *opening* the business would be the hard part.

"Penny for your thoughts," he said as the silence between us stretched on.

"I was just wondering if I was making a mistake." I'd uprooted my whole life to move back to Cedar River, and had sunk every dollar I had managed to save into opening the shop with my sisters. If we failed, we wouldn't just be back to square one. We would be in debt, with a room full of vinyl records and nowhere to sell them.

"You're a smart cookie, Juni," Teddy said, laying a comforting hand on my knee. "We all make mistakes. The key is to learn from our mistakes and do better next time."

His advice reminded me that taking a chance on my family wasn't, and would never be, a mistake. Sure, we would go through hard times, but we would make it work, somehow. I turned toward him. "You are very wise, my friend."

"So I've been told," he replied with a chuckle. He pulled up in front of Tansy's house. Lights were on over the porch and in the kitchen. My mother's little cottage was dark. I presumed she was out with Marcus, or at one of her many organizations. "See you later?"

"Yup." I got out of the Jeep, then leaned back in. "Tell your mom thanks again for dinner. And for helping with the Buttercup situation."

"Don't thank me, we got a free cow out of it."

Teddy waited until I was in the house before driving away.

There was a note in the kitchen saying that Tansy had gone out, but there was soup in the fridge. I probably should have let her know that I was eating supper at the Garzas. I wished my sister was home, though. I had a dozen ideas flying around in my head and no one to bounce them off.

I was so deep in thought I didn't even notice that I wasn't alone in the dark house.

CHAPTER 16

I flipped on the light and shrieked when I saw a man on my couch.

"Juni!" he said, pressing his hands to his ears. "Take it down a notch, will ya?"

It took a second for my pulse to resume its normal rate. "Uncle Calvin, what are you doing sitting in the dark?" I sagged into the wingback chair that was catty-corner to the sofa.

Tansy's living room had been decorated by multiple generations of cast-off furniture from various family members, as well as everything that didn't fit in Mom's cottage but she couldn't bear to part with when she sold her house. Grandpa's leather chair sat near the fireplace, and the walls were covered in old family portraits and an oversize wooden spoon and fork set from the sixties. A potted ivy hung in a macramé planter in the corner, and a string-art owl watched over us from its mounting above the light switches.

"What? A man needs a reason to visit his favorite niece?" he asked, leaning back into the soft cushions.

His hair was mussed and his voice was rough as if he'd been snoring. I assumed he'd fallen asleep waiting for me. I didn't blame him. Like everything else in the room, the couch was a hand-me-down that had seen better days, but it was comfortable. I could remember falling asleep on it during many family movie nights. Draped across the back was a blanket crocheted by my great-grandmother.

"I thought Tansy was your favorite niece," I pointed out.

He nodded. "She is. So is Magnolia . . ."

"*Maggie*," I corrected him. I didn't know why it was so hard for him to call her by her preferred name. "You know she hates it when anyone calls her that."

"But Magnolia is such a pretty name," he insisted.

"You call me Juni like everyone else does," I pointed out.

"You've been Juni since you were a wee baby. Magnolia didn't change her name until she was a teenager."

"That was almost twenty years ago. When Mom married Dad, you had no problem calling her Bea Jessup instead of Bea Voight, and you've known mom since she was a baby," I pointed out.

He shrugged. "I like Magnolia."

"Well, Maggie doesn't. And it won't kill you to extend the teeniest bit of courtesy to one of your favorite nieces." I scowled at him.

"Fine. I'll try. You got any beer?"

"Yeah, we got beer," I said. "You know where the kitchen is." But instead of expecting my uncle, a guest and my elder at that, to serve himself, I got up and came back with two Shiner Bocks, a local Texas brew. I handed him one and opened mine after I sat back down. "To what do I owe the pleasure of your visit?" I asked, trying to get the conversation back on track.

He toyed with the label of his beer. Instead of answering, Calvin looked up at me. "Did I ever tell you about the camels?" Without waiting for me to answer, he plunged into his story. "Back in the eighteen hundreds, the army was having problems patrolling Texas on horseback because even the best horse is going to tire out in this heat. So an enterprising fellow by the name of Major Wayne imported a pack of camels into Texas. They could walk for days without a drop of water, but camels are stubborn creatures. You can loop a horse's lead over a branch and they'll still be there in the morning. Not so with a camel."

"What does this have to do with anything?" I asked.

"I'm getting there. Whole platoons would wake up and find themselves stranded in the middle of nowhere because their camels had wandered off in the night. Before long, there were packs of camels roaming free around Texas. Everyone figured they died out eventually, but I was driving to El Paso in the summer of ninety-six, and what do you know—I found myself surrounded by a herd of wild camels running down the highway."

I smiled. I'd heard the story a dozen times. Most folks didn't believe him, but his best friend Samuel Davis had been in the passenger seat that day, and he swore up and down that it was true. "I remember, Uncle Calvin. I just don't understand what that has to do with you scaring me half to death."

"It just goes to show that no matter how weird life seems sometimes, it can always get weirder."

"You can say that again," I agreed.

Never one to pass up the opportunity for a punchline, Calvin grinned and repeated, "No matter how weird life seems sometimes, it can always get weirder." Then his face grew serious. "I thought maybe you could use some cheering up. I heard you've had a rough couple of days."

I sighed and took a sip of the cold beer. "That's the understatement of the year," I admitted. Everyone had come at me wanting to know details of Mayor Bob's death. Anyone who asked if I was okay did so as an after-thought. To be fair, it was a lot worse for Mayor Bob and his wife, Faye, but I wasn't exactly hunky-dory about the whole thing. Finding a dead body was traumatic. And I should know.

"I'm sorry you had to go through that."

"No need to apologize," I told him. "Unless you killed him. You didn't, did you?" I joked.

"Was tempted, a couple of times, but I never did."

"Oh yeah?" I asked. I scooted to the edge of my chair. Maybe it was people being hesitant to speak ill of the dead, but almost everyone I'd talked to had acted like Bob Bob-bert had been universally beloved. Sure, Mickey had complained about Mayor Bob selling off town land with-out bringing it to the board first, and Leanna had accused him of neglecting his mayoral duties, but even they didn't seem to hold a grudge. "Tell me about it."

"Bob was a stubborn old goat," he started.

"How so?" I encouraged him. I didn't normally have to drag a story out of my uncle. On the contrary, it was usu-ally all I could do to get a word in edgewise.

"You know that he was obsessed with the bank robbery back in 'fifty-six, right?" Before I could do anything more than nod, he launched into one of his typical lectures. "In the middle of the Bluebonnet Festival, the First Bank of Cedar River was hit by a crew of four notorious bank rob-bers."

"I know all this," I said, interrupting before he could go off on a tangent and explain the origin of the word rob-ber or the history of the Bluebonnet Festival. "What does this have to do with Mayor Bob?"

"He was just a kid when the robbery happened. Maybe that was why he was consumed with figuring out where the loot ended up."

It seemed like such a long time ago to me, but there were plenty of people alive and well today who had lived in Cedar River back in 1956. "And how old were you, Uncle Calvin?" I asked.

"Shush girl. I wasn't even a gleam in your grand-pappy's eye in 'fifty-six and you know it. But I grew up here, didn't I? While other kids were playing with their fire engines, those of us who grew up here pretended to be cops and the Cedar River Bank robbers. Other kids our age collected baseball cards, but we collected stories and souvenirs from that day at the bank."

"Everyone needs a hobby," I said. I understood the desire to collect. In fact, I was banking on it. At least half of the sales at Sip & Spin Records came from collectors. How was collecting memorabilia from a pivotal event any different than collecting vinyl albums?

He nodded. "I never grew out of it. It was another thing me and your dad had in common. If we weren't talking about football or cars, we were trading theories about the heist. But nowadays, with the internet and eBay and everything, word of the mystery has spread. There're dozens of sites dedicated to the robbery, and there's always something new going up for auction."

"Please tell me you're not blowing all of your money on artifacts from the bank robbery," I said.

"Don't I wish? Every time something new pops up, some jerk outbids me. A few years ago, I made a friend in a Facebook group about the robbery, and come to find out he was having the same problem. He's a little more tech savvy than me, and he managed to dig up that the guy who kept outbidding us went by the username MayorB1956."

"Mayor Bob," I said.

My uncle nodded his head. "One and the same. Seems like our dear mayor has been beating the rest of us to all the good stuff. A while back, an old map of Cedar River came up for sale. It showed how the town looked before the bank robbery. I'll tell you what, it was a treasure-hunter's dream."

"Why?" I asked, taking another sip of beer. "What's so important about an old map?"

"Think about it. Where this very house stands was probably part of a ranch's back forty back in the day. Old buildings have been torn down and new buildings erected. Even the river has changed course over the years. If some-one is looking to figure out where that money was buried, it sure would help to know where everything was back then."

"Wouldn't any map from the fifties do the trick?"

"This one was rumored to be special. But Bob just wanted to own the map for the map's sake, just like the bluebonnet paperweight that came up for auction a few weeks ago."

"A bluebonnet?" I asked. "A single bluebonnet?"

"Yup. According to the provenance, this very blue-bonnet was stuck to the shoe of one of the robbers when he was gunned down. It was logged into evidence and everything. The lead detective had the bluebonnet set in resin to preserve it and kept it as a paperweight on his desk until he retired. When he passed, rest his soul, the paperweight was sold with his estate. I'm a simple man, Juni, but I would have traded my right arm for that paper-weight. So me and this fellow I'd met on Facebook made a deal with each other. We'd pool our resources and bid as high as it took."

"You didn't," I sighed. Uncle Calvin wasn't a man of means. He owned his house outright, and his 'eighty-six Bronco. He also had a slice of Sip & Spin. But he'd never been great with money. The moment he earned more than a nickel with one of his get-rich schemes, he'd bet it on the ponies. The idea of him spending an exorbitant sum on a paperweight containing a flower that may or may not been connected to a bank robbery that happened almost seventy years ago made my head hurt.

"No, we didn't. Even with Marcus and me working together, the esteemed Mayor Bob outbid us, like he always did. Even had the nerve to display it on his desk at Town Hall like it was a trophy."

"Good for him," I said, and I meant it. "As much as I want you to be happy, you can't afford to go throwing money around like that." I toyed with my half-empty beer bottle. "Wait a second, your partner—what was his name again?" I took a sip.

"Marcus. Marcus Best. Runs a few used car dealerships around here. Maybe you've heard of him."

I almost spit out a mouthful of beer. "You wouldn't have happened to introduce this friend of yours to Mom?" I asked.

Calvin had the sense to look sheepish. "Uh, maybe. I don't recall."

"Cut the act. She introduced us to her new boyfriend this weekend. How long have you known she was dating someone?"

"What my sister does is her own business," Calvin said.

But I wasn't worried about him keeping secrets from us right now. There was nothing more annoying than having to admit that Maggie might be right about something. When she got a bad feeling from Marcus, I assumed it was because she couldn't stomach the idea of Mom dating anyone other than Dad. But I was wondering if there was more to it. Mayor Bob's office had been starkly decorated. I would have noticed if there had been a bluebonnet paperweight on his desk. There hadn't been.

"This map you were talking about, was it in a real

elaborate antique frame hanging in Mayor Bob's office?" I asked.

"Sure is," he said. Calvin sat up straight and set his now-empty beer bottle on the coffee table. He didn't use a coaster. "Hey, you think the widow Bobbert might be willing to part with that map?"

"I hate to break it to you, but I think someone stole that map out of his office this weekend."

"Wait a second? This weekend?"

I nodded solemnly. "When I found Mayor Bob on Saturday morning, the map and the paperweight were both gone. I think maybe whoever killed him took them."

Calvin held up his hands. "Well, it weren't me. I wanted them bad, but not that bad."

"I know you weren't involved," I told him.

We wrapped up the evening. I cleared the empty beer bottles and put them in the recycle bin. I went around to make sure all the doors and windows were locked—Tansy had her own set of keys—before going to bed. The whole time, I had one single thought going around in circles in my brain.

Calvin was innocent, but could the same be said about his partner, Marcus Best?

CHAPTER 17

I didn't get much sleep that night. The next morning, I lay in bed wondering what I should do. I knew I should inform Beau about the connection to the bank robbery and the missing map. I'd love to ask him if a certain bluebonnet paperweight had been logged into evidence. The right thing to do would be to tell him about the link, no matter how tenuous, between Marcus Best and the murder victim, but I couldn't. Because anything I told Beau would implicate my uncle as well.

Whatever liberties Beau might afford me did not extend to my immediate family. He wouldn't go easy on my uncle any more than he'd cut my mom a break on a speeding ticket.

When my phone buzzed with an incoming call, I glanced at the screen and was unsurprised to see it was Beau. Not only did we seem to have some kind of annoying psychic connection where he always popped up the minute I started thinking about him, but he was pretty much the only person in the world who called me instead of texting. Well, him and my mom.

I picked up. "Hello?"

"Morning, Junebug. Hope I didn't wake you."

I sat up in bed. "Nah, I'm up."

"Since we missed our date last Saturday, can I take you out to lunch today?"

I blinked at my clock. He called me before nine a.m. for that? "I've got errands to run this morning, and I'm working the afternoon shift at the shop." I deliberately didn't mention that Maggie and I were long overdue for a serious conversation with our mom's new boyfriend. If we managed to dig up any dirt on him that didn't also lead back to my uncle, I'd be happy to share it with Beau, but not a second before that.

"And you close at, what, seven?" he asked.

"Yup."

"Okay then, I'll pick you up at seven."

"Huh? What?"

"For our date," he said. "See ya at seven." He disconnected. I didn't even remember agreeing to go out on a date with him tonight. Beau was either annoyingly smooth or smoothly annoying—I just didn't know which.

I got ready for the day and considered making breakfast, but since I planned on hitting the bakery on the way to work, I would pick up something there instead. I took my time picking out my outfit—but not because I had a date with Beau tonight. No, siree. I selected my white and yellow R.E.M. Out of Time concert shirt. It was one of my favorites simply for the fact that it was the softest, and it didn't hurt that now I'd be humming "Shiny Happy People" to myself all morning. I dug through my collection of glasses to find my rainbow ones since they were the only pair I owned with yellow on them.

There was a line at the bakery, which was probably a good thing since if I'd been the only customer, I'd be tempted to buy one (or two) of everything. By the time it was my turn at the counter, I was ready to eat the entire display case. "Good morning!"

I didn't recognize the person behind the counter, but they recognized me. "You're Juni Jessup, right?"

I didn't ask how they knew that. It was a small town, and if there was any question as to my identity, I'd parked my lime green adult tricycle out front in full view of the person behind the counter. "Yup."

"You're the one that found him, aren't you?" they asked.

"Yup," I said again. I braced myself for the worst. What wild theory would I have to debunk this morning?

"Is it true that he was mauled by an animal? I mean, I don't want to believe all the stories about werewolves in these parts, but if we've got jackalopes and chupacabra, why not werewolves, right?"

I stared at them, trying to figure out if they were being serious or not. I think they were. "For the record, jack-alopes are a joke someone invented to prank tourists." Jackalopes were created by mounting a small rack of deer horns onto a large taxidermied jackrabbit. "Even if chu-pacabras were real, we're way too far north. Can you imag-ine them trying to take down a fifteen-hundred-pound longhorn? And as for werewolves, you know those don't exist, right?"

They shook their head. "Man, that's just what *they* want you to believe."

"Uh-huh," I said to save time. I was curious who they thought had gotten to me. Big werewolf, maybe? But I wasn't curious enough to get into a debate with them before I'd even eaten my breakfast. "Can I have a dozen assorted cookies? And three of your biggest bear claws." What could I say? The more I thought about werewolves, the more I wanted a bear claw.

Traffic was light on Main Street. I set the pastries in the basket, looked both ways, and pushed my trike as I jaywalked across the street to Sip & Spin. We wouldn't open for a few minutes, but I caught a glimpse of Tansy inside. I knocked before using my key to unlock the door so I didn't startle her. "Don't you ever sleep?" I asked as I locked the door behind me.

"I didn't get home that late last night," she protested. "But I did get up early to go to the gym. Leanna's been coming in at six o'clock and she always hogs the good treadmill, so I wanted to get there at five thirty."

"Seriously? Aren't there like a hundred treadmills at your gym? And the track at the high school is open to anyone, not to mention the sidewalks."

"It's the principle of the thing," she said. She looked at my bakery bag. "Do I smell coffee cake?"

"Better. Bear claws." I pulled one out with the wax paper wrapper and handed it to her. "Careful, or I'm gonna call your gym and tattle on you."

"Oh please. They put out donuts on Wednesday and pizza on Fridays. They know it keeps us coming back." She peeked into the bag. "You're not planning on eating all of those, are you?"

"Of course not." I took my bear claw out and set the bag aside. Daffy jumped up to explore what was in the bag, but I guess cookies didn't smell as good as cat food, because he quickly lost interest. "Hey, I wanted to talk to you about something, but I'd rather wait until Maggie gets here so I didn't have to repeat it."

"Then you're in luck," Maggie said, appearing from the narrow hall that led to the back of the shop. She had a dust rag in one hand and a spray bottle of her favorite cleaner in the other. Yes, my sister had favorite cleaners. Today, she was wearing her usual outfit—a shin-length dress covered in tiny blue flowers on a field of yellow. "Hey, we match!"

I looked down at my yellow and white concert shirt,

and then over at Tansy, who wore a pale yellow sweater twinset over gray slacks. "Well, look at that, we do," I agreed. I didn't own a dress. Maggie didn't own a single pair of jeans. And Tansy didn't own even one T-shirt. "Or at least, we complement each other," I amended my statement. My sisters and I couldn't be more different when it came to personal style, but we got along when it counted. "Bear claw?" I offered.

"Sure," Maggie said. "What's this big news you've got to share?"

"I was talking with Uncle Calvin last night, and he said that he, Marcus Best, and Mayor Bob are all obsessed with the 1956 bank heist. Apparently, there was a heated competition between them on who could acquire the most mementos from it, and they're always outbidding each other. Interestingly enough, two of those mementos are missing—a paperweight and the map that used to hang in the frame that Tansy and I found in the dumpster yesterday."

"Oh my goodness, how many times has Calvin told us the story of that bank robbery?" Tansy asked. "I'm not surprised to hear that he's obsessed with it."

"To be fair, our uncle knows an awful lot about a bunch of different subjects," I pointed out. I remember one time we'd gone out for pizza. He'd regaled me with the entire origin of pizza and the history of red pepper flakes. By the time he'd finished, his pizza was cold.

"Wait a second, Marcus Best? As in Mom's Marcus Best?" Maggie asked.

I nodded. "Caught that, did you? I'm sorry I flaked on you yesterday."

Maggie reached into the pastry bag for her bear claw. "Tansy told me all about the cow. What did you do with her anyway?"

"I took her to the Garza farm. They're going to add her to their dairy herd."

"Sounds like you found a great home for her," Maggie said. "And you managed to dig up some leverage on our friend Marcus, too. Speaking of which, are you ready to go interrogate him?"

"Yup." I bent down to pet Daffy, then straightened and picked up the bag of cookies. "But first, we need to drop these by Faye Bobbert's."

♪ ♫ ♪

The Bobbert house looked like something out of a fairy tale. It was two stories with a sharply peaked gray-shingled roof, and had a huge bay window overlooking the massive, green front lawn. It was a white-on-white-on-white color scheme with old wood shingles, white filigree trim, and white railing on wide balconies that circled each story of the house, with a matching white gazebo over-looking a lush rose garden on one side and the river on the other.

The rose garden was a particular point of pride for Faye Bobbert, who won the Best Garden in Cedar River award every year, except for the time when aphids destroyed her prize-winning roses the day before judging. This year there was no sign of the aphids, and the gorgeous roses were in full bloom.

Due to the relatively early hour, there was only one other car in the circular driveway. Maggie and I walked up the long sidewalk lined with frosted white balls that probably lit up at sunset and added to the magical appear-ance of the house.

We knocked, and Jen Rachet—the last person I ex-pected to bump into this morning—opened the door.

"Yes?" she asked, blocking the door as if she were on sentry.

Ignoring the fact that yesterday's encounter with Jen had been unpleasant, I plastered my friendliest smile on my face and lifted the pastry bag. "Howdy. We just wanted to offer our condolences," I said.

Jen reached for the bakery bag. I snatched it back. "I'll let Faye know you dropped by," she said, holding out her hand expectantly.

"Oh, Jen, aren't you sweet?" Maggie asked, sweeping her up into a hug. "I'm sure Faye appreciates you so much. Don't you agree, Juni?"

"Of course she does," I said, following my sister's lead. Being nice to Jen when she'd never been anything but mean to me was difficult, but she wouldn't let us through the front door if we behaved as rudely as she did.

"Tansy didn't bake those did she?" Jen asked once she untangled herself from Maggie's embrace.

I bristled at the unspoken accusation that my sister might have tampered with the cookies, like Jen alleged my oldest sister might have poisoned the mayor's coffee. "Nope, bought them fresh this morning at the bakery."

"Oh," she sniffed. "Store-bought. How quaint. Well, I guess you might as well come inside. I'll tell Faye you're here."

She moved back and I stepped inside the fairytale house. It was as beautiful as I'd always assumed it would be. The white marble floor shone. A white gently spiraling staircase led to the second floor. The white walls were bare of ornamentation except for a subtle white-on-white pattern in the wallpaper. The windows that sparkled so brightly from the outside flooded the foyer with light, which bounced off a heavy chandelier and cast tiny rainbows into the corners.

We followed Jen into a sitting room furnished with light blue upholstered furniture that would have been more at home on the set of Bridgerton than in a house on the outskirts of Austin. Instead of her normal bright colors, today Faye was decked out in gray and black. She sat on a plush, high-backed chair. If she had puffy eyes or splotchy skin from crying, it was expertly disguised under a thick layer of makeup. "Oh, hello," she said, looking between my sister and me as if trying to remember our names.

"Maggie Taggart and Juniper Jessup came by to bring you some cookies," Jen announced.

Faye's face lit up. "From the bakery?"

I nodded.

"Oh thank goodness," she said. "I couldn't bear to look at another casserole."

Good thing my mom had talked me out of bringing one.

"We wanted to tell you how sorry we are for your loss," Maggie said solemnly. "Mayor Bob will be missed."

"Won't he?" Faye absently twisted the wedding ring on her finger as if it was an old habit, which I supposed it was—the Bobberts had been married for fifty years.

Jen brought the cookies out, arranged on a plate, and handed smaller plates all around. We each took a cookie before placing the rest on a low coffee table adorned with matching crystal vases, both filled with roses from the garden. We sat in awkward silence for a moment before I asked, "How was Alaska?"

Faye visibly brightened. "It was lovely. My sister and I always talked about taking a cruise together, but she hates the tropics. Cynthia, that's my sister, lives up in Boston, and I don't get to see nearly enough of her anymore." She nibbled on her cookie, then set it on the plate she'd balanced on her knees.

"I understand completely," Maggie said. "It was so hard having Juni in Oregon. We're all so happy to have her back home." She reached over and squeezed my hand.

I agreed wholeheartedly. I didn't realize it until I moved back, but what had been missing in my life was being close to my family. And now that I lived with one sister and worked with both of them, I saw them almost every day. I would have thought that I'd get sick of them by now, but it hadn't happened yet. "Is that where you're from? Boston?" I asked, realizing I knew next to nothing about Faye Bobbert outside of her being the mayor's wife, now the mayor's widow.

"Born and raised," she said. "Met Bob there, at Boston College. He was pre-law. I was poli-sci. But his family was all down here, so after graduation, we moved to his ancestral home." She looked around. "Here." Faye stared out one of the expansive windows overlooking the river. "I've been on him to retire for years. He promised me one more term, and then, well, this." She drew a handkerchief out of her pocket and dabbed delicately at the corner of her eye.

"What were your retirement plans?" Maggie asked, trying to direct the conversation onto more solid footing.

"Move back to Massachusetts, for starters, closer to Cynthia. Then, I want to travel. See the world. Maybe get an RV and drive around the country, visiting family and seeing all the national parks. I just can't take another Texas summer," Faye said.

"I don't know, I've always kind of like Texas in the summer," Maggie said. I turned to her, flabbergasted. Don't get me wrong, I loved my home state, but Texas summers were brutal. From June to September, temperatures could stay in the triple digits for weeks at a time with little or no rain in sight.

"You can't possibly be serious," Jen said. "What would become of your roses if you left?" Faye was well-known in Cedar River for being militantly protective of her roses. No one was allowed near them, not even the gardeners who took care of the rest of the property. Rumor had it she even mixed her own proprietary blends of fertilizer and weed killer because she didn't trust the stuff they sold down at the feed store.

"All things come to an end, eventually," she said. Then she heaved a sigh. "Now Bob won't ever have the chance to retire."

"Poor Bob," Maggie said.

"Poor Bob, indeed." Faye moved her plate to a table near her elbow. More than half of the cookie still remained. I'd gobbled my cookie within minutes. She turned her attention to me. "Juniper, dear, can I ask you a question?"

"Of course," I said. I was getting tired of the questions, but Faye was Bob's wife. She deserved answers. If I could give them to her, I would.

"When you—" She stopped herself. "That is to say, in Bob's office, did you . . ." Her voice trailed off. She twisted her handkerchief. "Did you happen to notice a bluebonnet paperweight on his desk?"

Out of hundreds of questions she could have asked, I was not expecting that one. "No, ma'am, I did not. To be fair, I wasn't looking for it, though." I wish I had known about the paperweight at the time. I racked my brain. Had it been on his desk and I'd overlooked it? I didn't think so. Desperate to distract myself from looking at Bob, I'd studied every inch of that office. I hadn't noticed a paperweight.

"Will you do me a favor?" she asked.

"Yes, ma'am. Anything," I promised. I felt so bad for her and everything she was going through.

"You let that nice detective of yours know if he finds the paperweight, he should throw it in the trash straight-away."

"Why?" Jen asked. "Bob loved that paperweight. He wouldn't stop talking about it."

"It's nothing but bad luck." She stood and smoothed her long, dark gray skirt. "If you'll excuse me, I have arrangements to make."

"Anything I can help with?" Maggie offered.

"Thank you, but no. I'll see you at the service on Thursday, though? All of you?"

We all nodded dutifully. "Of course," Maggie said, and I echoed her.

The three of us headed to the door. As soon as it was shut behind us, Jen asked, "Can you believe that nonsense?"

"Nonsense?" I asked.

"About Bob planning to retire after the next term. And leaving Texas? Never. He's a lifer."

"Are you sure?" Maggie asked. "It sounds like they had plans up north."

"And when I talked to Leanna Lydell-Waite the other day, she mentioned that Mayor Bob hadn't decided whether or not he was running for reelection come November," I added.

"Horsefeathers," Jen said. "I am, was, on his reelection fundraising committee. He was running. I guarantee it."

I looked at Maggie. I didn't want to ask it aloud, not in front of Jen, but hadn't Marcus Best contributed to his campaign fund recently?

"Why not retire now? Look at all this," Maggie said, gesturing at the fairytale house surrounded by the perfectly manicured lawn. "It's not like Mayor Bob needs the salary. He's the richest person in Cedar River. If anyone can afford to stop working, it's him."

"Wrong again," Jen said with an air of authority. "I heard it from Carole, who heard it from Joyce down at the bank, that the Bobberts are flat broke. And while I was helping Faye straighten up, I may have noticed a whole stack of overdue bills. Such a shame, isn't it? Goes to show you never really know." She shook her head before splitting off from us to head to her car.

CHAPTER 18

"Do you think it's true?" I asked Maggie as we got into her car and we drove away. "The Bobberts are broke?"

"I don't know what to believe, but Jen was right about appearances being deceiving. Look at this car. Look at my house. We bought one of the biggest houses on the block and lease nice cars because J.T.'s clients expect a successful lawyer to live in a nice house and drive a good car. But all of our money is tied up in his law office or the record shop. We're one bad month from losing everything."

I frowned. "I'm sorry. That's rough." I was also all in on the shop, but I had nothing to lose. I didn't have a car or a house, but I also didn't have a car payment or a house payment to worry about.

"But if Jen is right, and that's a big if, then Bob couldn't afford to retire anytime soon. Faye had to know that," Maggie said.

"Not necessarily. You're the most organized person I know, and a whiz with math. You've kept the books at J.T.'s legal firm since it opened, and since you're a regular bean counter—no pun intended—you manage all the finances for Sip & Spin. I assume you pay the household bills, too?" It wasn't a question exactly, but Maggie nodded in the affirmative. "Mom said it's not like that in the Bobbert house. With Bob in charge of the finances, she might not have realized that they were in trouble."

"Good point," she said, merging on the highway. "But Faye didn't come off as worried. A little resentful, maybe."

"You picked up on that too? I was surprised she wanted to throw his paperweight in the trash. To hear Uncle Calvin talk about it, that paperweight was one of Mayor Bob's prized possessions. Why would she throw it away?"

"People grieve in different ways," she reminded me.

"True." I watched out the window as we sped down the highway. It was a lovely day.

It's hard to describe exactly what made the sky in Texas so spectacular. It's blue, that's true. But it's blue most places, at least some of the time. Even in Oregon, where it seemed to rain almost every day, the sky was generally blue. It just wasn't this blue. Or this big. How was that even possible? The sky was the same size and shape no matter where on earth you viewed it from, but in Texas it just seemed bigger somehow; bigger and bluer than anywhere else.

As my sister drove, I replayed our conversation with Faye in my head. When our dad passed, Mom locked herself in her room and refused to come out for two weeks. Faye, in comparison, was accepting company and might as well have been planning a vacation as arranging a service. And for that matter, was it wise to hold a service so soon after Bob's death? If he'd been murdered—and all signs pointed to that—then would she even be allowed to bury him yet? But Maggie had a point. Everyone had their own journey after a loss.

"Did you know Bob was a lawyer?" I asked Maggie, remember how Faye had told them about them meeting in college.

"Of course. He wasn't practicing anymore, but he and J.T. ran in the same circles."

"Is being a lawyer a prerequisite for running for mayor?" I asked.

"As far as I know, there are no prerequisites. I mean, I'm sure you have to be a citizen of Cedar River. There's probably some kind of minimum age, and a background check, I assume."

"Background check?" I asked.

"To make sure you're not a felon or something," she answered. "Why are you so interested? You're not thinking of running for mayor, are you?"

I shook my head. "No way. I'd make a lousy mayor."

"I don't think that's true," Maggie said. "You'd do a great job. You care about people. You go out of your way to make things right. Just look at you now. You don't need to be running around investigating a murder, but of course you are, because you can't help yourself. You've always had a strong sense of right and wrong."

"For the record, the only reason I'm 'running around' as you put it is that the sooner we can prove that Tansy didn't poison Mayor Bob, the sooner business can pick back up."

"So you're doing this for purely selfish reasons?" she asked.

"Of course not. I want to see the person who killed Mayor Bob brought to justice."

"Then why not let the police do their job?"

I rolled my eyes. "Please. No offense to Beau and his crack squad, but I literally have as much experience solving murders as they do."

Maggie chuckled. "Exactly."

"If anyone could run for mayor, even me, then why has no one run against Bob? He's been in office for ages and, as far as I can tell, he hasn't actually *done* anything."

"He hasn't offended anyone, either," Maggie said. "He's kept the lights on and the roads paved. Anything beyond that, he's bound to make enemies. I mean, just look at this land deal. Cedar River had a few acres that no one was using, so he sold Rawlings Hollow to a developer. Sounds like a win, right? Then why are people so angry?"

"I went past that land the other night, with Teddy," I told her. "It's not just undeveloped, it's wild. Pristine. Turning it into a parking lot ought to be a crime."

"See? That right there is why everyone in Cedar River was perfectly happy reelecting Mayor Bob over and over again. As long as nothing ever changed, no one ever had anything to be upset over."

"Then why, after over a decade in office, did Mayor Bob finally do something controversial?" I asked.

Maggie pointed a finger at me. "That's the million-dollar question. Was he planning on retiring and had nothing left to lose? Or was he going to run again and needed some extra political capital? Was he doing what was best for the town, or did he have his own self-interest in mind? If Jen Rachet was telling the truth, the Bobberts are in financial trouble. He wouldn't be the first mayor to abuse his office for financial gain."

"Like a kickback?" I asked.

She pulled into a parking lot. We got out of the car. "I don't know. But then again, maybe I'm not the best person to answer that question."

"Who is?" I asked.

Maggie gestured at the building in front of us. It was a squat brick building, with the front made of glass. Inside, I could see people wandering around a showroom of cars. Beyond the building was an enormous parking lot filled with even more cars. And over the door was a sign the size of a billboard advertising Best Used Cars, featuring the face of Marcus Best with a cartoon bubble coming out of his mouth announcing, "If you need a car, you need the Best."

A salesperson approached us in the parking lot before we could even touch the front door. "Howdy, ladies, how can I help y'all?" He was tallish, with a beer belly, slicked-back hair, and squarish gold-framed glasses. His blue polo shirt was untucked, and there was a stain on the hem of the shirt. He sized us up, then glanced over at my sister's Lexus. "Let me guess, you're looking for something high-end."

"Actually, we're looking for Marcus Best," Maggie said. "Is he in?"

"Sure is." He opened the big glass door and held it as we walked through. "Can I get y'all anything while you wait? Coffee maybe?"

"No, thanks," I told him. I didn't like to think of myself as a coffee snob. I'd certainly always had my favorite shops, but before my sisters and I opened Sip & Spin Records, coffee was coffee. But now that customers relied on us to pour rich blends and perfect combinations, I'd gotten much pickier about what I drank.

We waited in the showroom. There were no chairs. The front and back walls were almost entirely made of glass, so there was nowhere to lean. We had no choice but to browse the cars. As far as purpose-built design went, it wasn't awful.

Marcus approached and held out his hand. "Girls, good to see you again." Like his salesperson, he was wearing a polo, but his was tucked into jeans and stain-free and was covered by a sports jacket. "Did no one offer you any coffee or refreshments?"

"We're good," I assured him.

"I don't blame you. After having the stuff y'all serve, I wouldn't drink the swill we have here, either." I glanced at Maggie. When had Marcus visited the shop? She shrugged. She didn't know, either. Oblivious to our silent conversation, he plowed onward. "I'm assuming you're here to take me up on my offer to get you in a previously owned car or truck? What kind of budget are we working with here?"

That question made me uncomfortable. There was something about a stranger asking how much money I had to spend that made my toes curl, and not in a good way. Then again, I suppose it was his job.

"Can we talk in your office?" Maggie asked.

"Why, sure. Why don't y'all follow me?" He led us down a hallway.

Unlike Mayor Bob's, Marcus's office was not so much cluttered as homey. Instead of standard office chairs, we sat in comfortable, mismatched armchairs. Mine had a throw pillow on it that for some unknown reason featured the face of Nicolas Cage. The desk was covered in model cars, and the rug was a kid's play mat of a fake road. He tossed each of us a small squeeze toy in the shape of a car with the Best logo emblazoned across the hood and doors. "Aren't these just the darndest things?" he asked.

"Sure are," I agreed, giving it a test squeeze. It had a nice squish to it.

On the walls behind Marcus's desk hung a large flat-screen that showed a rotating slideshow of happy customers signing contracts, holding up keys, and driving away in shiny vehicles. But as decorated as it was, there were no personal touches in the office. It was playful, but at the same time it was literally all business.

"Now, normally I wouldn't mention this, but we are

having a sale next month. No money down, top value for your trade-in, and skip the first two payments on any vehicle you finance through us. It's our best deal of the year, and by the end of the sale, there won't be but two cars left on the lot. Because you girls are practically family, I'll let you look through current inventory and find your perfect ride, but I won't process the paperwork until next month, which means you qualify for the sale. Plus you'd get an extra month payment-free. Who can say no to a deal like that?" He sat back in his chair looking satisfied.

"Um, I'll have to think about that," I told him. I didn't need a car. I couldn't afford a car. More importantly, I didn't *want* a car. "I was talking with my uncle Calvin yesterday, and he mentioned that you were also interested in the 1956 bank robbery in Cedar River."

He looked surprised by the change of topic. "Why yes, I am. That's actually how I met Calvin. Real good guy. Horrible taste in cars, though. Don't you think it's time for him to upgrade?"

"Calvin loves that Bronco of his," Maggie said.

"More like Break-o. Am I right?" Marcus asked.

"What's your interest in the bank robbery?" I asked, trying to refocus the conversation. "I mean, you're not from around here originally, are you?"

"Grew up just outside of Dallas," he admitted.

For the record, there were several big cities in Texas, multiple regions, and even two time zones. But in a very real way, there were two Texases: the real Texas, and Dallas. Don't come at me, I don't make the rules.

"I remember hearing the story when I was a kid and it caught my imagination."

"Is that why you moved here?" I asked. His flagship dealership was north of Dallas, but he had used car lots all up and down I-35.

"Yes and no. I was in San Antonio at a car auction a few years ago, and on my way home I was going to stop in Cedar River just to have a poke around like I always do when I'm down this way. I saw this lot and it was love at first sight, I tell you what. And the *Best* is history," he said, laughing at his own pun.

"How did you discover the lot out in Cedar River? You weren't driving by that, not unless you were really lost," I said.

"The Cedar River lot?" he asked.

"You know, Rawlings Hollow? That overgrown bit of land by the Garza dairy farm on a dirt road so far away from anywhere that it would take a surveyor's map, a professional guide, and a good hound dog to find it?" I clarified.

"Oh, that lot." Marcus flashed us a toothy grin. "That's not car related. Speaking of cars, am I right about you being a truck person? Or are you more of a flashy two-door model? Something with a little get-up-and-go to it?"

"What do you mean, not car related?" Maggie asked, trying to direct the conversation back on topic. "If Rawlings Hollow isn't slated to be the newest location of Best Used Cars, then what do you need it for?"

"Why does anyone need anything?" he asked. "It's a beautiful spot, don't you think? Absolutely pristine, if a bit rural. If I ever decide to build anything bigger than a hunting blind on it, it would take the Army Corps of Engineers, but I couldn't pass it up. You know what they say, girls, they're not making any more land."

"Technically that's not correct," I said.

"Juni, shush," Maggie said.

"Well it's not," I insisted. "Sea levels are dropping. Volcanic activity is at a high. The ice shelf is receding. Dust storms on the African continent are dumping so much sand in the tropics that beaches are expanding. New land is being made every single minute." Maggie gave me a look that said that I needed to shut up, and I realized that I had meandered away from our interrogation. Maybe I had more in common with my uncle than I'd realized. "But yeah, I know what you mean," I finished, meekly.

"So you're a hunter, Mr. Best?" Maggie asked. "And you're planning on putting a deer blind out on Rawlings Hollow?"

He shook his head. "Call me Marcus. To be honest, the only thing I hunt is bargains. Speaking of which, I've got a sporty little all-wheel-drive Juke that has your name written all over it, Juni. Let's get out of this stuffy office and take it for a spin. What do you say?"

I glanced at my sister. We weren't getting much out of Marcus. "Maybe some other time." We both stood.

"Oh come now, girls. I can't let you walk out of here without a test drive. Won't take but a few minutes. Now if I can just take a copy of your driver's license and get a credit check started, we'll have you behind the wheel in a jiffy."

"Gee, look at the time," Maggie said as she tugged on my arm. We speed-walked back to her car, dodging two more salespeople as we made a dash for the exit. "Oh my goodness, I didn't think we were getting out of there without signing something."

"Right? He's like a dog with a bone. And did you catch how he kept calling us 'girls'?" I asked.

"So cringy. What does Mom see in him?" Maggie asked as we pulled out of the lot, half expecting another salesperson to step in front of her car to keep us from leaving.

"I mean, I want her to be happy." I turned around in my seat and studied the car lot as it receded behind us.

"He's a successful businessperson, plus he's friends with Calvin."

"You know I love our uncle with my whole heart, but you have to admit he's not exactly the best judge of character," Maggie countered.

"Even if he's not, Mom is," I said.

CHAPTER 19

We rode in silence for a while, each of us lost in thought. I was replaying our conversation with Marcus Best in my head, looking for any potential clues. A few miles before our exit, Maggie pulled off the highway and found a spot in a parking lot that was already crammed full of other cars.

Food trucks ringed the lot, their generators humming loudly as people lined up at the windows to order. In front of the trucks were several picnic tables, each with their own umbrella. Like the sound of ten different radios all blaring from ten different kitchens, the smell of a dozen different cuisines all baking, frying, roasting, and grilling was at once jarring and exciting. It was like the food at the Bluebonnet Festival, only dialed up to ten.

"What is this magical place?" I asked.

"I knew you'd like it," Maggie said. "Tuesday Truck Day. Why don't you go grab something and we'll meet back at one of the picnic tables?"

"Uh-huh, sure," I agreed, barely paying attention to her as I scanned the colorful trucks, squinting to read their menus from afar. My glasses were good, but they weren't that good. I'd have to examine each truck up close before making my decision. Or decisions. I wondered if they had samples.

"We don't have all day, Juni. Just pick something, okay?"

"I'm not good at picking just one thing when the choices are this good," I said.

Maggie made a harrumphing sound. "Like I don't know that. You've got five minutes to order something or I'm leaving without you."

"Whatever," I said, hurrying toward closest truck. Five minutes? That wasn't nearly enough time. I was ninety-nine percent sure Maggie wouldn't leave me like she threatened. Besides, we weren't that far from Cedar River. I could always order an Uber.

I chose a falafel wrap and chips at the second truck in the row. While I waited for my food, I wandered around taking mental notes. I would have to come back next Tuesday, and maybe every Tuesday after that until I'd tried everything there was to try.

Don't get me wrong, I loved living in a small town. It's safe. It's quiet. Everyone knew everyone. On a mild day, I could ride my tricycle from one end of town to the other without breaking a sweat. But the food options were, at best, limited. There was United Steaks of America—an expensive steak house—Betty-B-Que, and the diner. That was it. If I wanted anything else, I had to make it myself or borrow a car and drive to Austin. I had to get on the highway just to go to Sonic. This was closer, and the selection was mind-altering.

By the time I'd picked up my food, Maggie had already sat down at one of the picnic tables. "What did you get?" I asked as I stepped over the picnic bench to sit across from her.

"Oh no you don't," Maggie said, circling her arms protectively around her burger and fries. "You have your own food."

"I do," I agreed, and started peeling the foil off my lunch. It was crispy falafel balls, chopped lettuce, diced tomato, and sliced cucumbers wrapped in a thick, fresh pita and slathered with tzatziki sauce. The chips were homemade, still warm from the fryer, and dusted with just the right amount of seasoned salt. It was a simple meal, and yet so delicious.

Maggie put her burger down, and made sure that her fries were out of my reach. Rude! As if I didn't have my own homemade chips and needed to steal off her plate. She pulled a notebook and pen out of her bag and flipped to a clean page. "We need a list of suspects. Bob was too inoffensive to make enemies, but someone out there wanted to kill him. We should start with the obvious." She wrote Marcus' name in block letters and underlined it twice. "Who else?" she asked.

"If Tansy were here, she'd add Leanna Lydell-Waite, so we might as well. I suppose she has motive—if she wanted the mayor's job. She was in Town Hall that morning, but wouldn't tell us why. That's opportunity." Personally, I thought that my oldest sister had been barking up the wrong tree, but looking at her on paper, Leanna was a viable suspect.

"What about Pete Digby?" I asked. "He was there the morning of the murder. Did he let a murderer into Town Hall by accident or is he a willing accomplice?"

"That's hard to swallow," Maggie said. "If we're gonna add Pete, we might as well add Tansy."

"What? No!" I was so upset, I almost dropped my falafel wrap.

"Obviously she didn't do it. But unless we write her name next to the others, it makes her look guilty."

"I don't care. We already know she's innocent. Even

Beau knows that. We don't need to prove that. We just need to find out who *did* do it. Yes, Tansy had access to Mayor Bob's coffee but she had no reason to kill him. And where would she even get poison?"

"Exactly," Maggie agreed. "That's why we should add her to the list."

"No way." I reached across the table and covered the pad of paper with my free hand, accidentally smearing tzatziki sauce on the page. "How would you feel if it was your name, and you found out that Tansy and I wrote you down as a suspect?"

"I'd feel awful," Maggie admitted.

"Which is why we're not doing it."

"Okay. You win. Who else do we add?"

"I don't know," I said. "Faye Bobbert? Jen Rachet?"

Maggie wrote down Faye's name. "Faye, I get. The spouse is always a suspect. But why Jen Rachet? Is this because she doesn't like you? Because, to be honest, she doesn't like anyone."

"She seems to know just a little bit too much about Mayor Bob's death. And why was she at Faye's house this morning acting like she owned the place? Very suspicious, if you ask me."

"Fine, I'll add her," Maggie said. "I don't know where Jen was at the time of death—the festival, I suppose—but Faye was on a cruise in Alaska. The Bobberts always seemed like such a happy couple, but I guess you never really know what's going on inside of someone else's marriage. Even if she did have a motive, she's got the perfect alibi."

"A little too perfect," I muttered ominously.

"You've been listening to too many true crime podcasts," Maggie said. She tapped the top of the page with her pen. "Marcus has motive. He and Mayor Bob were rivals when it came to collecting the bank robbery memorabilia."

"If that's reason to kill someone, we might as well look at Uncle Calvin, too." Maggie started to write. "Don't you dare," I said. "He's had enough police suspicion to last a lifetime. Marcus and the mayor competed against each other on the auctions, but Marcus contributed to his campaign fund and Bob sold him the plot of land. Those aren't the actions of mortal enemies."

"Unless Marcus's campaign contribution was a kickback to get the land cheap," Maggie suggested. "But he paid fair market value, so I guess it's not that great of a motive."

"It doesn't make sense. People have gotten killed over business deals gone bad, but this one went through. It was quiet, but aboveboard, so there's no reason for Marcus to kill Bob to hush him up," I said between mouthfuls of warm, salty chips.

"Unless Mayor Bob was threatening Marcus."

"With what? To sell him more land?" I shook my head. "Friendly rivals don't poison each other in self-defense."

"Poison is historically a woman's weapon, though," Maggie said. "Which is another strike against Leanna."

"And Faye, and Jen," I pointed out.

"When I asked Marcus if he was a hunter, he changed the subject, instead of talking about his guns and trophies like most hunters would have. Maybe he doesn't own a gun, which is why he used poison to kill Mayor Bob."

"Come on, Maggie, you're reaching. Marcus doesn't work for the town. He lives in Austin, not Cedar River. He'd have no access to Town Hall while it was closed and locked." Then I corrected myself. "Except the doors were unlocked. I walked right in. But I bumped into Pete

Digby, the security guard, almost immediately. He let me go back to the mayor's office, but only because he knew me."

"If Marcus has been buying property in Cedar River, he had to go downtown to file his paperwork. Maybe Pete felt like he knew him, too."

"Yes, but Pete said he hadn't seen anyone else come or go," I said.

"Unless he was lying about that," Maggie said.

"Unless he was lying," I agreed. "That morning at the festival, I saw Mom walking around with a man I only later realized was Marcus. If he was with Mom, he didn't have a chance to murder anyone."

"We can ask her," Maggie said, "but what if she lies to protect him?" She reached for one of my chips, and I snatched the paper basket away from her.

"You have your own fries!" I protested.

"Yeah, but those chips are a perfect golden brown. Please?"

I sighed. Of course I would share with my sister. I always had and always would. I pushed the basket of chips between us. "I forgot to get ketchup. Can I have some of yours?"

"Yeah, sure," she said, moving her ketchup-laden fries into easy reach. Then she turned the notebook sideways so we could both read it.

Not counting Tansy or Calvin, which I absolutely wasn't, we had five possible suspects: Marcus, Faye, Leanna, Pete, and Jen. None of them had a strong motive. Only Leanna and Pete had a reason to be in Town Hall, but security was a joke. And as for the means? I had no idea. "Mayor Bob was poisoned, but do we know what kind of poison killed him? Was it fast acting or slow? Hard to come by or natural?"

"Natural?" Maggie asked.

"Like a mushroom or something."

"A poisonous mushroom would make you sick before it would kill you. Even bluebonnets are poisonous, in enough quantity."

"They are?" I asked.

"Sure. Every year at the start of bluebonnet season, the state puts out a warning not to let your pets or babies put bluebonnets in their mouths. But you'd have to eat a whole bunch of them to do any damage, and supposedly they taste horrible. Plus, no self-respecting Texan I know would pick a single bluebonnet, much less enough to kill a grown man," she explained.

I looked down at the table and realized that we'd eaten everything. I started gathering the wrappers. "I probably should have taken it easier. Beau's taking me out for dinner."

Maggie wiggled her eyebrows at me. "Well, that's just perfect." Out of everyone in my family, she was the only one who'd come around to the idea of me dating Beau. I guess it's because she's a romantic at heart, and the idea of a second chance on love was too much for her to pass up. Then, she surprised me by adding, "You can grill him at dinner. Ask if they've got any suspects. Find out what you can about the autopsy. Ask him what kind of poison killed Mayor Bob."

"I am not talking about an autopsy over appetizers," I declared.

"Dessert, then."

"I'm not ruining a perfectly good dessert. Besides, Beau won't tell me anything—not on purpose at least—but I think I know someone who will." I pulled out my phone and dialed. When a voice answered, I put it on speakerphone. "Kitty? It's me, Juni. My sister Maggie's here too."

"Oh, hey, Juni. Hi, Maggie."

"I was just curious. Did the medical examiner figure out what kind of poison killed Mayor Bob yet?"

"Hold on." I could hear voices in the background growing fainter as footsteps echoed in a small space.

While we waited, Maggie put her hand over the microphone. "Kitty? As in J.T.'s cousin, Kitty? What does she have to do with any of this?"

"She works at the hospital," I reminded her.

Kitty came back on the line. "Okay, get this. The killer went old school. Cyanide. I mean, how cool is that?"

I swallowed hard. Kitty was an EMT. She was used to dealing with sick, injured, and even deceased people. I wasn't. "Cool?"

"I don't mean *cool* cool. Obviously. Just I've been on the job for a couple of years now, and most of my patients OD on fentanyl, not cyanide."

"I guess if you put it that way," Maggie said doubtfully.

On the other end of the phone, I could hear Kitty talking to someone else before she returned and said, "Sorry, gotta run."

"Okay, thanks!" I said, but she'd already disconnected. I looked at my sister. "She's right about it being old school. How do you even get cyanide?"

"I have no idea," she said as she pulled out her phone. "Is this going to get me on a watch list or something?"

"Probably," I told her.

She read quietly for a minute, slowly scrolling past the information on her screen. "Apparently cyanide is in a bunch of stuff. It's got a bunch of legit uses, including taxidermy and film developing. Next time we see Marcus, we should ask if he's got a darkroom at his house."

"I don't know about Marcus, but Tansy took a photography class recently with one of her Groupons. Do you know who else was in the class? Leanna."

Maggie made a note of that. "Out of all of our suspects so far, only Leanna had means." She scrolled a little more. "Aha! Cyanide is used in all sorts of pesticides and weed killers. Who do we know that just bought a huge plot of land that is certainly overrun with bugs and weeds? He could buy barrels of this stuff at Home Depot and no one would bat an eye."

"Yeah, but how does he get into Town Hall? And how does he convince Mayor Bob to drink pesticide?"

"It's just a theory," Maggie said, and made a note under Marcus's name. "What about the others?"

I shrugged. "Everyone has access to weed killer, I guess, but I'll bet you a month's pay Faye has never pulled a single weed in that gorgeous lawn of hers. She has an army of gardeners."

"Not fair," Maggie complained. "You don't have a paycheck coming in right now." None of us did, not until Sip & Spin started turning a profit. It was a sacrifice we'd all agreed to make. Although, at the time, we hadn't anticipated all the bad luck we would run into.

Cedar River hadn't had a single murder in almost fifty years. And now, there had been two in the short time since I'd moved home. If I didn't know any better, I'd write my own name on the list of suspects.

We cleaned up after ourselves. As soon as we stood up, a family swooped down and claimed our seats. Now that I knew this place existed, and that it was this popular, I would come earlier next Tuesday. We drove back, and

Maggie dropped me off at the shop so I could relieve Tansy.

Unfortunately, there didn't appear to be much to relieve her from. Annie Lennox was singing to an audience of one as my sister busied herself with reorganizing our stock. Daffy was sunning himself in the front window. While that was an enviable activity, it was a bad sign. The skittish cat wouldn't be casually dozing in a beam of sunlight if we had any customers.

"Has it been this quiet all day?" I asked, looking around at the empty shop.

"We had a lady come in earlier, but it turns out that her kid just needed a restroom. But what about y'all? Did you and Maggie learn anything interesting?"

"I don't know about interesting, but it feels like we made some progress. Hey, before I forget, you took a photography class with Leanna last week, right?"

"Not *with* Leanna, but Leanna was there," she confirmed.

"And it was all film, right? Not digital?"

"Yup. The class was more focused on how to develop film and print photos than how to take good photos, but it was still annoying that Leanna ruined my film just so she could be better at something than I am." She shook her head. "But, because I had such a bad experience, the instructor gave me a free pass to come back and I got a refer-a-friend-for-half-off coupon. Why don't you go with me some night and we'll take the class together?"

"Sounds like fun." I'd never been terribly interested in photography, unless I counted posting hastily composed photos on my Instagram grid without any thought to theme or consistency. But spending an evening with my sister, not at the shop? That would be great. "Wait a sec.

If you got a coupon to refer someone, did you get referred by someone?"

"Yeah. It was, um . . ." Tansy tilted her head back and tapped her chin with one finger. "Jen. Jen Rachet."

My eyes got big.

"Why? What does that have to do with anything?"

"We added her to the suspect list, practically as a joke, but now she has means."

"How so?" Tansy asked. "Mayor Bob wasn't killed with a camera."

"No, but he was killed with cyanide, one of the chemicals used in film development."

Tansy paled. "How does that help me? I had access to those same chemicals. You're supposed to be proving I didn't kill Mayor Bob, not that I did."

CHAPTER 20

Before I could reassure my sister that no one was accusing her of killing Mayor Bob, the front door opened and a man walked into Sip & Spin. He was average height, a few pounds overweight, and white. He had light-colored short hair and a bulbous nose. He wore slacks with a polo and had a messenger bag slung around his body. For a second, I was paranoid that one of the salespeople from Best Used Cars had followed me to work to give me the hard sale. Again.

"Howdy," I greeted him. "Welcome to Sip & Spin Records. We've got the best selection of new and used records in all of Cedar River, and we specialize in local Austin bands. We also make a killer cup of coffee." I paused. Considering what had happened to Mayor Bob, I might want to tweak my pitch. "Today's special is All My Expressos Live in Texas, made from a rich local bean with just a hint of pecan flavor."

"Actually, I'm looking for Tansy Jessup," he said.

Tansy stepped forward. "Hi. I'm Tansy. Can I help you with something?"

He looked at me, and then back at my sister. I've been told that all three of us Jessup sisters bear more than a passing resemblance to one another. Personally I didn't see it, but folks that didn't know us well claimed we looked enough alike to be clones. But by the way he was looking at us with confusion on his face, I guess there was something to that. "A friend of mine is hardcore into vinyl, and he told me if I was ever in the neighborhood, I should look you up."

"I love to hear that. Anything particular you're looking for?" Tansy asked.

The man looked stumped at the question. "He gave me a list of artists to start with, but now that I'm here, I can't think of a single one of them."

"That's okay," Tansy said with a smile. "I'm sure I can recommend albums you'll love, and you can check them out over there." She pointed at the listening stations.

"No, no, that's fine. I don't want to waste your time. I'm meeting up with my friend later, and then we can come back. How long are you open?"

"We'll be here until seven," she said.

"Great. Thanks." He hurried out.

"Did that guy strike you as odd?" she asked me.

"Very," I agreed.

Instead of gathering up her things and leaving me alone to work the afternoon shift, Tansy poured a beverage for herself. "You want an All My Ex-pressos Live in Texas?"

"I'd love one. But aren't you off work?" I asked as she started preparing my drink.

"Got nothing better to do." She sat the coffees down on one of our café tables and took a seat. "You might as well take a load off."

After another hour of no customers, it became clear that Sip & Spin was done for the day. Tansy fed the cat as I cleaned the barista station. Then we closed up early and headed home.

As we pulled into the driveway, I noticed that the front

door was open. "Tansy, look at that," I said, pointing it out. I glanced over at Mom's cottage. The lights were off, the shades were drawn, and her car wasn't parked out front. "Do you think one of us forgot to close the door?"

"I doubt it. And if we had unexpected visitors, they wouldn't leave the door open for the air-conditioning to get out. Think we should check it out?"

I gave my sister a sidelong glance. "As the baby of the family, I shouldn't be the one making the smart decisions, you know." I pulled out my phone and called Beau.

"Junebug, you better not be calling to cancel on me," he said in lieu of a greeting. I could picture him leaning back in his chair with his cowboy boots propped up on his desk. "I've been looking forward to our date all day."

"Tansy and I just pulled up to the house, and the front door's wide open."

His flirty banter voice was replaced by his all-business one. "Where're y'all at now?"

"In the car," I said. "In the driveway."

"Pull out and leave. I'll be there in just a minute."

I relayed his instructions to Tansy, who backed out of the driveway. She drove past three houses and parked against the curb on the other side of the street, where we still had a view of the front of the house. "We're just supposed to wait? What if someone's inside right now? Or worse yet, what if no one's inside and we panicked for nothing?" She let the car idle.

She had a point. The other night when I came home and found Uncle Calvin on my couch, I just about jumped out of my skin. I'd been on edge lately, ever since I found Mayor Bob in his office. "Better safe than sorry, right?"

"I guess there are perks to dating a cop," Tansy said. "Which, for the record, I still think is the Titanic of bad ideas."

"Your objection has been noted, counselor," I replied sarcastically.

A police car pulled up in front of our house and an officer I didn't know got out of the driver's side. As he walked around the perimeter of the property, Jayden Holt emerged from the passenger side. She headed straight up the walk and through the open door with her flashlight in her hand. A minute after they arrived, Beau's truck parked behind them. He headed into the house and met Jayden at the door. After exchanging a few words, he turned around and headed for us.

I rolled down my window as he approached. He leaned over so he could address us both. "Afternoon, ladies. I've got good news. No one's in the house, and it's safe to enter." When I reached for the door handle, he put a hand on mine. "Bad news is it looks like you did have uninvited company earlier, and they ransacked the place."

"They what?" Tansy exclaimed.

"I'm gonna need y'all to walk me through the house and tell me if anything's missing."

Tansy maneuvered around the police cars to park in the driveway. A few seconds later, Beau joined us on foot. She'd driven only a few yards, but it said something about my sister's state of mind that she hadn't even thought to offer him a ride.

We entered the house and I stifled a gasp. Tansy had never been as meticulous as our sister Maggie, but she was neat. Tansy dusted and vacuumed every week. Maggie vacuumed daily and routinely dry cleaned her curtains. I was happy if my dirty laundry was in a basket instead of on the floor.

The living room looked worse than I'd ever let my room get, even when I was a sullen teenager. Couch cushions were slashed and their fluff tossed around willy-nilly. Pic-

tures had been ripped off the walls. The plant that had
been hanging in the macramé was on the ground in a
pile of dirt. Tansy's hope chest was open, and quilts were
strewn about the floor.

The kitchen was much the same. The refrigerator door
stood open, its contents spilled onto the floor. A tub of
Blue Bell Blackberry Cobbler ice cream was melting on
top of a half-empty bottle of ketchup and a container of
leftovers. The cabinets hung open, and dishes were stacked
on the counter tops. Even the silverware drawer had been
yanked out and emptied.

"I think you interrupted them," Beau said gravely as
we surveyed the carnage. "Either that, or they found what
they were looking for and left, because the bedrooms are
untouched. Well, Tansy's wasn't tossed. With Juni's, it's
impossible to tell."

"We would have seen them leave," I said, ignoring
his dig on my housekeeping skills. I had more important
things to worry about. Some stranger had come into our
house and riffled through it. Or, at least, I hoped it had
been a stranger. The mere thought that someone we knew
might have done this was too much to bear.

"The back door was wide open," he said.

From our parking spot a few houses down, we would
have seen someone leave through the front door, but not
the back. "Have you checked Mom's cottage?" I asked.

He jerked his head at Jayden, who was hovering behind
him.

"On it," she said. Tansy followed her out the door.

"Why would anyone do something like this?" I asked
him.

"Money. Drugs. Revenge. Boredom. Pick one," he replied.

"We don't have any money, or drugs for that matter.

We don't have any enemies that I know of. You mentioned boredom. Have there been a lot of break-ins like this in the neighborhood?" I asked, even though I was certain I knew the answer. I might not be the town gossip like Mom or Tansy, but if there had been a string of burglaries in Cedar River, I would have heard about them.

"Nope. Do you lock your doors?"

"Always." I know that there's a perception that no one locked their doors in small towns, but my family had locked our doors as long as I'd been alive. It was a habit so deeply ingrained in both Tansy and I that there was no way one of us forgot to lock them this morning when we left the house.

"Is anything missing?" Beau asked.

"Other than our security, dignity, and peace of mind?" I looked around and shook my head. "Impossible to tell in all this mess."

"You haven't upset anyone recently, have you, Junebug?" he asked, eyeing the mess as he wandered from room to room.

"Me? Not that I know of," I said, trailing after him.

"You haven't been, and I'm just spitballing here, sticking your nose somewhere it didn't belong? Asking too many questions? Interviewing murder suspects?"

I felt myself go pale. "Of course not?" It came out sounding like a question.

"Good to hear. Because someone capable of killing the mayor might be capable of hurting a sweet record shop owner, too."

Tansy and Jayden returned before I had a chance to think too hard about that. "Mom's not home, and they didn't touch the cottage. Ran out of time, I guess," Tansy said. "I called her, told her everything. She wanted to come home immediately, but I told her it might be better if she spent the night with a friend. Just until we straighten things up. We can straighten up, right?" She directed this to Beau. "It's not like an active crime scene or anything?"

"Of course. Officer Holt, if you've gotten all you need, y'all can go. I'll stick around here for a little longer."

"Sure thing, Detective," Jayden said. Then to me, she said, "Sorry about all this."

I smiled at her. "Thanks for coming so fast."

"And thank you for calling us instead of dealing with it on your own," she said. Then she and the other officer left.

Beau led the way into the kitchen. "I know this looks bad, but we'll have everything set to rights in no time." He reached inside the pantry and grabbed a broom.

"If y'all have the kitchen, I'll get started on the living room," Tansy said.

"Give a shout if you need a hand," Beau told her. Several bottles that had been in the refrigerator had shattered on the floor, and he began sweeping up the broken glass.

"You don't have to do that," I told Beau.

"What do you think they were looking for?" he asked.

"I have no earthly idea." I reached past him to get a dust pan, and held it so he could sweep the remnants of a bottle of cherry salsa that I hadn't even opened yet into the pan.

"That jerk," I muttered. I'd been looking forward to trying that salsa.

"More likely 'Those jerks,'" he corrected me.

"What makes you think so?" I asked. It was hard enough coming up with one person who disliked Tansy or me enough to do this, but multiple people? My mind boggled.

"Look at your refrigerator. Whoever went through it just tossed stuff around. But the cabinets were emptied without so much as a chipped plate."

"Great," I said with a sigh. The thought of two strangers standing side by side in my kitchen, poking into every crevice gave me the creeps. "I think I'm gonna need another raincheck on that date tonight," I told Beau. "Sorry. This is getting to be a habit."

"No worries. I'll order us some pizza." He double-checked the fridge. Almost everything was ruined. "And beer." He pulled out his phone and placed an order. Our local pizza place didn't deliver, but we had a service called Roadrunners that would. "And before you argue, I'm staying here tonight, just in case they come back. Don't worry, I'll sleep on the couch."

"Do you really think they might come back?"

CHAPTER 21

"I don't *not* think that they'll come back," Beau said. "If I'm right that you interrupted them, they might have unfinished business."

Unfinished business. I didn't like the sound of that.

"It could be worse," Tansy said, coming over to grab a garbage bag. "I'm just happy they didn't go after the shop. Yes, they made a mess, but it's still better than them trashing our inventory."

"At least Sip & Spin has an alarm, and security cameras," Beau said.

Tansy and I looked at each other.

"You don't think . . . ?" I asked.

"Yeah, I do think," she replied.

"What's going on here?" Beau asked.

"This weird dude came into the shop an hour or so before we got home. He asked specifically to speak with Tansy, but he didn't seem to know anything about music, and didn't have any questions."

"I distinctly remember him asking when we closed," Tansy added. "I got a weird vibe off him, like he was casing Sip & Spin, but now I wonder if he was just trying to verify we wouldn't be home anytime soon."

"I'm going to need your security footage," Beau said.

"Of course," Tansy agreed. "Juni, you have access on your laptop, don't you?"

"Yup." We automatically backed up all the footage to the cloud. As the most tech savvy of us sisters, I was the one who had remote access. "It's in my room. I'll go get it."

When I reached my bedroom and opened the door, I had to admit that Beau had a point that an outsider might have a hard time telling if my room had been tossed by whomever had searched the kitchen and living room. My room was chaos, but I liked it that way. I found my laptop right where I'd left it and hugged it to my chest. At least the intruders hadn't taken it.

Beau joined me in my room, and I cleared a spot for him on the bed. "You okay, Junebug?" he asked as he sat. "I know how disconcerting this can be."

"'Disconcerting' is one word for it," I said, sitting cross-legged next to him. My laptop booted up. I bypassed the password with my fingerprint on the scanner before logging into the video feed. I jumped through the footage. It wasn't hard locating the strange man with the bulbous nose since we hadn't had many customers today. I passed the laptop to Beau.

After watching the footage a few times, he said, "There's not much to go on. He didn't do or say anything threatening?"

I shook my head. "He gave me the willies, and the timing is suspect. That's all."

"I don't think I can put out an APB because some guy gave you the willies, but when we catch these guys, this could be evidence. I'll need a copy of this."

"I'll email it to you," I said, taking my laptop back. I checked the website's email. We had several online orders. At least the scandal hadn't affected the online store yet. I was expecting cancellations for the upcoming Arts &

Crafts Night, but there were none. Either people would rather not default on the price of admission, or they were so invested in learning how to make picture frames out of old vinyl that they were willing to risk spending a few hours with a possible murderer.

"You don't have to stay here tonight," I blurted out.

"It's no biggie," he said. The doorbell rang. Beau stood. "That's probably the pizza." He went to answer the door, leaving me alone in my bedroom. After putting my laptop away, I followed him.

Beau, my sister, and I sat around the kitchen table eating pizza and sipping cold beer straight from the bottle. "What kind of person would break into someone else's home and empty their freezer?" Tansy asked between bites.

"You'd be surprised," Beau replied. At our expectant stares, he continued. "People hide stuff in the weirdest places. I've found drugs in fake beer cans in a refrigerator, an urn stuffed with cash on a mantle, and a priceless stamp collection hidden in a family-size box of Cheerios. You don't even want to know all the things that can be stashed in a cookie jar. People store contraband in their freezer, evidence in their toilet tank, and stolen goods in their fireplace all the time. You're just lucky you came home before they started prying up floorboards and smashing holes in the walls."

"They wouldn't," I said.

"They would," Beau said. "And that's why I have to ask again. Do you have any idea what they were looking for?" I shook my head. "Anything at all?" he asked Tansy.

"No. We don't keep cash in the house. Or artwork. Or jewelry," she replied.

"There is another possibility," Beau said slowly, as if he wanted to make sure we didn't miss a single word. "Someone's trying to scare you."

"In that case, it worked," Tansy said.

"I'm not kidding," Beau said.

My sister stared at him from the opposite side of the table. "Neither am I."

"Ladies, I'm not an idiot."

My sister muttered, "Could have fooled me."

Beau continued as if she hadn't said anything. "I know y'all. You're out there playing detective, and someone doesn't like it. Maybe if you'd share who you've been talking to and who's on your suspect list, I can check their alibis and see who might have done this."

"I have no idea what you're talking about," Tansy said.

"You're lying," Beau countered. He turned to me. "Junebug, talk to me."

I glanced at my sister. She shook her head. I jiggled my leg under the table, and Beau put one hand on my knee to still it. I could never betray my sisters. But I couldn't lie to Beau, either. Not Beau, my friend, and certainly not Beau, the detective. But there was a thin line between lying and bending the truth. "We're not investigators."

"But you've talked to people," he prodded.

"Of course we have. I mean, it's a small town. People talk. That's what they do."

"Fine. Then tell me everyone you've talked to in the past few days."

"That would be impossible," Tansy said. "We run a popular business. Plus, with the Bluebonnet Festival, it would be easier to list all the people we *haven't* talked to."

"Tansy's right," I agreed.

"Fine. We'll do this the hard way. I'm guessing you've talked to the widow?"

"Maggie and I brought her cookies this morning when we stopped by to offer our condolences," I admitted.

"And the town council?" he mused. "Or were you at

Town Hall to interrogate Leanna Lydell-Waite specifically?"

"We were checking up on a friend," Tansy said.

"Nonsense. We've already established that you and Leanna aren't friends," Beau said.

"We could be," she argued.

"And who else? Pete Digby? Hank Akers? Jen Rachet? Samuel Davis?"

"What do Hank or Samuel have to do with this?" I asked, leaning forward and taking mental notes. I knew Samuel wasn't involved. My honorary uncle wasn't the killing type. I didn't know Hank well enough to tell one way or another. I had no idea how either of them might be connected, but I was determined to find out.

"Nothing," Beau said. "But now you've confirmed that you *have* spoken with Pete Digby and Jen Rachet."

"I've also talked to Esméralda Martín-Brown, Miss Edie, Marcus Best, and pretty much everyone at the Garza dairy farm."

"Marcus Best? The used car dealer?" he asked, leaning toward me. "What did he have to say?"

"Other than trying to get me to buy a Juke? Not much," I said.

"He's dating our mom," Tansy volunteered.

Beau leaned back in his seat. "I didn't know your mom was seeing anyone. Maybe we could double date some time."

Tansy let out a distinctly unladylike snort. "That's quite possibly the worst idea I've ever heard in the entire history of bad ideas," she said. She finished the last bite of her pizza crust, got up, and rinsed her hands at the sink. "Now if you'll excuse me, I have some cleaning to get to."

"Sometimes I get the impression that your sister doesn't like me," Beau quipped.

"Oh no, you're wrong about that."

He lifted one eyebrow. "I am?"

I nodded. "Tansy doesn't dislike you. She hates your guts."

"Gee, that makes me feel better." He stood and carried our empty plates to the sink and started on the dishes.

"Don't you have something better to do?" I asked him, leaning against the counter while he washed. "Like catching killers or whoever did this?"

"It's my night off," he said. "And I don't have any plans since my date flaked on me." He turned off the water and turned to face me. "Junebug, don't get your hopes up. Most home invasions aren't solved unless the perp is caught in the act."

"And the murderer?" I asked.

"Him, we'll catch."

"Him?" I asked, wondering if I'd missed something.

"Him or her," he corrected himself. "Or them. Can't discount the possibility that there are two or more people working together."

"Like the people that broke in here," I prodded.

He nodded solemnly. "I know it looks like I'm doing nothing, but while we're waiting for reports and results and computer searches to come back, I'm doing exactly what I'm supposed to be doing."

"Babysitting me and my sister in case the burglars come back?"

"Doing dishes," he answered. He handed me a damp plate. "Unless you want to wash and I'll dry?"

I chuckled. "Nah I like it this way. Wouldn't want to ruin my manicure." I held up my hands. My fingernails were short and uneven, with flakes of blue polish on my right pinky. The rest of my nails were bare and could seriously use some attention. If I ever had the free time, or the free money, I might worry about them, but for now they were fine.

While I put away dishes, Beau went back to work on the fridge. Tansy turned on music and the house started to feel more like a party and less like a crime scene. By the time everything was back in order, it was getting late. I stifled a yawn. "You don't have to stay, you know," I told him again.

"I know." He got one of the remaining beers out of the refrigerator and untwisted the top. "You thirsty?"

"Yeah," I said.

He held out a Shiner, and as soon as I reached for it, pulled it back. "First, promise me something, Juniper."

I grimaced. Beau didn't call me by my full name unless he meant business. "What?"

"Promise me you'll stop looking into Bob Bobbert's murder. I know you're worried about your sister, but you running around interrogating people is just painting a target on both your backs. If anything, it's making Tansy look guilty when you and I both know she isn't, and while I can't prove that your not-so-friendly intruders were here because of your nosiness, I can't prove they weren't, either."

"What do you want from me?" I asked.

"I know I'm asking too much, but promise me you'll be careful."

"Deal," I told him. I reached for the beer, and this time he let me take it. "Want to watch TV or something?" Since Tansy was still organizing her hope chest in the living room, we set up my laptop between us on my bed and streamed nature documentaries on Netflix until I fell asleep.

CHAPTER 22

The next morning, when I woke up alone in my bed, it took me a minute to realize that anything was wrong. Then I remembered that I'd fallen asleep next to Beau, and I bolted upright. My phone and my glasses were on the nightstand next to me. The other side of my bed was empty.

I found a note from Beau in the kitchen, taped to the coffee maker, with half a pot of coffee warming on the plate. His handwriting was neatly printed. "J—Try not to make any enemies today. X, Beau." There was a clean mug with sunflowers on it sitting next to the pot, waiting for me. I poured a cup before starting my day.

Despite not being on the schedule to work until Arts & Crafts Night started this evening, I got dressed for work in the Gin Blossoms shirt Teddy had found for me, distressed denim pants, and my pink glasses. Then I got on my trike and pedaled downtown. Maggie was already at Sip & Spin, and she was struggling to carry a large piece of wood out the front door. "Here, let me help," I said. The board wasn't heavy, but it was awkward.

It turned out to be one of the sandwich boards we'd set out for the grand opening but hadn't needed since. Up until this week, we'd had a steady enough stream of customers that it hadn't seemed worthwhile to block part of the sidewalk for advertising. Sip & Spin Records was printed at the top, with a vinyl record glued in the corner. The chalkboard part still read "Grand Opening Tonight!"

"You do anything fun last night?" Maggie asked. I must have looked guilty at the question—despite not having done anything I should feel guilty about—because she clarified, "Tansy called me last night to tell me all about the break-in. And for the record, I'm very hurt that you didn't invite me over for the cleanup party."

"I know how much you love to clean, but we had it under control."

"Oh come on, Juni. Under control?" She winked at me. "I know Beau spent the night."

"It's not like that," I protested. "Really, it wasn't. We watched TV. He got up early and left. That's the whole story."

"Uh-huh." Maggie erased the message. "What should we write?"

"Something cheerful."

"Something that doesn't scream 'We might have accidentally murdered someone but we probably won't murder you,'" she added.

"Don't Worry, Be Frappé?" I suggested. "Tansy and I wanted to create a special to honor Mayor Bob. He was a huge Bobby McFerrin fan, so I think he'd like that."

"Perfect," Maggie agreed. "What's going into it?"

I thought about it for a second. I wanted complementary flavors without overwhelming our customers. "Espresso made from Hawaiian beans. Add a splash of almond milk, a pump of amaretto-flavored creamer, and for that tropical kick, how does dairy-free coconut ice cream sound?"

Maggie nodded. "I can't wait to taste this."

"I'll run to the grocery store and pick up the coconut ice cream. Anything else you need while I'm out?" Daffy chose that moment to meow loudly as he trotted down the stairs.

"In case you don't speak cat, that's a request for dolphin-safe tuna," Maggie translated for him.

"Coming right up," I promised them both before heading to the store.

The only market in Cedar River was well-stocked, if small. It carried all my favorites, at a markup. Shopping local small businesses wasn't cheap, but it was worth it. Much of what we made at Sip & Spin we bought wholesale, but this was an emergency. Besides, with as few customers as we'd had recently, I didn't want to get stuck with too much coconut ice cream. If we were going to partner with Mrs. Garza, we would need to save freezer space for her locally made flavors.

Purchases safely tucked away into the basket mounted behind my trike, I made my way back to the shop. On the way, I passed Leanna, who was jogging down the sidewalk with a giant Great Dane trotting beside her. I pulled my trike over so I could say hello. "Lovely morning for a run, isn't it?" I asked her.

"Sure is," she agreed. The dog came over for an enthusiastic sniff. He butted me with his enormous head, demanding pets. If I had been on a bike instead of a tricycle, I might have fallen over. "Be gentle, Hammy," she admonished the dog.

"Hammy? Cute name for such a big dog," I said.

"Short for Hamlet, you know, like the play?" she explained.

"You named a Great Dane after *the* Dane? Clever." I chuckled.

"My wife's idea. She's a theatre nerd. Out for some exercise?" she asked.

"Actually, I'm on my way back to work."

Leanna nodded. "You should come running with me sometime."

I shook my head. "Thanks but no. Running is more Tansy's thing." I didn't know if it's this way in every family, but in the Jessup household, we had a strict rule that we could never like the same thing. Tansy liked lattes, so Maggie drank tea, and I preferred mocha. Maggie liked softball, so Tansy was into running and swimming, and I stuck with my computer games. Tansy had a hamster growing up, so Maggie got a lizard. I wanted a ferret, but Mom vetoed that. I loved Taylor Swift, so Maggie listened to Korn, and Tansy was obsessed with Aretha Franklin.

It's a miracle the three of us got along as well as we did.

"In that case, tell Tansy to give me a call sometime. We'll go jogging together."

I couldn't imagine Tansy accepting that offer but then again, she was competitive enough that she might take that as a challenge. "I'll pass along your message," I promised.

"Well, I don't want to hold you up, and I have ice cream in the basket, so I've got to get going."

"See ya," she said, waving before she and her enormous dog jogged away.

Back at Sip & Spin, I fed Daffy his tuna—I knew how to prioritize!—before blending up a few test drinks. It took more tries than usual to balance the nutty flavors into something tropical and refreshing, but once I figured out the right combination, it was delicious. As predicted, the morning was slow, but the sign worked. Slowly, customers started to trickle in to order the special of the day and stuck around to browse our collection.

In honor of Mayor Bob and Don't Worry, Be Frappé, Maggie and I took turns selecting island albums. Mine was anything featuring Hawaiian musicians Israel Kamakawiwo'ole and Don Ho. Maggie preferred Gregory Isaacs' Jamaican sounds. By the time Tansy came in to relieve us, we'd sold most of our Reggae, Ska, Calypso, Caribbean, and island music. I'd had to go back to the market for more coconut non-dairy ice cream.

"This is a nice turnaround," Tansy said as she stashed her purse under the counter and came over to watch me make the drink special.

"It is," I said. "Luckily, Cedar River loves their tropical frappés and aren't afraid of a little murder. That, and Sip & Spin is the latest gossip hot spot." Everyone had questions about either the intruders last night or Mayor Bob. I didn't particularly want to talk about either of those things, but I wasn't in a position to turn down free publicity.

"For the record, this drink is amazing," Tansy said, sipping on the sample I poured for her. "Your idea or Maggie's?"

"Both, and you helped too. It was your idea to come up with something Mayor Bob would have liked."

"Well, you did an absolutely splendid job. Got plans this afternoon?" She lowered her voice. "You going investigating?"

I shook my head. "Beau asked me to back off."

"And?" Tansy asked. "Since when did you take orders from Beau?"

"I don't. But look around. Business is back to normal. Better than ever, even. You don't have anything to worry about because you didn't kill the mayor. Maybe Beau has a point. Maybe we should leave this to the professionals."

"If you say so," Tansy said, though she didn't sound

convinced. "You're gonna be back later for Arts & Crafts Night?"

I nodded. "Yup. I'll be back early enough to set help set up."

"Great. Now shoo," she said, accompanying it with a matching shooing motion. "You and Maggie both. Get out of here. I've got the afternoon covered."

Before I got on my trike, my phone rang. It was Teddy. "Hey, what's up?"

"Not much. I just wanted to let you know that the vet gave Buttercup a clean bill of health, so we introduced her to the rest of the herd."

"How's she doing?" I asked. "They're not bullying her because she's different?"

"Juni, I swear, you're one of a kind, aren't you?"

"I'm just worried about her fitting in, that's all," I said.

"In that case, what are you doing this afternoon?"

"Nothing. Just got off work, but I need to be back by six to help set up for Arts & Crafts Night." We stayed open later than usual on event nights. Between the event fee, and the additional coffee and record sales, it was well worth it. Plus, it was drawing in new customers. Last month, we made vinyl roses and we had customers come from as far as San Antonio, an hour and a half away.

"You still at Sip & Spin?"

"Yup," I told him.

"In that case, I'll pick you up in a few."

"What for?" I asked.

"So you can see for yourself that Buttercup is just fine."

A few minutes later, Teddy's familiar Jeep pulled up to the curb and I climbed into the passenger seat. "I Only Want to Be with Brew," I told him, handing him the black drip coffee I'd made for him. "You sure you don't have better things to do?" I asked him.

"Better than spending the afternoon with you? Nah. But be warned, if I bring you home for supper more than twice in the same week, Mamá's either gonna adopt you or force me to marry you."

I nodded. "Thanks for the heads up. But I can't stay for supper. I've to get back to the shop."

"Mamá's gonna be awful disappointed," he said.

"Only your mama?" I asked with a grin. "Not you?"

"Speaking of mothers, how did yours take the news of the break-in last night?"

"You heard about that?"

"Of course I heard about that. It's my job to visit every house and business in Cedar River every day, and it's all anyone's talking about."

"Mom's taking it in stride," I told him. "Which is surprising, really. I thought that when Tansy told her what had happened, she was going to rush over and then insist on standing guard with a shotgun all night."

"That's hardly necessary when you have your own personal bodyguard, don't you think?" Teddy asked. His words were teasing, but his tone was dry.

"Does that bother you?" I had expected the local rumor mill to pick up on the break-in. A home invasion in Cedar River was capital-B Big, capital-N News. But the fact that tongues all over town were wagging because Beau slept over last night was disconcerting.

"That your ex spent the night at your place last night? Should it?"

"Nothing happened, if that's what you're wondering. But Beau's more than my ex. You know that," I admitted. "I'm not sure exactly what he is, though."

"If you're worried about me, don't be," he said, carefully keeping his eyes straight forward and his hands at ten and two on the steering wheel as he bumped down the unpaved road that led to his farm. "You're too smart to make the same mistake twice."

"You'd think that," I said. "But sometimes I wonder if I'm really as smart as everyone thinks I am."

"You are, Juni." Teddy took one hand off the wheel to pat my knee. Then he flipped on the radio. Alanis Morissette was playing, and he started to sing along in a loud falsetto. I joined in, channeling everything I had into the raunchy song.

Once we reached the farm, we traded the Jeep for an ATV. With as much acreage as the Garzas had, it was impractical to walk everywhere. If we were spending a few hours in the fields, we would have saddled up a pair of horses. If we were delivering feed to the livestock, there were several trucks capable of traversing the rough terrain. Even Teddy's Jeep could handle even the worst of it in a pinch, but the ATVs were faster, and more fun.

Bouncing along at speeds that bordered on reckless, I held on to Teddy's waist as we shot through the first meadow. He slowed to a stop near a gate, and I jumped off to hold the gate open. He motored through and I jumped back on. There were multiple pastures broken up to keep the herd from overgrazing. We headed to the far field, the one the cows used in the summer. It had a small creek that we used to splash around in on brutally hot August days, and plenty of scrubby trees that were less than ideal for climbing but provided welcome shade.

We were taking an unfamiliar path though, swinging wide to the west instead of making a beeline to the creek. "Why are we going this way?" I asked, having to raise my voice and lean in to be heard over the wind and the ATV's loud engine.

In response, Teddy angled the ATV toward the more well-worn tracks I remembered using the last time I'd been out here, which must have been a decade ago. Generations of using the same route had created a natural road, wide enough for a truck pulling a stock trailer and almost as smooth as the dirt road leading to the farm. He slowed and gestured at a lush coating of bluebonnets that had taken over the pasture, shouting back, "Don't want to crush the flowers."

Once we reached the herd, he slowed to a stop and jumped off. "The bluebonnets encroach a little more every year, which is a good thing. Until they go to seed, we try to leave them alone."

Teddy offered me a hand. I was perfectly capable of dismounting from an ATV on my own, but I took the help anyway, mostly because my lower half was numb from the lively ride across the rough land. The last thing I wanted to do was take a misstep and land on my face in a cow pasture.

The cows were grazing not too far from us. They were used to the noisy ATVs and other farm vehicles, but it was less stressful for them if we parked a few yards away and approached on foot. "I thought bluebonnets were poisonous," I said, remembering what my sister had told me.

"They are," Teddy. "But cows are too smart to eat them unless they're desperate, and there's plenty of good grazing they have access to."

"How do they know?" I asked. "That bluebonnets are poisonous," I clarified.

"Well I'm not a botanist, but I suppose they smell or taste bad."

Remembering Beau plucking a snake out of a thick patch of bluebonnets, I carefully checked my surroundings before kneeling to get a good whiff of the flowers. I smelled dirt and grass. Bees and butterflies flitted between the blooms, undeterred by their poisonous properties, but

I supposed the poison didn't come from the nectar. "I don't smell anything."

Teddy shrugged. "Maybe cows smell something you don't."

"How many bluebonnets do you think it would take to kill a man?" I asked. I knew that babies tended to put anything within reach into their mouths, and if they ate a bluebonnet, they could get sick, but it would be hard to trick a grown-up into eating enough bluebonnets to poison themselves if they tasted bad.

Instead of answering, he said, "You make me nervous sometimes, Juni. Come on, let's go say hi to Buttercup."

I traipsed after him, glad that today was one of the rare days that I'd worn cowboy boots to work. They might not be the most comfortable when standing on my feet all day, and they were awkward to pedal my tricycle with, but they afforded my ankles protection against snakes, bug bites, and gopher holes.

"Where is she?" I asked. Buttercup was a black and white Holstein, which meant she was nearly half again as big as the Garza's reddish brown Jersey cows. She should have been easy to spot in the herd of smaller cows.

"I'm sure she's around here somewhere," he assured me.

He led me to a narrow bend in the creek and helped me jump over without getting wet. As we walked, the bluebonnets grew thicker. We stepped carefully to keep from trampling them. Eventually, we reached the far border of the Garza farm. Where there should have been barbed wire separating the properties, I saw fence posts that had been knocked over.

"Uh-oh," I said.

"Don't worry, I'm sure she didn't go far," Teddy assured me. He pulled out his phone and dialed the main house, where he explained the situation and requested reinforcements before disconnecting.

"I'm sorry Buttercup knocked down your fence."

"It's not her fault, Juni." He pointed to the fence posts on the ground. "Looks like they've been down for a while." He shook his head. "Someone wasn't doing their job very well if they missed that. There's no telling how many cows have gotten out."

The downed fence was in a thick section of underbrush. "Watch your step," Teddy warned me. "Don't want you stepping on barbed wire or a rattler."

"I don't want to step on those things either," I assured him. We pushed through the tangled thicket, passing several No Trespassing signs nailed to scrubby trees. "Are you sure we should be out here?" I asked, a little nervous. Texans didn't take kindly to trespassers.

"No worries. We're in Rawlings Hollow, which belongs to your future father-in-law. I don't think he's going to shoot you."

I cringed. "Wow, you really are up on the latest gossip, but please, don't call Marcus that."

"Sorry, I didn't realize it was a sore subject."

I shrugged. "I'm trying to be happy for Mom, but I'm still on the fence," I admitted. "No pun intended," I added. It was nice of Marcus to help us load up the other night, but spending time in his office yesterday didn't exactly endear him to me. Maybe I'd like him better in a more neutral setting. "Now that the cat's out of the bag, when Mom invites him to family dinner, would you come too, as a buffer?" Teddy had been a fixture at family dinners growing up from kindergarten until about midway through high school when we'd drifted apart, about the same time that Beau started coming around.

"Sure. Just let me know when, and I'll be there," he

agreed. Teddy led me through a thicket of trees. He cocked his head. "Do you hear that?"

I strained to listen. I'd been hearing a low humming noise since we'd arrived, but I'd dismissed it as a residual effect of riding the loud ATV. "Chainsaws?" I suggested.

Teddy frowned. "Doesn't sound like it." Unlike his sister, Teddy had never shown any interest in working the Garza farm. He wasn't involved in day-to-day operations, but he still lived there, and was invested in his family's livelihood. "Besides, no one is supposed to be back here. Let's go check it out."

We cleared the thicket that served as a natural border between Rawlings Hollow and the Garza farm. Stretched out in front of us was a sun-drenched field blanketed by bright bluebonnets. It looked like a painting that should be hanging in a museum, right down to the big black and white dairy cow, calmly munching on a patch of spring-green grass.

"Buttercup!" I exclaimed. "There you are!"

Hearing her name, she looked up at me and mooed a greeting before returning to her meal.

"Do you see any other . . ." My voice trailed off as I scanned the field looking for any other wayward cows, but saw something else instead. In the middle of the bluebonnets was a small backhoe diligently destroying the most pristine patch of wildflowers in all of Texas. In addition to the hole they were currently working on, there were mounds of earth peppering the field. They'd been busy.

Without stopping to think, I ran toward the backhoe, waving my hands over my head like I was a shipwreck survivor trying to flag down a passing plane. "Stop!" I yelled, even though I knew the operator couldn't possibly hear me over the engine. As I sprinted past Buttercup, toward the destructive equipment, I noticed a heavy-duty truck hauling a flatbed trailer parked nearby. Crossing the path it had carved through the field, I noticed hundreds of bluebonnets crushed in its tracks.

It might not be illegal to pick bluebonnets anymore, but in my mind, they were sacred. "Stop! Cut the engine!" I yelled, and then tripped over a mound of dirt I'd missed in my rush. I would have fallen into the hole if Teddy hadn't caught me.

"Whoa, Juni," he said, hauling me back from the edge. I looked down at a neatly excavated hole in the earth, a few yards wide and several feet deep. The roots of hundreds of murdered bluebonnets stuck up out of the mound of dirt.

"What on earth are you doing?" a loud voice asked us. Behind him, the backhoe rumbled to an idle as an enormous man strode toward us with no regards to the flowers he trampled. "You guys can't be here!"

Between the run across the field, my anger at the senseless destruction of so many bluebonnets, and my near miss with the deep hole, my pulse was pounding in my ears. "Neither can you!" I replied.

Teddy's grip on me tightened, and I remembered that we were trespassing. I counted four of them to the two of us. I couldn't tell if they were armed or not. As far as I knew, Teddy wasn't. I certainly wasn't.

"Howdy," Teddy said, his drawl a sharp contrast from the nasal stranger's "you guys." "Didn't mean to disturb y'all. We're the neighbors." He jerked his thumb over his shoulder at his family's farm. "Out looking for a stray cow." Buttercup's curiosity must have gotten the best of her, because she'd followed our dash across the field and now butted the back of my shoulder with her huge head, demanding attention. "Didn't realize anyone was working out here today."

"Well, we are," the stranger said, crossing his arms over his chest in a threatening pose. He seemed deeply suspicious of Teddy's friendly attitude.

"Whatcha excavating?" Teddy asked. He stepped forward, deliberately putting himself between me and the big man. Buttercup mooed in my ear. "You'll never hit water with one of those." He gestured at the backhoe. "And if you're planning on clearing the whole field, you're going to be here all year with something that small."

"No offense, but I don't see how that's any of your business," the man said, leering at us.

He was focused on Teddy, so now that I'd caught my breath, I studied the men around us. The large man in front of us was white, mid-forties, and wearing a Boston Red Sox ballcap. I couldn't make out much about the backhoe operator from this distance, other than the fact that he was wearing shorts. Another white man, this one scrawny and dripping with sweat, leaned against a shovel. A large metal detector rested against the truck where a fourth man studied a large piece of paper spread out across the hood, held down in the corners by rocks.

That fourth man seemed familiar. He carried a few extra pounds and had short, dirty blond hair and a large nose. Despite working under the hot sun, he wore a polo shirt. "I know him," I whispered to Teddy. "The guy by the truck. He's one of the guys that broke into my house yesterday."

CHAPTER 23

Teddy tensed. "Give us a second, please," he told the man in front of us. Without taking his eyes off him, he whispered back to me, "You sure?"

"Maybe," I told him. I was certain it was the man who'd come into Sip & Spin. I'd watched that clip of video often enough that I'd recognize him anywhere. I couldn't prove that he was casing us so he and his friends could toss Tansy's house, but I had a bad feeling about him. "I think so?"

Teddy took another step in front of me. I used his body as cover to take out my phone. I only had one bar, but it was more coverage than I'd expected this far out of town. I wouldn't be surprised if the Garzas had erected their own cell phone repeater to improve coverage on their property. I texted Beau, "@ Rawlings Hollow. Robber here?" I hit send before slipping my phone back into my pocket.

While I'd texted Beau, Teddy had been talking, trying to distract the big man. "What are y'all lookin' for?" His smile was wide and welcoming, but I recognized the stiffness in his shoulders.

The man shrugged. "We just go where we're told. And we were told no one else was allowed out here."

"Uh-huh," Teddy said, affably.

I strained to see around them both. The truck had no distinguishing features or signs advertising a construction company. The trailer and backhoe both sported stickers from a local rental agency. The big man in front of us was dressed in khaki pants and a button-down shirt that had been unbuttoned to reveal a sweat-stained undershirt. Even if he was a crew chief, it didn't explain why the other men in his crew were dressed more appropriately for a backyard barbeque than for manual labor.

There were plenty of people in Cedar River who would jump at a job clearing a field like this. And most of them had their own equipment better suited for the work. There was no reason to bring in out-of-towners in polo shirts for something like this. "Who hired you?" I asked.

"The town," he replied in an annoyed voice. "This is Cedar River property. Now, scram, if you know what's good for you."

He turned and started to walk away, and I let out a sigh of relief that the confrontation was over.

"Actually," Teddy said, "this is private property. But y'all would know that if you were hired to, do what exactly?"

The big man stopped in his tracks and turned back around to face us. "What? Nope. You're mistaken. Look, if you have any questions, you can take it up with the mayor."

"The mayor?" I asked, my voice raising an octave as a shiver went down my spine. "The dead mayor? The recently murdered mayor?"

Teddy poked me with his elbow, warning me to keep my mouth shut. We were outnumbered and outmatched. Maybe this was one of those times when I should be quiet.

"What? When?" the big man asked, looking genuinely shocked. "Hey, Jimmy, get over here." The blond man with the bulbous nose joined us. "Tell him what you just told me."

Up close, I was certain that Jimmy was the same man who'd come into Sip & Spin yesterday afternoon. I wondered if he was the one who'd trashed our house, or if it was some of these other guys. He didn't seem to recognize me, but then again, I was half hidden by Teddy and overshadowed by a large, friendly cow who was entertaining herself by nibbling on my hair.

"Y'all friends of Mayor Bob?" I asked, reaching over my shoulder to pull my hair out of Buttercup's mouth. Eww.

The new guy gave an unenthusiastic shrug. "That old so-and-so? I guess you could say that. Convinced the old blowhard to give us a permit to dig here, didn't we?"

The first man elbowed him. "Bob's dead."

"Dead?" Jimmy asked, but he didn't look surprised. "You don't say."

"I do say," Teddy said. "You claim you've got a permit to dig, but this isn't town property."

"Sure it is," Jimmy said.

Teddy shook his head. "No, it's not." He pulled out his phone. "I'm just gonna give the rightful owner a shout, have him come down here and sort this all out." He looked at me. "You got Marcus's number?"

Before I could reply that I didn't, the first man scowled. "Marcus? Marcus Best? I should have known he'd try to beat us to it."

"To what?" I asked.

Jimmy spoke up. "To the treasure, okay?" Neither of us needed to ask what treasure he was referring to. He obviously meant the bank robbery loot. "Let's cut to the chase. Everybody knows it's buried somewhere in Cedar

River. Bob Bobbert was bragging that he had a map that led right to it."

"You're the ones who stole the map from Mayor Bob's office," I blurted out, realizing that the map must be the large piece of paper spread across the truck's hood.

"We didn't steal nothing," the big man insisted.

"How did you get past Pete Digby?"

"Who?" the man with the bulbous nose asked.

"Pete? The security guard at the town hall?" I clarified.

"When I came in, the front door was unlocked. I didn't see no security guard, so I headed back to Bob's office. Look, I swear he was already dead when I got there!"

"What?" the first man turned to him.

"Look, I didn't want to say anything and freak everyone out," Jimmy admitted. He turned to him. "Butch, I know, I should have said something sooner."

Then he addressed us. "We had an appointment that morning, Bob and me. He was going to sell me the map. I'd already paid for it. He told me to meet him in his office on Saturday morning. When I got there, Bob was at his desk, dead. I panicked, okay? I grabbed the map off the wall and took off. I heard someone coming, so I ran out the back door."

I wondered who he'd heard in the building. Pete Digby? Leanna Lydell-Waite? Marcus Best? Me? "Once you were outside, you tossed the frame in the dumpster and took the map with you," I guessed.

"I didn't want to draw any attention to myself," he said.

Neither would I, if I were running away from the scene of a murder carrying stolen property. "Why didn't you call the cops when you found the body?" I asked. Jimmy was quickly becoming one of my least favorite people. Even if he hadn't been the one that broke into my home, if he'd reported Mayor Bob's death, then I wouldn't have had to be the one to find him like that.

"You've got to believe me, I thought about it. But with Bob dead, how was I gonna get the map? I'd already paid for it, fair and square. It was mine." He pulled out his phone, logged into Venmo, and showed me a payment from him to Bob Bobbert.

"You paid that much for a map?" Teddy asked, staring at the screen.

Jimmy shrugged and put his phone away. "Like I said, that map was rumored to show where the treasure was, and now it's mine. Here's proof. It wasn't my fault the old man croaked before he could give it to me."

"He didn't croak," I said, correcting him. "He was murdered."

"He was what?" His face was sunburnt from a long day spent outside, but even so, some of the color drained from it. He looked at Butch. "Did you know this?"

"Did I know this? I didn't even know the man was dead. You didn't bother telling me."

I scanned the destruction of the field. "You dug all of this up because some old map told you to?"

"What can I say?" Jimmy asked. "We had the tip of a lifetime."

"How exactly was Mayor Bob's map the clue to unlocking a decades old mystery?" Teddy asked.

"Unfortunately the map alone isn't enough, as you can see," Butch replied. He swept an arm at the dozen or so holes in the field, each with a corresponding lump of dirt beside it. "There's still a piece of the puzzle missing that would pinpoint the search."

"And you thought that missing piece was in my freezer?" I asked, glaring at him.

"That was your house?" Jimmy asked. "I thought you

looked familiar. You're one of the girls from the record shop."

"Yeah, I am." I glared at him.

"Hey, sorry about that," Butch said. "We got carried away. I'll pay for any damages."

"Well?" I asked. I wasn't about to forgive them anytime soon, but my curiosity was piqued. "What was it? The missing piece of the puzzle?"

Jimmy hung his head. "We didn't find it. All we know is that the money was hidden at the Bluebonnet Festival fairgrounds."

"Rawlings Hollow isn't the fairgrounds," I corrected them. "You're digging up the wrong side of town."

"Actually, Juni"—Teddy interrupted me—"back in the day, it was. The festival didn't get moved to Cedar River Memorial Park until the year after the robbery."

"That's why the map was so special. It pinpoints this field as the old fairgrounds," Jimmy said. "But as you can see, it's still a lot of land. We needed the final clue to narrow down the exact burial site."

"And what made you think the final clue was hidden in my house?" I asked.

"A few years ago, Clint bragged that he had it."

"Clint?" I felt my breath catch in my throat. "Clint Jessup? You knew my dad?"

"Clint Jessup was your father?" He studied my face. "I don't see the resemblance."

"I take after my mom," I said with gritted teeth. My sisters and I all did. It had been a constant source of irritation with my father that he had three kids and not a single one looked like him in the least. We had our mom's coloring, her face shape, even her eyes—except I inherited his bad eyesight. Lucky me. "And you assumed it was hidden in my house?"

"Well, it wouldn't be out in plain sight, would it be?" Butch argued.

"The map was," Teddy pointed out.

The blurt of a police siren interrupted us as two marked sedans and Beau's familiar pickup raced toward us. As they approached, the scrawny man with the shovel and the one in shorts who'd been in the backhoe jumped in the truck and took off. Butch shouted at them to come back. Jimmy, looking terrified, ran after them. Butch, realizing his crew had deserted him, took off in the other direction, toward Teddy's house.

The getaway truck hit one of the mounds of dirt they'd left. The truck jerked then dropped, hood first, into one of the holes. The closest police car stopped short behind it. Jayden Holt jumped out and ran around to check on the occupants. She hauled one man out of the hole and clicked handcuffs on his wrists as another uniformed officer pulled the scrawny man out of the other side of the truck.

Jimmy had changed direction when the truck crashed, but on foot, he couldn't outrun the second police cruiser as it bounced over the field, mowing down bluebonnets with abandon. Realizing it was futile, he gave himself up and was bundled into the back of the police car.

Beau's truck stopped beside us and he rolled down his window. To my surprise, Marcus Best was seated in the passenger seat beside him. "Is that all of them?" Beau asked.

"Another one took off that way," Teddy said, gesturing toward where we'd come from.

I turned, expecting to see Butch fleeing into the thicket. Instead, he was walking back toward us. Behind him, Shelton, one of the farmhands, was prodding him along from his ATV. "Y'all lose something?" Shelton called out as they got closer. He pulled up alongside us, and I realized he was brandishing a cattle prod at Butch.

"Thanks, but you can put the cattle prod away," Beau told him, getting out of his truck. "I'll handle it from here."

"How'd you know he was a bad guy?" I asked.

Shelton took off his dusty cowboy hat and let it dangle from his hands as he leaned over the handlebars of the ATV. "Teddy said he needed help rounding up some stray cows. I was on my way when I heard the police sirens and saw this guy running for the hills." He glanced over at Beau. "I don't suppose there's a reward for this fella?"

Beau shook his head. "I don't suppose there is."

"Look, you guys, this is all a big misunderstanding," Butch said. "I'm not a bad guy."

"Did you break into my house?" I asked.

"Yes, but . . ." Butch sputtered

"And were you trespassing?" Marcus asked, getting out of the passenger side of the truck. "And destroying my private property?"

"Well, I was, but . . ."

"And did you run when the police showed up?" Beau asked.

Butch hung his head. "I'm gonna need a lawyer, aren't I?"

Beau grinned at him. "You have the right to an attorney. If you cannot afford an attorney, one will be provided to you. While we're at it, I might as well go through the rest." He handcuffed Butch as he cited his Miranda rights. When he was done, he glanced at me. "What am I gonna do with you, Junebug?"

"What? I didn't do anything," I protested.

Careful to avoid the holes in the field, the police cruisers returned to where we stood. One of the officers loaded Butch into the back of the cruiser next to Jimmy.

Teddy turned to Beau. "That Jimmy guy says he bought it fair and square, but he admitted to taking the map out of Mayor Bob's office after the mayor died. He and Butch both confessed to breaking into Tansy and Juni's house. Didn't speak with the other two, but they were both digging when we got here, and I wouldn't be surprised if they were in on the break-in, too."

Beau pursed his lips. "Take them to the station," he said told the other cops. "I'll meet you back there."

As they took off toward town. I saw something fluttering out of the corner of my eye and looked up to see Buttercup eating Mayor Bob's map. "Give me that," I told her, and pulled the map out of her mouth. It was missing a small chunk out of the bottom but was otherwise intact.

"I'll take her," Shelton offered, getting off the ATV.

"You're not going to use the cattle prod on Buttercup, are you?" I asked.

"Wasn't planning on it," Shelton said. He took a coil of rope off the back of the ATV, and tied it around the cow's neck.

"Thanks, Shelton," Teddy said. "Don't worry about the ATV. I'll take care of it." Shelton nodded and settled his dusty hat back on his head before leading Buttercup away. "Let me get this straight," Teddy said to me. "You get upset at the thought of him using a cattle prod on a cow, but you had no qualms about him pointing it at Butch?"

"Buttercup didn't break into my house and turn it inside out," I said. "Sorry if she's a troublemaker."

"Oh please. I like troublemakers." Teddy bumped my shoulder with his. "Besides, if she hadn't wandered away from the herd, we never would have found the guys who broke into your house."

"Exactly," I agreed. Then something in the field glinted in the waning light, catching my eye. I walked over to where the metal detector lay. Next to it in the dirt was a paperweight with a bluebonnet suspended in it. I held it up. "This is the paperweight that went missing from Mayor Bob's office," I said.

"How'd you know about the missing paperweight?" Beau asked, appearing beside me with his hand outstretched. I gave him the paperweight. "I didn't tell you about it." He shook his head. "You know what? I don't think I want to know."

"Uncle Calvin might have mentioned it to me," I said. It was hard to remember what I had and hadn't shared with Beau. It would probably be easier if I was more open with him in the first place, but that would introduce a whole separate set of complications.

"How's your uncle wrapped up in all this?" Beau asked, his eyes narrowing.

"He's not," I said hastily, as the complications I'd been worrying about reared their ugly head. My first priority was protecting my family. Beau's was solving the crime. Sometimes that put us at odds. "Faye mentioned it was missing, too. And Marcus might have, also." I looked over at him and he shrugged, neither confirming nor denying my story. "So many people were talking about this paperweight and this map, I can't keep track." I rolled up the map Buttercup had been chewing on and passed it to Beau.

I turned my attention to Marcus. "You never intended to put a car lot on Rawlings Hollow, did you?"

"I told you I didn't," he said.

"Not exactly. You just changed the subject when I asked. So why did you buy it?"

He shrugged. "Why do you think?" He glanced over at the torn-up field. "There's a fortune buried out here, somewhere. I was going to wait until after bluebonnet season was over to start excavating, but I guess Butch and his boys did me a favor. At least now I know a few places that the treasure ain't."

"Sounds like you know a lot more about this than you've been telling me, Juni," Beau said, sounding disappointed. "You can fill me in while I give you a lift back to town." He opened the passenger door of his truck and held it for me.

I glanced over at Teddy. "Go ahead, I'll see you later," he told me.

"Okay," I replied. I climbed into Beau's truck and scooted over to the center of the bench seat to leave room for Marcus next to me.

"You promised you were gonna stay out of trouble," Beau commented as he started the truck.

It suddenly felt very crowded in the cab. "I was just checking on Buttercup."

"Those men could have been dangerous," Beau said.

"They could have been," I agreed. "But no one got hurt." They had broken into my house and trashed Rawlings Hollow. I was glad they were in custody. Maybe under different circumstances I would have been more nervous confronting them, but I had Teddy by my side and I knew that Beau was on his way.

"Your mom would have my hide if anything happened to you on my land," Marcus added.

"You're not gonna tell her, are you?" I asked. "I'd hate to worry her."

Marcus grinned at me. "Sorry, but I don't keep secrets from Bea." He patted my knee. "Don't worry about it, I'm sure she'll be happy just to have you back home safe and sound."

"You don't know her mother very well if you think that," Beau mumbled.

I turned my attention to Beau. "I hope you don't mind that I texted you."

Beau looked surprised. "Why would I mind?"

"The other day, you gave me a hard time about calling you instead of 911."

"I was teasing you, Junebug. You can call me anytime."

I squirmed in my seat. There was no way to sit without pressing up against either Marcus or Beau. I chose Beau. "Thanks for responding so quickly. I wasn't sure the text would go through. Reception is sketchy out here."

"Yup." Beau took one hand off the wheel and draped it over my shoulder. "Guess you got lucky this time."

I thought about it. He was right. After a rough couple of days, things were finally looking up. The ride smoothed out as we hit the paved road, and I felt relief that the worst was behind us.

CHAPTER 24

Beau dropped Marcus off at his car, which was parked at the municipal lot, and offered to give me a lift home. I told him I was headed to the record shop. He double-parked in front of Sip & Spin Records, but made no move to shoo me out of his truck

"Now that those four are in custody, think you can catch me up on the case?" I figured I knew the answer already, but it didn't hurt to ask.

"Which case?" Beau asked. "The mayor's murder, the break-in at your house, or those guys tearing up Rawlings Hollow?"

"Aren't they all connected?"

"How so?" he asked.

"Mayor Bob, Uncle Calvin, Marcus Best, and those four guys were all after the Cedar River bank heist treasure. They all knew each other online. They even knew my dad. Bob beat Calvin and Marcus out on an auction for that bluebonnet paperweight, but then he sold Rawlings Hollow to Marcus and his prized map to Jimmy. Jimmy claims he already paid for the map, so when he found the mayor dead, he took off with it. He didn't tell his friends that Mayor Bob was dead."

"That's interesting," Beau said.

I don't know what made Beau change his mind about sharing information, but as long as he was in a generous mood, I was going to lay all my cards out on the table. "Right? Leanna Lydell-Waite was the only other viable suspect we had up until now, and I don't think she cares much about the treasure. Faye Bobbert didn't share her husband's obsession, if her comment about destroying the bluebonnet paperweight is any indication, so she'd probably be over the moon to find out that Bob was selling off his collection. Maybe now they could get out of debt."

"What makes you think the Bobberts are in debt?" he asked.

"Faye told me." Or was it Jen? Maybe Leanna was the one that mentioned it. "Bob drained their savings looking for that treasure. I guess it finally got bad enough that he had to sell something to stay afloat."

"Rawlings Hollow wasn't part of his collection," Beau pointed out.

"No, but it belonged to the town, and Bob practically ran Cedar River. He knew that land was connected to the heist, and was his best chance of ever recovering the fortune, but he sold it to his rival anyway. Why do you think that was?"

"Because he already knew there was no treasure in Rawlings Hollow?" Beau suggested.

I nodded. It was the only option that made sense. "He could have dug up that entire field a bit at a time over the years, and as long as he filled in the holes afterward, no one would have been the wiser. If he did it after the bluebonnets went to seed, that would explain why they were so thick in that field. Since he knew the treasure wasn't out there, he was free to sell the map for a profit and turn around and sell the land to Marcus for a campaign donation kickback."

"Assuming you're right, if Marcus or the other four treasure hunters found out that Mayor Bob already knew there was no treasure to be found in Rawlings Hollow and he took their money anyway, that might be a motive to kill him."

"Wait a second. Butch, Jimmy, and the other two didn't know exactly where in Rawlings Hollow to look," I said, leaving out the part where my own father might have gone to the grave with the final clue. "They were using a metal detector to pinpoint places to dig. If they'd known that the field was a bust, they wouldn't have wasted all that time and effort digging."

"You make a good point." Beau drummed his fingers on the steering wheel. "Even if they weren't in on the murder, we have them for unlawful trespass, breaking and entering, destruction of private property, and failure to report a dead body."

"Is that a crime?" I asked.

"Sure is," he confirmed. "But they didn't need to kill Mayor Bob if he'd already sold them the map, and they didn't know that the map was worthless or they wouldn't have torn up that field."

"That's about it," I agreed.

"They're not the killers," he murmured, more to himself than to me.

"Looks that way."

"But Marcus Best didn't know that Rawlings Hollow was a dead end. I'm gonna need to go back and have another chat with him before he heads out," he said.

Uh-oh. Once Mom found out that I was the one who sicced the police on her boyfriend, she was going to be seriously disappointed in me. On the other hand, if it turned out that Marcus was involved with the mayor's death, I was saving my mom from getting serious with a murderer.

And if I was real lucky, Beau would arrest him before Marcus had a chance to tell Mom about my adventures tonight.

"I gotta get going, but Junebug? Can't you at least try to stay out of trouble?"

"I'll try," I said as I climbed out of the truck. "But no promises." I smiled and blew him a kiss before hurrying into the shop.

With all the excitement at Rawlings Hollow, I'd stayed out longer than I'd anticipated. Sip & Spin was already starting to fill up with Arts & Crafts Night participants. We had a lot of unfamiliar faces, along with our regulars. I even noticed Teddy's sister, Silvie, milling around. "Those coupons were a great idea," I told Maggie as I found my sister in the crowd. "This place is packed. Sorry I'm late."

"No biggie. Your Don't Worry, Be Frappé was such a success, the market ended up running out of coconut ice cream. So tonight, we decided to switch it up and go with Sweet Chai O'Mine."

"Good idea," I agreed. It was a much easier drink to make. The reduced caffeine and reduced sugar in the spiced tea made it ideally suited for an evening crowd.

As Maggie and I finished setting up, Tansy rang up the participants. When we were ready to begin, Tansy walked everyone through the process. She started with the milk crates filled with albums. "Everyone gets to pick out a record. It doesn't matter which one you select because we'll be discarding the center, but feel free to pick through what we have. Once you've got your record, make sure it's clean." She held up a dust rag. "Now you'll either go to the cutting station first, or head over to me to mount your photo on the backing with the hanger already attached." We'd already cut out circular foam boards the same size as the records. It didn't matter if they cut their record or mounted their photo next, and we figured by giving them two options it would split the line.

"My sister Juni will help you decide how big you'll want to cut the hole. Juni, can you show them the options?" I held up three albums that we had prepared ahead of time, and demonstrated by holding each album over the same photo to show how the finished product would look. This week, my station was the easiest. I had two cutters set up and it was easy to adjust the size. All our crafters had to do was select the correct setting, center their record on the template, and press a button. The machine did the rest.

"If you want to add vinyl stickers, you can start at that station if you want," Maggie explained. She held up a few brightly colored sheets of sticky-backed vinyl sticker paper, not to be confused with vinyl records. "We have a few options to choose from." She held up pre-cut shapes of the state of Texas, the year, silhouettes of bluebonnets, the words Cedar River in a fancy script, hearts, and stars. "Choose the color you want and what shapes, and we'll help you run them through this cutting machine," she said, patting the paper-cutting craft machine.

"Or, if you bought the deluxe package, once the center is cut, bring your album to the detailed design station." There, we had two more machines, each hooked up to a tablet. "You can choose between three designs. This one's my favorite." She held up a record with a silhouette of a bluebonnet on both sides and the year on the bottom. The other options were six star shapes equally spaced around the circle or "I ♥ Texas" cut out of the bottom of the record.

"We'll show you how to assemble everything here." She tapped on the final table. "And there's lots of markers if you want to add your own message." There were several areas that might cause bottlenecks, but we hoped that we could keep people moving between stations without having to wait too long. We had a selection of music set out at the listening stations to encourage the customers to play DJ for the evening, and a set up to serve Sweet Chai O'Mine to anyone who wanted a cup.

As expected, the first few minutes were chaotic. One person took forever selecting their record and another couldn't decide what color vinyl stickers she wanted, but soon the shop was filled with happy voices, good music, and the sound of vinyl being cut and shaped. I made sure to compliment something about each picture I saw, which was easy when the subject was people and pets having fun in bluebonnets. The festival's photographer was great at her job. She was the same photographer who had held the photography workshop that Tansy had attended with Leanna, so in a way, everything was coming full circle.

Silvie came up with a selfie of her and her mother surrounded by bluebonnets, instead of one of the portraits taken at the festival. I recognized the background as the Garza farm blanketed in bluebonnets. She'd chosen the star cutouts for her frame. "That's a great picture," I told her.

"Gracias. I hope Mamá likes it, too."

"I'm sure she will," I assured her.

"I hate to admit it, but you were right about the records," she said. "I got here early and was playing a few albums. The sound quality is much better than what I get on my phone."

I grinned, knowing that we had another convert. "I'm glad you think so. If you need help getting started with a collection, you know where to come."

"I sure do," she said. "Hey, there's finally an opening at the marker station. I'm gonna try to grab the silver paint pen. See you later."

"Sounds good," I told her.

By the time that the last customer put the finishing touches on their framed bluebonnet picture—they'd meticulously outlined all the cutout shapes with a metallic blue marker and added "Best day ever!" in silver script—my sisters and I were exhausted. "It's too late to put all of this away tonight," Tansy said when Maggie automatically started cleaning and setting things back to normal.

"It won't take but a minute," Maggie argued.

"It'll still be here in the morning when we're not as tired," I said, making sure all the markers were capped and the machines were off. "How'd we do?"

"Pretty good," Tansy said. Maggie handled the shop's books, but since Tansy had checked everyone out, she had a better idea than either of us how much we'd made. "Enough to make up for a few days of slow sales this week. Plus, we had a ton of customers today."

I let out a sigh of relief. A few more nights like this, and we were on our way to success. We locked up the shop. Tansy offered to give me a lift, but I'd ridden my tricycle this morning and I wanted to ride it home. "I don't know," Tansy said with a frown. "After the break-in at the house last night, I'm worried about you being out here alone."

"Didn't I tell you?" I asked.

"Tell me what?"

"They caught the guys."

"I thought Beau said not to get our hopes up," Tansy said.

"Well, technically, Teddy and I caught the guys. We stumbled onto them tearing up Rawlings Hollow."

"What on earth?" Maggie asked. "What do you mean you caught them?" Tansy asked at the same time.

I gave them a quick rundown, concluding with, "In any event, they've all been arrested. I'm sure we'll get an update in the morning."

"Good. Maybe I'll sleep soundly tonight. We're not expecting any company, are we?" Tansy asked me.

"Nope," I told her. As much as I appreciated Beau offering to stay over last night and keep an eye on us, we
didn't need an around-the-clock guard.

The trike ride home did me good. Other than sleeping
and showering, I hadn't been alone for more than a few
minutes in a while. When I lived in Oregon, I worked
from home a lot, made meals for myself, and even went
to the movies alone sometimes. I had friends. I had co-
workers. I even had a few dates, but after growing up in
a three-bedroom house with two sisters, I had learned to
appreciate a little alone time. Of course, now that I was
back and surrounded by friends and family, I wasn't sure
how I'd ever survived without them.

I pedaled through the quiet neighborhood. It wasn't
terribly late, but this was a working-class neighborhood
where people put their kids—and themselves—to bed
early. The days were getting hotter, but it was cool tonight.
The pedaling kept me pleasantly warm. Having this time
to myself, my thoughts kept returning to Mayor Bob's
death.

With Butch and his crew cleared—at least as far as
Beau or I were concerned—Faye Bobbert was the most obvious suspect. If I'd learned anything from watching true
crime shows, the spouse was almost always the killer. I'm
sure that every marriage had its own challenges, but Faye
and Bob seemed like such a happy couple. With Mayor
Bob selling off some of his bank heist memorabilia, they
could pay off their debt and start looking forward to retirement. But even if they'd been at each other's throats,
Faye had a rock-solid alibi.

I waivered back and forth about whether or not Leanna
Lydell-Waite was a viable suspect. She had access to Bob's

office, true, but so did Jimmy the treasure hunter and Pete Digby the security guard. So did I, for that matter. Cedar River Town Hall wasn't exactly Fort Knox. Power was a good motive for murder, but if Mayor Bob was retiring in a few years, all Leanna had to do was be patient. Who knows? Maybe Leanna had a decent chance at defeating him in an election. The fact that he never did anything made him vulnerable to an ambitious challenger.

Then there was Marcus Best. He was jealous of Mayor Bob's collection. He'd dropped a lot of money to contribute to his reelection campaign. He'd also invested in a plot of land, thinking it was the site of buried treasure that turned out to be a bust. If he found out that he'd been had, he'd be furious. Was that motive enough to kill someone? His business was booming and he had a great girlfriend. Why would he risk all that to get revenge when he could have just demanded his money back or gone public? A scandal could have ruined the last few years of Bob's political career.

I couldn't outright dismiss Pete Digby, either. I'm not sure what motive he had, if any, but he had all the opportunity in the world. As the security guard for Town Hall, he had the keys and he knew when the building would be empty. Even if he didn't commit the murder, he might have helped someone pull it off. But Pete and I went way back. He had no reason to pin anything on me or my sisters, unless we were just convenient scapegoats.

As I pulled up to the house, I noticed every light was blazing inside. I guess Tansy still felt uncomfortable being home alone, even after I told her that the invaders had been caught. Maybe I should have rode home with her, for her peace of mind if not my own. I parked my trike under the overhang where it would be protected from the elements, but my mind was still trying to sort through what we knew about Mayor Bob's death and who might have killed him.

Not that I was investigating. No, siree. That would be breaking my promise to Beau. I was curious. There was no law against that. It would be nice to have the killer caught and any suspicion against Sip & Spin removed, but I could leave that to the police. I had a family to care for and a shop to run. And tomorrow, when I attended Mayor Bob's service, it would be to show my respects, not to solve a mystery.

CHAPTER 25

I slept in on Thursday. Mayor Bob's service was at eleven and everyone in Cedar River would be there, so there was no point in opening the shop until after it was over. After I showered, I stared at my closet in frustration, willing a grown-up's wardrobe to miraculously appear.

Instead, a closet crammed full of boxes glared back at me. Since moving back home, I'd been so busy setting up the shop that I hadn't fully unpacked yet. I'd packed in such a haste that any given box might have a stack of well-read paperbacks, a beloved stuffed animal from childhood, a pair of tennis shoes, and a stack of dishes cushioned in a towel. It wasn't well-organized, but it had been efficient at the time.

The problem was, I now had no idea which box might hold my one and only professional suit, or even if all the coordinating pieces had even made the final cut. I pretty much lived in jeans and vintage concert T-shirts these days, and hadn't seen the need to dig out professional clothes, until now.

I pulled out the first box, broke the tape, and opened the flaps. Inside were POP! figurines, the spare cell phone charger I'd been looking for, a tea kettle, a handful of dried-out pens, and a fluffy pink robe. I tossed the robe and charger on my bed and started on the next box. Thirty minutes later, I had a pile of stuff on my bed, no place to walk, and most importantly, no suit.

There was a knock on my door followed by Tansy sticking her head inside. "What happened in here?" she asked. "Not another home invasion, I hope."

"Funny. Just looking for something more funeral appropriate than an old Rolling Stones shirt," I groused.

"In that case, ta-da!" She nudged one of the boxes aside so she could open the door a little wider, and flourished a dress on a dry-cleaning hanger.

"No, no, no," I said. It looked suspiciously like one of Maggie's dresses. It was black with tiny yellow flowers on the top and larger yellow flowers on a skirt that would likely hit me right below the knees. It had quarter sleeves and a heart-shaped neckline. It would look adorable on my sister, but it wasn't my style, not at all. "I can't wear that."

"Maggie dropped it off this morning on her way to the shop."

"Shop's closed," I said.

"If you don't think our dear sister would miss the chance to jump at a mess like we left last night, you don't know Maggie very well. While she's there, she'll feed Daffy. Now hurry up or we'll be late for the service."

With Daffy and Sip & Spin in good hands, I could focus on what was important. If I wore that dress—and it didn't look like I had any better options—I couldn't go to the service in a hasty ponytail and no makeup. I would need to wash and straighten my hair. I would even need to shave my legs.

I took my time getting ready. Normally I wrapped my long hair up in a towel and hoped for the best, but today, I grabbed a hair dryer and set about the arduous process of straightening it. With a little spray and a lot of patience, I got it to lay almost as flat as Tansy's super short hair.

There was a knock at the bathroom door. "Am I taking too long?" I asked, opening it.

"No worries," Tansy said, holding out a small hard-sided case about the size of a purse. "I thought you might need some makeup."

"That's great!" I couldn't remember the last time my sister and I had shared makeup. Tansy was taller and thinner than I was, so swapping clothes had always been a no-go. We had the same coloration and skin type, but I don't think Tansy had ever forgiven me for using her eye shadow palette as finger paints when we were little. In my defense, Tansy was eight years older than I was. When she was thirteen and experimenting with makeup for the first time, I was only five.

Tansy sat on the edge of the tub. "Need some help?"

"Thanks, but I'm good." I opened the makeup case and scanned the contents. I didn't wear much makeup. Tansy was right in guessing that I had no idea what box in my room hid what little makeup I did own, and I had a feeling it was expired. One of the drawbacks of being the baby of the family was that by the time I showed any interest in makeup, both my sisters were grown and out of the house. Thank goodness for YouTube makeup tutorials.

With a running commentary from Tansy—"That shade looks good on you." "You need to blend that a little more." "Where on earth did you learn to put on blush?"—I applied my makeup. I ran a brush through my hair one more time before putting on the dress and realizing I had another problem I hadn't accounted for.

I liked shoes as much as the next person, but my taste leaned toward comfy sneakers, scuffed cowboy boots, and funky Doc Martens. I didn't have anything that would go with this dress. Tansy came to the rescue again, this time supplying a pair of black and yellow cowboy boots that perfectly coordinated with Maggie's dress.

For the record, cowboy boots were perfectly acceptable footwear for dresses, according to the Texas state bylaws. They were appropriate for weddings, mucking out stalls, going to Walmart, funerals, horseback riding, and anything in between. They were versatile like that.

When I stepped back and examined myself in the mirror, I liked what I saw. I'd gone with simple black-rimmed glasses that didn't hide my—if I may say so myself—fantastic eye makeup. "Ready?" I asked.

"Yup." My sister was wearing black pants with a black and silver ombre twinset. She'd pinned back one side of her hair with a silver butterfly comb and topped off her look with an oversize necklace.

"You look nice," I told her as I followed her to the car. As I locked—and then double-checked that it was locked, even though I knew the men who'd ransacked our house were in police custody—I glanced over at Mom's cottage. "Should we see if she needs a ride?"

Before Tansy could answer, a shiny dark blue Dodge Charger pulled up to the curb. It had Best Used Cars temporary tags on it. Marcus got out of the car. "Morning, girls," he called out. "Your mother ready?"

"I'll go check on her," Tansy said, and cut across the lawn to knock on Mom's front door.

Alone with Marcus, I realized this was a good time to pump him for information. "I'm surprised that you're going to Mayor Bob's service. Uncle Calvin made it sound like y'all didn't get along."

"Oh, Bob and I go way back," he said. "A little friendly competition would never change that, Maggie."

It took me a minute to realize that he'd mistaken me

for my sister, just because I was wearing a dress. "It's Juni, actually," I corrected him. "Why did you contribute to his reelection fund, even though you're not a Cedar River resident?"

"Where'd you hear that?" he asked.

I thought about it. Where had I heard that? Leanna Lydell-Waite? Jen Rachet? One of my sisters? I couldn't remember. "So, you didn't make a donation?"

"I didn't say that. I was just wondering who told you."

I tilted my head slightly, trying to get a better read on him. "Campaign contributions are public record. It's not hard to look up," I bluffed. I had no idea how to go about doing such a thing, but I'm sure I could find out.

Marcus gave a hearty, if slightly forced, laugh. "Aren't you just a firecracker? Yes, I donated. While Cedar River isn't my primary place of residence for now, I own Rawlings Hollow, and I feel like it's my civic duty to pay attention to local politics. I presume, as a small business owner yourself, you're also active in the community."

"What do you mean Cedar River isn't your residence for now?" I asked. "I thought you already had houses in Dallas and Austin. Are you moving here?" If he was planning on putting down roots in my hometown, maybe things were more serious with my mother than I'd assumed.

"Yoo-hoo!" Mom called. She emerged from her cottage waving at us. "If we don't get going, we'll end up in the cheap seats."

"I don't think there are any cheap seats at a funeral, Mom," Tansy said.

"Oh, you know what I mean." She joined us and looped her arm around Marcus's waist. "You'll have to forgive Juni," she said, giving me a loving smile. "I'm afraid she's as quiet as a mouse, that one."

"Really?" Marcus asked. "And here she was, talking my ear off. Come on, hon, let's go."

As he steered my mother toward his car, I contemplated what my mother had said. I used to be the quiet one in the family, sure. With an outgoing mother, a boisterous father, and two older sisters, it was hard to get a word in edgewise. I'd started coming out of my shell in college, but I don't think I'd really found my voice until I moved to Oregon. I'd grown up, but I'd done it so far away that no wonder no one in my family had noticed yet.

Tansy came over to stand shoulder to shoulder with me as they drove off. "What do you think?"

"I don't know," I admitted. "Mom likes him."

"Maggie doesn't."

"Honestly, I thought her dislike of him was clouding her judgment, but there's something suspicious about him. Why buy Rawlings Hollow and not build on it? Why team up with Uncle Calvin to bid against Bob in the auctions if they're such good friends? Why spend money on an election he can't even vote in? And what did he mean by he doesn't live here *yet*?"

"That's a lot of questions," Tansy said. "Would you rather stand around and talk them through or shall we head out before the cheap seats, as Mom called them, are all that's left?" Since the answers weren't going to be found in Tansy's yard, I followed her to her car.

Mayor Bob's widow had arranged a traditional funeral service, except instead of holding it in a church or funeral home, it was set up in the big meeting room in Town Hall. The room was packed for the occasion. Tansy and I hovered at the open doors, taking in the scene. At the far end of the room where the council members usually sat in a semicircle on the raised dais, was a coffin draped in flowers. "I'm surprised the police released the body so soon," I whispered.

"They haven't," Tansy whispered back. "I'm assuming the coffin's just for show."

I shivered at the thought, and concentrated on the details of the room to distract myself. Fresh flowers covered the dais. A podium stood on one side of the empty coffin. In front of it was a blown-up photo of Mayor Bob and Faye propped up on a wooden easel. Faye herself stood nearby, greeting mourners.

Music played over the speakers, but it didn't sound like anything we carried at Sip & Spin Records. We had an eclectic collection that might at any time include guitars, pianos, drums, flutes, bagpipes, or even one song that featured kazoos. But if there was a harp and organ section in the shop, I didn't know about it.

It was hard to hear the music over the crowd. "I think the whole town turned out," I noted.

"And then some," Tansy agreed. She pointed to cluster of people huddled in one corner wearing dark suits and stern expressions. "Isn't that the governor?"

I adjusted my glasses so I could get a better look. "I think so. I guess Mayor Bob was more connected than I realized."

Now that I was here, I also saw what my mom had meant by the cheap seats. The galley was filled with folding chairs, the same as it would be for any town event, but there appeared to be half as many chairs as there were residents milling around. Most of the chairs had already been claimed. I wondered if the murderer was in the room, hiding in plain sight.

"Looks like standing room only," Tansy said.

A dark-haired man on the third row turned around, and I saw that it was Teddy. He waved to get our attention before patting the seats next to him. "Looks like we have a reservation," I said. I took a step forward but stopped abruptly when a hand closed on my upper arm. I looked over to see Beau, dressed in uniform. "I'll be right there," I assured Tansy.

As she went in to claim our seats, I let Beau lead me away from the doors. "Hello to you too," I said as he tugged me down the hallway.

He opened a door that led to one of the smaller meeting rooms and pulled me inside. As the motion-activated lights flickered on, I glanced around. There were posters on the wall advertising community resources and a calendar with room reservations written on it. The back wall, where the chairs were normally stacked, was clear. Every free chair had been repurposed for Mayor Bob's service.

Beau flashed that lethal smile of his that frankly should only be used with a permit. Then he took a half step back and held me at arm's length. "I like the dress."

"It's Maggie's," I told him.

"Figured. Looks good on you, but I think I prefer the T-shirts."

"You do?" I asked. I'd be lying if the idea of bumping into either Teddy or Beau at the service hadn't crossed my mind while I was getting ready. I never in a million years would have thought that Beau, of all people, would prefer my more relaxed look to a pretty dress and makeup.

"Don't get me wrong, I love this. I do." His hand still gripped my arm, but now his thumb softly rubbed my skin. "But it's not very you, now, is it?"

I shook my head. "I feel like I'm playing dress-up in my sister's clothes. What's up?"

"I was about to ask you the same thing. Why are you here?"

"Showing my respects, like everyone else in Cedar River," I said. "Did you know the governor is here?"

"Yup. Their office called this morning to give us a heads up."

"Is that why you're in uniform?" I asked. As awkward as I felt in Maggie's dress, I could only imagine that Beau was more uncomfortable. His uniform was dark blue bordering on black, with long sleeves stretched over a protective vest. He wore a tactical belt and had a walkie-talkie clipped to his shirt, over the lapel patch that identified him as Det. Russell. He wore his ever-present cowboy hat, and had shaved for the occasion. I missed seeing the dark stubble on his face. He looked years younger without it, more like the Beau I remembered from high school.

"Among other reasons," he said.

The room got quieter, and I realized that the crowd next door had fallen silent. "The service is starting," I said. "I should go take my seat."

"Come find me after." He let go of my arm. He walked with me, and held open the door. "And Junebug?" he asked as I brushed past him. "No investigating. Please."

I smiled. "I'm gonna be late."

Without waiting for the inevitable lecture that Beau had prepared, I hurried down the hall and slipped into the big meeting room. Leanna Lydell-Waite, in her capacity as acting mayor, was at the podium, introducing the governor. I worked my way through the people unlucky enough to not have snagged seats. They grumbled as I passed.

The chairs were packed in tightly, forcing the other people in the third row to half rise to let me get to my seat between Tansy and Teddy.

"You okay?" Teddy asked.

I nodded.

"What did Beau want?" Tansy whispered.

I jerked my head toward the podium, where Leanna was shaking hands with the governor. "Shh," I told her.

The service was predictably long. The governor didn't stay for all of it. They slipped out with their entourage between speakers. People took turns at the podium, each extolling the virtues of Mayor Bob and praising the work he'd done for Cedar River during his years in office. I soon found my mind wandering.

I scanned the crowd. Teddy had gotten us seats near the front, so I could only see the people in front of me. Beau, on the other hand, had worked his way through the crowd and was now standing near the very front of the room, on the far side of the dais, facing the guests. I caught his eye and he smiled. To my right, Tansy shifted in her seat. The metal chairs were uncomfortable, and squeaked loudly anytime someone adjusted. To my left, Teddy's attention never wavered from whomever was speaking, but he reached over to squeeze my hand.

Mom and Marcus had managed to snag seats in the second row. Marcus had one hand draped over the back of her chair. The man seated behind me muffled a cough, and elsewhere someone sniffled. Several people had tissues at hand but for the most part, the audience was too busy chuckling over one anecdote or another that the speaker was sharing to need them.

The longer the service drew on, the more I realized that I hadn't known Mayor Bob well. He'd made the commencement speech at my high school graduation, but I hadn't had much interaction with him before the Bluebonnet Festival. I was embarrassed to admit that I hadn't ever voted for or against him, since as long as I'd been voting age, he'd always run unopposed. The stories that people were telling about him at the podium made him come alive for me.

Several people mentioned Mayor Bob's love for his wife, his dedication to civic service, and his passion—bordering on obsession—for anything related to the 1956 bank heist. When Uncle Calvin stood up to speak, I braced myself. Calvin was known for his long, rambling lectures that could at any moment split off onto a tangent about the historical origins of a word or correcting what he thought was a common misconception.

"We all loved Mayor Bob. We respected him. And more importantly, we liked him. He was a good ol' son-of-a-gun." There was a nervous chuckle in response to this. "But we're not gathered here today because of how great he was. We're all here because he was murdered. And I'm gonna tell you who killed him."

CHAPTER 26

Teddy's hand involuntarily closed around mine. My mother turned to me and hissed, "Do something," at me, presumably because I was closest to the aisle.

"It was the year 1956," my uncle started. "The annual Cedar River Bluebonnet Festival was still in its infancy, but it was starting to draw guests from all over Travis County. Now, of course, when we say bluebonnets, we're actually talking about several different but related varieties of *Lupinus* that are unique to Texas."

"He's your brother," I hissed back. "*You* do something." Even so, I knew that unless someone did something, and fast, we would all still be here an hour from now when Uncle Calvin finally got around to making his point— which I did want to hear, just not in this particular forum. I began making my way down the row, people grumbling as they had to stand so I could pass.

"Bluebonnets, as we all know, grow in two distinct regions—the Blackland Prairies, the vast stretch of flat plains that runs up I-35 from San Antonio to Dallas, and the Edwards Plateau, otherwise known as Hill Country, which covers most of the area between Austin and the Mexican border. Cedar River, at the intersection of the prairie and the plateau, is prime bluebonnet country."

The funeral attendees were packed in so tightly, it was hard to make any headway. I was just glad there wasn't a fire or other emergency. We'd never all make it out of the room safely. I came to a bottleneck where the other guests couldn't—or possibly wouldn't—make way for me, when a hand reached out and I grabbed it.

I let Beau part the crowd. I clung to his hand as he pulled me closer. Accustomed to my uncle's long-winded, rambling speeches, Beau said, "You need to get him away from that podium. If anyone drops dead from boredom, I'm charging your uncle with manslaughter." But one look at his narrowed lips and I knew that he wasn't worried about my uncle boring the crowd as much as what Calvin might be working up to.

"What do you think I'm trying to do?" I asked.

My uncle continued his lecture. "Texas is so large that it is almost an ecosystem to itself, and since bluebonnets only grow natively in this state, it's important that we protect them. That's why, in 1933, we passed the Wildflower Protection Act, which, until its repeal in 1973, made it illegal to pick bluebonnets. Since, unlike nearby Austin, Cedar River is still undeveloped enough to have vast swaths of untouched land, bluebonnets grow like, well, wildflowers around these parts."

While Calvin spoke, Beau crossed his arms over his chest. Since I was still holding his hand, I found myself with one arm wrapped around his waist. "Hold on," he told me, and pressed forward. Beau wasn't the biggest man in the room. That distinction quite possibly belonged to my rambling uncle. But he was able to shoulder his way through spectators who refused to budge lest they lose their prime spots up front. His bullish determination, coupled with the uniform, was enough to propel us to the podium.

"Which is why people came from far and wide to

our revered Bluebonnet Festival, long before other towns jumped on the bandwagon. Now, bluebonnets aren't the only thing that Cedar River got going for us. In 1956, the oil companies were making a killing."

Beau maneuvered me in front of him and boosted me up on the dais, where I hurried over to Uncle Calvin. "Okay, that's enough," I told him.

"Oh hey, Juni. My lovely niece, Juni Jessup, everyone. Aren't you just as pretty as a picture?" he said into the microphone, and I blushed. "Now, I was just getting to the good part."

"Calvin, we need to go sit down," I begged him, tugging on his sleeve like I'd done so many times as a little girl.

"Shush, sweetie," he said, the mic picking up every word. "And don't you worry none, I ain't gonna tell them that Tansy killed Mayor Bob."

A collective gasp rose from the crowd, and I bit back a groan. My uncle turned his attention back to them. "No, no, you see I'm trying to tell you that Tansy didn't do nothing. I mean, yeah, sure, she made the coffee that killed him, but she wouldn't hurt a flea. Would you, Tansy?" he addressed my sister directly. "Tansy, why don't you come up here and tell everybody you're innocent?"

When I snatched the microphone out of his hand, there was a smattering of applause completely inappropriate for a funeral service. As soon as I took the mic, I realized my mistake. Now that I was holding it, I was going to have to say something. In public. In front of a packed house.

I should have stayed in my seat and let my uncle make a fool out of himself. Or better yet, I should have stayed home and let someone else have my spot on the third row. But now that I was here, all the should haves in the world wouldn't save me. Someday I was going to get over my stage fright, but today wasn't looking like my day. "Tansy didn't kill anyone. End of story," I croaked into the microphone. "Who's next?" I asked, waving the microphone around.

Faye Bobbert came to my rescue, nearly tripping up the stairs in her rush to replace us at the podium. I ushered Calvin off the stage and steeled myself to have to push back through the crowded room, but Beau materialized at my side and ushered us out a side door instead.

"What was that, Juniper?" my uncle asked sharply. "I can't believe you interrupted my speech like that."

"Cut her a break," Beau said.

"You don't talk for her," he told Beau.

"Guys, guys, chill out. Uncle Calvin, you were about to say who murdered Mayor Bob, and I suppose you know why, as well."

"I was going to explain everything, until you gave me the bum's rush."

"Please, Mr. Voigt," Beau said, but Calvin waved a hand at him.

"What's up with this Mr. Voigt nonsense? Boy, you've known me since before you were old enough to shave."

"Fine. Calvin," Beau started again.

"That's better. Now what was so dang-gum important that you had to interrupt me? If you'd let me talk, I would've told you everything."

"Uncle Calvin," I interjected, "we all know that if we'd just let you talk, you'd still be talking next Tuesday. Why don't you save us all a lot of time and tell us—" Beau cleared his throat, and I remembered that I'd promised that my days of investigating were behind me. "Tell Detective Russell what you know about the person who killed Mayor Bob."

"Well see, there's only one problem with that." He scratched his head. I couldn't help notice that my uncle was wearing a pair of jeans with an old checkered shirt that fastened with mother of pearl buttons. If I had known that I could get away with wearing blue jeans to a funeral, I never would have gotten dressed up in Maggie's cute little dress.

"And the problem is?" I prompted. That's my uncle in a nutshell. Half the time, I couldn't drag information out of him with a herd of wild mustangs, and the next, I couldn't get him to shut up. "Just spit it out. Twenty words or less."

"The problem is, I don't exactly know who killed him. The murderer always returns to the scene of the crime, right? So I figured they'd show up at the funeral. Only I got there and the place was packed to the gills. I put myself down as saying a few words so I could get in front of everyone and look every single person in the eye until I knew who done it."

"You were going to stare at everyone who came to the funeral until an 'I'm guilty, ask me how!' sign appeared out of thin air, pointing to the culprit?" I asked.

"That's about the gist of it," he agreed.

"That's the silliest thing I ever heard," Beau muttered.

"And what's so silly about it?" Calvin asked, puffing out his chest. "Bet you're just upset you didn't think of it first."

"Yeah, that must be it," Beau replied. He turned to me. "I need to get back in there. Can you can keep him out of trouble until the service is over?"

"I'll do my best," I promised. Beau stroked the top of my hair like I might pet Daffy, then returned to the service.

"I don't know what he's so grumpy for," my uncle said. "I was doing him a favor."

"I know you were," I told him.

"What do you say we should get a jump on the crowd

and start making our way back to the Bobbert house for the wake?"

"Sure thing," I agreed. I hadn't learned anything that I'd come here to learn and I'd made a fool of myself on stage, all while wearing my sister's dress. All things considered, it wasn't my best day. But I hadn't found any dead bodies—yet. Knock on wood—so it wasn't my worst, either.

It was eerily quiet when we reached the lobby. Everyone was at the service. Even Pete Digby was nowhere to be seen, but I noticed the back door was propped slightly open. He was probably out behind the dumpster, having a smoke. No wonder he hadn't noticed anyone coming or going the morning of Mayor Bob's murder—not even Leanna, Jimmy the treasure hunter, or Mayor Bob himself. He was never at his post.

Something was nagging me, though. Anyone could come and go as they pleased with security as lax as this, but who would have known that? Most people would assume, as I had, that Town Hall would have been locked up tight. Whoever snuck in and killed the mayor had to have known that Bob was in his office, and that they had free reign of the hallways without fear of being caught.

"A thief wouldn't expect to find Bob in his office when everyone's at the Bluebonnet Festival," I muttered, and heard an echo of the circumstances surrounding the 1956 bank heist in my thoughts.

Maybe Tansy was right about Leanna Lydell-Waite. But how could she poison the coffee without Mayor Bob noticing? I shook my head. It made no sense.

"You okay, Juni?" my uncle asked.

I realized what it must look like to him. I was standing in the middle of the lobby, shaking my head and talking to myself. "I gotta check something out real quick. Go on ahead. I'll meet you at your truck."

"Whatever you're up to, I'm coming along," he announced.

"Fair enough." After all, I had interrupted his speech and ruined his plan—not that it had been much of one. I led the way to Mayor Bob's office. A sliver of police tape clung to the doorjamb, but other than that, it looked like nothing had ever happened here.

"Should we?" I asked Uncle Calvin.

"In for a penny, and all that," he said. He twisted the door handle, and the door opened. "Does no one lock their doors in this town?" he asked, shaking his head. "You know, a lot of people assume the phrase 'In for a penny, in for a pound' is the equivalent of 'go big or go home,' but in actuality, the origins can be traced to the British penal system, where defaulting on a debt . . ."

"Calvin?" I interrupted him, stepping around him to enter Mayor Bob's office. The motion sensor lights flickered on.

"Yes, dear?"

"Really not the time."

"Maybe later," he agreed. "What are we doing here, Juni?" he asked.

"I don't know," I said. "I feel like we're missing something. I wish I knew what happened between the time that Mayor Bob left the DJ booth and when Jimmy showed up."

"Jimmy always was a sneaky one," Calvin said. I'd forgotten they ran in the same circles. He probably knew all the treasure hunters. "So I'm supposed to believe Jimmy bought the map, fair and square?" he continued.

"Where'd you hear that?" I asked.

"He was bragging about it on Facebook." He gestured

to the big empty spot on the wall where the map used to hang.

"He did have a Venmo receipt," I admitted. "And probably an email trail. Assuming he's the one that texted Mayor Bob and got him to leave the DJ booth on Saturday morning, there'd be a record of that, too. If he was trying to be stealthy, he did an awful poor job of it."

I walked around the desk and tried to see the room from Mayor Bob's point of view. "Jimmy walks in, expecting to pick up the map he's already paid for, but he finds the mayor dead instead. He panics and grabs the map. Even swipes the bluebonnet paperweight, figuring Bob didn't need it anymore. Seems like he's a thief, not a murderer."

Calvin scratched the back of his neck. "Truth be told, the map is worth a lot more than the paperweight. The paperweight is cool, no doubt, but the map unlocked a fortune."

I decided not to break it to my uncle that the map was probably useless. Mayor Bob would never have sold Rawlings Hollow to Marcus unless he'd already searched every inch of it and come up empty-handed. That was a good motive for Marcus to kill the mayor since he was the one who bought the land, but Jimmy had no idea that the map was worthless until after they'd destroyed the field.

"If Jimmy's telling the truth, Mayor Bob was already dead when he got here. That leaves a very narrow window between when Bob left us at the DJ booth and when Jimmy found him."

"You know, the more you pull on this thread, the worse it looks for you and your sister," Calvin pointed out. "It'd be simpler if this was a business transaction gone wrong or Bob interrupted a break-in."

"Even if you're right, poisoning isn't a heat-of-the-moment weapon. This was planned." I glanced down at where the trash can had been. "There were single-use coffee creamers in Mayor Bob's trash can when I found him."

"And?"

"They were fat-free amaretto-flavored," I said. "We didn't have flavored creamers at the DJ booth during the Bluebonnet Festival, only plain. We don't stock any flavored single-use creamer. It's expensive and wasteful. The blends we served last weekend didn't need it, but still, a few customers complained, including Jen Rachet and Mayor Bob."

"That Jen Rachet," he said, shaking his head. "If she didn't have anything to complain about, she'd make something up."

"True," I agreed. "Bob poured his own coffee, but where'd he get the flavored creamer?"

Calvin walked over to the mini-fridge and opened the door. "Amaretto, you say?"

I hurried around the desk and joined him in front of the fridge. There was a stack of sugar-free amaretto-flavored creamer cups inside. They didn't need to be refrigerated, but some people preferred them cold. The creamers were next to several cans of diet root beer soda and half a package of low-fat butterscotch pudding cups. Mayor Bob had quite the sweet tooth.

Not wanting to disturb the crime scene more than we already had, I leaned in and took a photo of the fridge contents with my phone. "Calvin, I think you might have just cracked the case."

"What?" he asked. "Who killed him?"

"You're asking the wrong question." I grinned at my uncle. It was nice to be the one with the answers for once. "The real question isn't who killed Mayor Bob, it's how they killed him."

CHAPTER 27

We slipped out of Mayor Bob's office and ducked out the front door before the service ended. My uncle's Bronco was easy to locate in the packed parking lot. In addition to the oversize tires that raised it up, the old truck's unique paint scheme made it stand out. It was blue on the top and down near the undercarriage, with a tan stripe running all the way around it. Except, the passenger side door had been replaced with one from a red and white Bronco and had never been repainted. My mom thought the truck was an eyesore. I thought it was like Uncle Calvin—unique and best not taken too seriously.

"I'll drive if you want," I offered holding out my hand. I'd driven the Bronco once without his permission and it hadn't ended well, but considering his previous legal troubles, I suspected my uncle didn't have a valid driver's license.

"Not on your life," he said, unlocking his door before reaching across to unlock mine. Not that there was anything of value to steal from the truck, besides what it might be worth melted down for scrap metal. "You wanna drive? Get your own car."

"Please, Uncle Calvin," I stood beside the driver's side door. "You could get arrested for driving without a license."

"Pshaw. Get in." I knew I wasn't going to win this

argument, so I did as I was told and buckled my seat belt. "Who's gonna arrest me? Every cop in town is at the funeral service." He chuckled to himself. "Reminds me of the 'fifty-six heist."

I'd been in the middle of composing a text to Beau to let him know what we'd found, but at the mention of the heist, Calvin had my undivided attention. Sometimes my uncle's rambling stories bored me to tears, but since everything kept coming back around to the bank robbery, maybe he knew something useful. "How so?" I asked, curious to see how it lined up with my earlier observation.

That was all the encouragement he needed. "You see, everybody was at the Bluebonnet Festival, including the local cops. The bank was operating on a skeleton crew—just the manager and two tellers for folks needing cash to spend at the festival. Now, this was way before ATMs—"

I interrupted, remembering what Tansy had said about not having ATMs. It was still hard for me to fathom a time without them. "You can fast forward through this part. I've already heard it."

"Oh yeah? But did you hear about the payroll?"

"I heard that the vault was full, but I don't think anyone told me why," I said, shaking my head. "If payday was on Friday, why would there be so much money on Saturday morning?"

"This was way before direct deposit, Juniper. Checks were handed out on Friday at the end of the shift, after the bank had closed for the night. The earliest folks could cash or deposit their paycheck was Saturday morning. Only that Saturday, all the good folks of Cedar River were getting their families ready for the festival."

I nodded, finally seeing where this was going. "Instead of cashing their checks right away, most everybody went to the Bluebonnet Festival. The cops were at the festival, and all that money was just sitting at the bank with a big, flashing neon sign pointing right at it." I stopped and thought about that. "But that's an awful lot of circumstances lining up just so. Real lucky for the robbers, don't you think?"

Calvin turned and grinned at me. I wish he hadn't. He'd already blown through a stop sign and almost hit a hydrant. It was a good thing everyone else was at the funeral, or I'd have to worry about pedestrians. "That's what I've been saying all along. There was an inside man."

"Or woman," I added.

"Or woman," he agreed.

"There were four robbers killed leaving town, right?" I asked.

Calvin nodded.

"And none of them were local."

"Right again," Calvin said.

"Which means they had a connection in town who didn't die in the shootout. Someone who knows where the money is buried."

"I didn't say that," Calvin corrected me.

"Okay, let's work backward. Did the tellers and the bank manager all have the same story?"

"Sure enough," Calvin said. He pulled up in front of the Bobbert house and put the Bronco into park. "They all reported seeing four bank robbers."

"Four?" I asked. "That doesn't make sense. These guys were professionals. They knew that the bank was understaffed because of the festival. So why risk putting all four men in the bank against three employees, and not having a lookout or getaway driver posted outside?"

Calvin grinned like he'd just won the lottery. "That's my girl."

"So there were five robbers. The four we know about, and their inside person."

"I used to think that, too. But if there were four robbers, then the fifth person, the local, would have known where the loot was hidden. They would have taken off with it the first chance they got."

"Who's to say they didn't?" I asked. "Just because they didn't get caught—"

Calvin made an annoying buzzing sound. "Close but no cigar. Trust me, Cedar River was even smaller back then than it is now. Anyone moving out of town or suddenly coming into a fortune would have raised eyebrows."

"So how did they do it?" I asked.

"That's the real question, isn't it?" Calvin said. He turned off the engine, got out of the car, and stretched. "Don't forget to lock the door after you."

We got out of the truck. "You were just buying time when you said you knew who the killer was?" I had a feeling I already knew the answer, but I had to ask.

He nodded. "Yup."

"And you have no idea who the fifth person was?"

"I have my suspicions, but I can't prove anything."

"A hint would be nice," I said.

"I've been puzzling this out since I was a boy, and you think I'm going to give everything away in a single afternoon? Speaking of which, do you know why we call puzzles 'jigsaws'?"

I recognized one of Calvin's infamous segues when I heard it. "Nope, but I have a feeling you're going to tell me."

He launched into a lecture about the history of jigsaw puzzles. I listened with half an ear while I tried to figure out how all the clues I'd found fit together. How did Mayor Bob's murder connect to the 1956 heist? What was I missing? I had a bunch of suspects with weak motives and few to no opportunities. Maybe, like with the bank robbers, there was another person involved who no one had ever suspected.

Calvin changed the subject, and was now talking about one of the many chess games he and his best friend Samuel had played, and was describing it move by move. I nodded at what I hoped were the appropriate times and tried to look like I was listening, but my heart wasn't in it.

I took a seat on one of the rocking chairs on the wide porch ringing the Bobbert home. The service must have wrapped up soon after we left, because guests were trickling in. The Bobberts had a big house, but if Mayor Bob's service had managed to fill up the enormous meeting room at Town Hall, I imagined that their living room would be shoulder to shoulder before long. Fortunately, it was a lovely day. Someone had set up a table on the porch with drinks and snacks, and the majority of the mourners were content to stay outside. Most wandered around to the back lawn that overlooked the river, but Teddy came over and claimed the rocker next to me.

"Have you seen Beau?" I asked him.

"Not since the service," he said, settling into the rocking chair. "I'm sure he'll be here soon enough."

I was anxious to tell Beau what Calvin and I had discovered in Mayor Bob's office, but Teddy had a point. Beau was on his way, and in the meantime, everyone in Cedar River—including everyone that had any reason at all to kill Mayor Bob—was right here. "What happened after we left?" I asked him. "Anything exciting?"

"After your eccentric uncle gave us a history lesson and then accused your oldest sister of murder in front of the whole town?"

I cringed. "Yeah, after that."

"Not much. That was pretty much the highlight of the funeral."

"You said because of your job, you hear stuff," I said.

"Yup," Teddy agreed.

"What are people saying?"

He shook his head. "You don't want to hear it, Juni."

"I do," I assured him.

"The consensus in town is that Tansy killed Mayor Bob. Now there are a few theories floating around as to why. Tansy wanted his job. He turned Sip & Spin down for a permit. Um . . ." He chewed on his bottom lip.

"Spit it out, Theodore," I said.

He winced at the use of his full name. "There's also a rumor that Tansy and Bob were, um, romantically involved. That Tansy murdered him in a fit of jealousy when he wouldn't leave his wife."

"Oof," I said, suppressing a shudder. "Bob's old enough to be our grandfather. Who started *that* one?"

Teddy looked uncomfortable. "Jen Rachet, I think. You know what, I shouldn't have said anything. Obviously, it's nonsense."

"Obviously," I agreed. I knew my sister wasn't having an affair with Mayor Bob, but that didn't mean someone else wasn't. Then again, if he was a cheater, who would have a better motive to murder him, his wife or his mistress? "Are we one hundred percent certain that Faye Bobbert was out of town when Bob was murdered?"

"I tried to deliver a package here last week. No one was here to sign for it, so I took it over to Mayor Bob's office. He accepted the package and told me that Faye was on a cruise with her sister," Teddy said.

"What about Marcus Best?"

"Your mom's new boyfriend? Even though he owns land next to our farm, he's not a Cedar River resident, so I can't tell you much about him. I deliver his flyers every few weeks and I've seen him on TV."

"And Leanna?" I asked. Out of everyone still on our suspect list, she had the most access to Mayor Bob's office.

"Acting Mayor Leanna Lydell-Waite? Why don't you ask her yourself? She's right over there."

"Hold my drink?" I handed the lemonade I'd picked up earlier to Teddy as I stood. Leanna was walking around the side yard. I turned the corner and almost bumped into my mother and Marcus, who were standing at the rail of the porch with their arms around each other's waists as they surveyed the guests milling around on the back lawn.

Below them, Teddy's parents were visiting with Rodger Mayhew, the owner of United Steaks of America. They all waved. But Mickey from the car rental agency saw me looking, and immediately turned their back on me to strike up a conversation with someone I didn't know but who bore a striking resemblance to a younger Faye Bobbert, so I assumed it was her daughter. I caught a glimpse of Esméralda Martín-Brown, whom I hadn't seen since the hole-digging contest. She wouldn't meet my eyes. Pete Digby, the security guard, was sitting with Miss Edie on lawn chairs overlooking the river.

Even paramedic Kitty Harris and her partner, Rocco, were there. Kitty smiled at me. Rocco leaned down and whispered something in her ear. She pushed him away and then walked off in a huff. In short, pretty much everyone I'd ever met in Cedar River was at the wake. Maybe I was being paranoid, but I got the feeling they were all talking about Tansy, and it wasn't good.

"Juniper," Mom said, "what's going on with you? You seem distracted."

"Is it just me, or is everyone staring at us?" I asked. I made eye contact with the passing Rocco, who quickly looked away and changed direction so he was headed for the river instead of the house. Once again, my family was at the center of a scandal, and I didn't like it—especially when we didn't deserve to be.

"If they are, it's because of how nice you look in that dress," Mom said. "Don't you think she looks nice, Marcus?"

Marcus nodded. "Lovely. Just like her mom."

"Uh-huh," I said even though I didn't agree. People were whispering about us behind our backs, and it had absolutely nothing to do with my outfit. "Have you seen Beau around?"

My mother pursed her lips. "He's probably busy setting up a speed trap for unsuspecting mourners." I guess she hadn't forgiven him yet for writing her a ticket.

Time to change the subject. "You two having a nice time?"

"Lovely," Marcus said.

"As nice as one can expect, at a wake," Mom said wryly. "Juni, you slipped out before I could say something, but you did a fantastic job of managing your uncle earlier."

"It was nothing."

"It was nothing," she repeated. She let out a dry laugh. "You convinced Cal to give up the spotlight without causing a scene, defended your sister's honor, and addressed the crowd without getting stage fright. I'm proud of you."

Considering how terrified I'd been to take the mic, that was a nice compliment, even if it was a low bar. Someday, I was going to prove to my mother that I wasn't a child anymore. "Thanks."

"I like to think Bob would have gotten a kick out of the service," Marcus said. "I know I did, but then again, I was sitting with the prettiest woman in all of Cedar River."

"Oh, stop," Mom said, nudging him with her hip.

That was my cue to skedaddle. Fortunately for me, my

timing couldn't have been better, because just a few feet away, Leanna had climbed the stairs onto the porch and was headed straight for the back door of the house. "I'll catch y'all later," I said, and hurried into the house.

It was crowded inside. Not as crowded as it had been at the Town Hall meeting room, but crowded nevertheless. I caught a glimpse of Jen Rachet holding court with Carole Akers and Joyce Whedon from the bank. They glanced my way, openly gaping at me, before returning to their huddle and resuming their animated discussion with new fervor. Great. It didn't take much of an imagination to figure out they were gossiping about me and my sister.

I didn't see Leanna, though, until I caught a glimpse of her heading upstairs. I followed her. There was a ribbon stretched across the stairs, tied to the banister on either side. A neatly hand-lettered sign reading 'Please respect our privacy' was threaded onto the ribbon, blocking the walkway. I ducked under it and continued, wondering what Leanna could possibly be doing upstairs in a dead man's house. I reached the top of the stairs and looked around. A hall stretched out in both directions on either side of me. There were more rooms than I could imagine the Bobberts ever needing, and all the doors were closed.

I knocked on the first door. When there was no answer, I opened it a crack. The room had the bland personality of a guest bedroom with its unruffled bed and generic artwork on the walls.

The next room was set up like a library, but instead of novels, the shelves were covered in knickknacks. I slipped into the room to get a better peek. Old ledgers took up one shelf. I pulled one out and flipped it open. The First Bank of Cedar River was on the cover and the date on the first page was January 2, 1956. The pages were filled with columns of numbers. I put it back and kept looking around.

There was an old pistol locked in a shadowbox, a police shield, and a glass jar filled with dirt. Another binder held what looked like original newspaper clippings about the bank robbery. If my uncle had known that Bob's collection of heist memorabilia was this extensive, he would have been terribly jealous. I wondered what Faye intended to do with it all now that Bob was gone.

The next door was locked. In the room after that, two small children were making colorful towers out of plastic blocks. A woman rocking a baby asked, "Excuse me, can I help you?"

"I, uh, was looking for . . ." I said, my mind drawing a blank at being caught snooping.

"Across the hall," the woman said.

"Huh?" I asked.

"The bathroom. It's across the hall. And please, don't slam the door. Darlene's almost asleep." Darlene was the baby, I guessed.

"Sure thing," I said, backing out of the room and closing the door softly behind me. I turned around and collided with Tansy. "What are you doing up here?" I asked my sister.

"I had to get away for a minute," she said to me. "Ever since Mayor Bob died after drinking the coffee I made, everyone in town's been looking at me funny. Uncle Calvin's speech just made things worse. If we don't figure out who killed Bob, and soon, I'm gonna have to move out of Cedar River and change my name."

I was about to share what I'd learned in the mayor's office when a door opened and Leanna stepped into the hall, stopping short when she saw us. She looked nervous. "Uh-oh, guess y'all caught me red-handed."

"Yup. Sure did," I said, even though I had no idea what she was talking about.

Tansy gave her a canary-eating grin. "Got something you want to confess?"

Leanna glanced behind her at the open bathroom door. "Just promise y'all won't tell anyone. We've been trying for a while, and after multiple rounds of IVF, it finally happened." She broke into a grin. "We were going to announce I'm pregnant at the Bluebonnet Festival, but with Bob's death, the timing felt off." She unconsciously shielded her belly with her arm even though she wasn't showing yet.

"That's the real reason you were in Town Hall on Saturday morning," I said, understanding dawning. I'd never believed her flimsy excuse that she was checking her email. It was probably also why she wouldn't drink the tea we'd brought her. And here I was thinking she was being rude. "And your craving for chocolate." It also explained what she was doing sneaking around the wake to find an out-of-the-way bathroom.

"Morning sickness," she confirmed. "Please, don't tell anyone yet."

"We can keep a secret," I assured her.

"Seriously?" Leanna asked. She looked over at my sister. "No offense, Tansy, but next to your mom, and maybe Jen Rachet, you're the biggest gossip in Cedar River."

"I am not," she protested. Leanna wasn't wrong, but with the whole town gossiping about my sister, I can see how she might be offended. "It's not my fault I'm easy to talk to."

"Ha!" Leanna scoffed. "Easy to talk to? I've been trying to befriend you since we were four years old and in the same Texas Tots pageant."

"You have?" Tansy looked confused.

"Oh my stars, really? I entered every pageant you were

in. I signed up for the yearbook in high school because you were on the staff. I even joined your gym in the hopes that you'd offer to train with me," Leanna said with an exasperated sigh.

"But why?" Tansy asked. "I thought you hated me."

"Hate you? I look up to you. Always have. Everything you do seems so effortless, and every time I see you succeed, it pushes me to work a little harder," Leanna admitted.

"I don't get it. You're a fabulous athlete, and you've got a wonderful wife and a successful career."

"I'm a part-time council member and a substitute teacher. You've got your own small business and everyone in Cedar River loves you," Leanna said.

"Everyone in Cedar River loves you, too," I pointed out. "Otherwise, you would never have gotten elected."

"Well, my political career is officially on pause as soon as we elect a new mayor and backfill my seat on the council," she said. "I love serving Cedar River, but there's no way I can hold down multiple jobs and raise a kid." She held up one finger, then turned and dashed back into the bathroom.

"I saw her wife downstairs," Tansy said. "I'll go get her, let her know that Leanna needs her."

While I waited for her wife to arrive, I realized that I could stand to use the restroom, too. There was no telling how long Leanna might be in there, and there was undoubtedly a line for the bathroom downstairs. Certainly, there was another bathroom upstairs in a house this large. I just needed to find it.

I continued down the hall. This time, I listened at each door before knocking. I didn't want to stumble across another of the Bobbert kids and have to explain why I was snooping around. The third door I opened hit paydirt.

It wasn't a bathroom. Instead, it was a large suite that stretched the width of the house. There was an enormous four-poster bed in the middle of the room and a love seat tucked into the curve of the bay window overlooking the river.

I let myself into the ensuite bathroom and closed the door behind me. Once the important business was out of the way, I washed my hands and checked my reflection in the mirror above the sink. My eyeliner was wonky, and I dabbed at it with a tissue. With that sorted, I stared at the mirror itself, wondering what secrets it might hold.

Riffling through Faye's medicine cabinet would be a huge invasion of privacy, but it was too tempting to pass up. I opened the hinged door, revealing three glass shelves packed with pill bottles. There was an assortment of over-the-counter painkillers and digestive aids, along with a bunch of prescriptions I didn't recognize. Feeling guilty, I closed the mirror and hurried out before anyone could catch me snooping.

Leanna was not in the hallway. The bathroom door was open when I walked down the hallway back toward the wake. I hoped this meant that Leanna was feeling better. I ducked back under the ribbon blocking off the stairs and returned to the crowd.

"Where have you been?" Maggie asked, materializing at the foot of the stairs. "Never mind. I need you. It's an emergency."

"What's wrong?" I asked. Even after Beau's repeated assurances that he believed in Tansy's innocence, a tiny part of me was afraid he'd shown up to the wake with a pair of handcuffs and a warrant for my sister's arrest.

"It's Mom," she said, and I felt the blood drain from my face.

The pills in Faye Bobbert's medicine cabinet were

a reminder that none of us were getting any younger. My mother wasn't quite sixty yet, but neither was my father when we lost him. "What happened? Is she okay?" I stayed right on my middle sister's heels as we circum-navigated the crowd.

"Is she okay? Seriously?" Maggie asked, looking at me with a disgusted expression. "No, she's not okay. She's making out with Marcus. In public!"

"Ew," I said before I could catch myself. My parents had always been affectionate toward each other. It had been a constant source of embarrassment growing up, but now that I was grown, looking back on it, it was kinda sweet. But that was with my dad. I couldn't imagine Mom kissing anyone else, much less at a wake.

When we reached the back door, I caught a glimpse of them. I wouldn't call what they were doing making out, but it was still too much PDA for me. "Mom!" I said.

She backed a half step away from Marcus and ran her hand through her hair to smooth it before turning to us. "Juni, Maggie. You needed something?"

"It's more what we *don't* need," Maggie said. "Get a room. No, on second thought, don't."

"Now, Maggie, don't be rude," Mom replied.

"Rude? I'm not the one—"

I nudged my sister, hard. There was no need to make a scene, not in this crowd. Not at a wake, and especially not when we were already under scrutiny. I said the first thing that popped into my head. "Mom, we're running low on lemonade."

"And?"

"Maybe we should make some," I suggested.

"That's very thoughtful," she said. She was no longer obscenely close to Marcus, but he still had his hand on her waist. "You should do that."

"I would," I said. "I mean, I will. But you make the best lemonade in all of Travis County. Everyone says so."

"They do," Maggie agreed, quickly backing me up.

"Well, in that case, it would be a shame to leave it to the amateurs, wouldn't it?" She kissed Marcus on the cheek. "Duty calls. I'll be back."

Maggie pushed me in the direction of the kitchen. "Let's get going then."

The Bobberts' kitchen, like the rest of the house, was spacious and very white. The cabinets were white. The appliances were white. The floor tiles were white.

"Maggie, find me a sharp knife, a cutting board, and a juicer," Mom ordered as she rummaged through the cabinets for a pitcher. "And Juni, grab lemons, sugar, and ice."

The lemons were easy to find. They were in a decorative basket on the counter acting as practically the only splash of color in the room. The sugar was in a white bowl next to the single-serving coffeepot and a stack of single-use sugar-free amaretto-flavored coffee creamer cups. I hit a wall with the ice, though. The freezer was filled with casseroles, and had no room for ice. I'd seen bowls of ice at the beverage station on the front porch, but I couldn't go grab the ice from there without arousing suspicion, so I looked in the refrigerator instead.

"Bingo," I said to myself, pulling out the chilled water filter pitcher. It wasn't ideal—good homemade lemonade required ice—but considering the lemonade emergency was just a made-up excuse to get my mother to come up for air for a moment, it would have to do.

As I closed the refrigerator door, I noticed two small glass vials where the butter should go. I leaned in to get a better look. I read the label. It was insulin. "Did Bob have diabetes?" I asked.

"He did, rest his soul," my mother said. I wondered if

my sisters knew that. I tried to recall his drink of choice. Everything was fat-free and unsweetened, but if we'd added the wrong ingredient, we could have accidentally contributed to his condition. Good thing he was drinking straight drip coffee the morning he was killed.

"Honestly I don't know how he managed it with his busy schedule," Mom continued. From what Leanna had shown us, his schedule wasn't nearly as taxing as everyone assumed, but I wasn't going to mention that today, of all days. She handed me a chopping board. "Now start cutting those lemons. Thin slices, please."

I closed the refrigerator door and sat the pitcher of cold water on the counter. I had to move the single-cup coffee maker over to make room for the cutting board. I guess in a household with only one coffee drinker, who has only one cup of coffee a day, or with people who couldn't agree on one type of coffee, it made sense, but I'd never own one. Now that I had easy access to a fancy barista machine and all the flavored syrups and creamers we had at Sip & Spin, I'd gotten spoiled.

Wait a second. I put down the knife and picked up one of the creamer cups. They were amaretto-flavored, the same as the ones in the mayor's office. It made sense, this being Bob's kitchen and all, but finally, everything clicked.

"Juni? Are you okay?" my mom asked. "You didn't cut yourself, did you?"

"I'm fine," I said. "Better than fine, actually. I know how to prove that Tansy didn't kill Mayor Bob."

CHAPTER 28

I rushed out the front door and scanned the crowd milling about on the lawn. Unlike at the funeral home, the music coming from the outdoor speakers wasn't quite as formal. I recognized the one of the lesser-known Beach Boys songs. It ended, and a Simon & Garfunkel tune took its place. I spotted Teddy talking with Esméralda Martín-Brown and hurried over to join them.

Teddy put his arm around my shoulder. "I was starting to wonder where you'd gone off to."

"Is Beau here yet?" I asked.

Esméralda shook her head. "I haven't seen him. If the rumor mill is to be believed, he's probably out looking to arrest your sister."

Teddy gave her a stern look. "You know as well as I do that Tansy's innocent." He turned to me and rolled his eyes. "Some people will believe anything. Beau was here a second ago. I'd check around the side if I were you."

"Thanks." I gave him a spontaneous kiss on the cheek. How had I had such a great guy under my nose for literal decades and never noticed until recently?

"No problem," he said with a wink. "If I see him first, I'll tell him you're looking for him."

Beau wasn't on the side lawn, nor was he around back.

I was about to head toward the back door again and brave the crowd inside when I heard his familiar voice behind me. I followed the sound and found a clump of men standing near the riverbank. They were drinking beer and smoking cigars.

Fortunately, Beau wasn't one of the smokers. Seeing me, he grinned. "Hey, Junebug. Just who I wanted to see."

"We need to talk," I said. "Can we take a walk?"

"Sure thing." He nodded at the other men. We followed a well-trodden path from the river back toward the house.

I pointed at the beer in his hand. "Drinking on the job?"

"Am I?" He glanced at the bottle before turning the label to face me. It was a non-alcoholic beer.

"Oh," I said, feeling a little foolish. Of course he was drinking a fake beer. Unlike me, Beau didn't do anything without thinking it through first. Everything he did was calculated. Even his ridiculous charm was usually part of some bigger plan.

"You wanted to talk?" he prompted. We stayed near the water's edge. The gurgle of the river afforded us a little privacy, but not much.

"Your lab tested our cups. Tested our coffee. Tested our carafe. There were no traces of poison. That's what you said. But did you test the empty creamer cups in Mayor Bob's trash can?"

"I may have received additional test results this afternoon," Beau said.

"I was right." I bobbed my head. "I knew it! The poison came from the creamer, not the coffee. Tansy and Sip & Spin are off the hook."

"Not so fast, Juni. Let's suppose, hypothetically, that we test a cup of coffee and a cup of creamer, and they both have trace amounts of the same poison on them. Did the poison go from the creamer to the coffee, or the coffee to the creamer?"

"Well, that's just silly. You pour creamer into coffee, not the other way around."

"Sure do," Beau agreed. "Unless, suppose in this hypothetical situation that everything in the wastebasket had trace amounts of poison on it. The scrap paper. A candy bar wrapper. A water bottle. A stir stick. The creamer cups. Did cross contamination happen in the trash can, or in the lab?"

"Shoot," I said.

Beau bobbed his head in agreement. "Hypothetically, if evidence is contaminated, the results get tossed. Including results that otherwise might be able to convict, or exonerate, a suspect."

"You're telling me that even if the creamer *was* poisoned, because the test was inconclusive, that information might never come out in court, even if it's proof that my sister is innocent?" I asked. My pulse raced as I thought about the implications. It was one thing for folks to gossip that she might be guilty, but for her to have to stand trial? She didn't deserve that. Even with a lawyer like J.T. on her side, there was always a possibility that she could be convicted for a murder she didn't commit.

"Hypothetically," Beau admitted.

"What if you had another non-contaminated sample to test?" I pulled up the picture I'd taken on my phone and handed it to him.

"Where did you take this?"

"There's a mini-fridge in Mayor Bob's office," I said. I zoomed in on the screen to enlarge the image. "Does that look like a puncture mark in the lid to you?"

CHAPTER 29

"Hmm. Does that look like a puncture mark?" Beau repeated, studying the screen. "Maybe. But before you get your hopes up, Mayor Bob's office was unsealed this morning. Acting Mayor Lydell-Waite requested it personally. Anyone could have tampered with the creamer at any time before or after his death. No chain of custody means they can't be used as evidence."

I grudgingly agreed that crime scene tape right down the hall from where the mayor's service was being held was unseemly, but in having it removed, Leanna unknowingly—or knowingly—ensured that the creamer cups Uncle Calvin and I had found in the mini-fridge didn't prove a thing.

"Don't worry, Junebug," Beau said, placing one hand on my shoulder. "We'll catch the killer." He paused, then clarified. "And by 'we', I mean the C.R.P.D. Not you."

"Right," I agreed.

He pursed his lips. Clearly, he didn't believe me. I didn't blame him. I guess we both had trust issues with each other. "I've got to get back to work. Stay out of trouble?"

I nodded. "Yup." He walked back the way we came from. I continued following the trail as it led back to the house, over perfectly manicured lawns. I paused to admire the award-winning rose bushes ringing the porch, and caught a glimpse of Faye Bobbert framed in one of the large windows.

The widow looked regal in a black dress and matching black hat pinned to her hair. She was surrounded by familiar faces, most of whom were on Maggie's suspect list.

Jen Rachet and Leanna Lydell-Waite both had access to chemicals containing cyanide from their recent photography class. Leanna would have had easy access to syringes during her last round of IVF, and she was in Town Hall on Saturday morning, but she had no reason to kill the mayor. Jen didn't have a reason to keep syringes on hand, and I assumed she was busy at the festival Saturday morning. As far as I could tell, the only reason she was involved at all was because she had to be at the center of everything.

Faye had to have needles in the house to go with the insulin I'd seen in the fridge, but she had an alibi and no access to poison. Marcus could have bought a container full of cyanide-laden pesticides to clear out Rawlings Hollow and no one would have batted an eye, but I'd seen him with my own eyes at the park that morning. As for Pete, I had no idea if he had access to needles or poison, but like Leanna, he was in Town Hall when Bob was killed.

I climbed the steps and made my way through the crowd, ignoring the suspicious glances thrown my way. "That was a lovely service," Mom was saying as I joined the clump of mourners surrounding Faye. Marcus had his arm around Mom's back.

"Thank you, dear," Faye said. Her voice wavered, and my heart went out to the widow. It couldn't be easy keeping it together in front of all these people after what she'd just been through. "It wasn't too much, was it?"

"Everything was perfect," Jen assured her. "He died

doing what he loved. It was only fitting to hold Mayor Bob's service at Town Hall."

"Despite his promise that this year's election would be his last, I always said that Bob would work until the day he dropped. I just wasn't expecting him to be so literal about it," Faye said, a hint of bitterness leaking into her voice. "I tried for years to convince him to retire, but you know Bob. He didn't know when to walk away." She looked around the crowded living room, meticulously decorated with her prized roses in crystal vases on every table, next to abandoned cups. "Although, I suppose, maybe this is a sign. No one lives forever, and I'm not getting any younger. Maybe it is time to move on."

"You can't be serious," Mom said. "You're really considering leaving Cedar River?"

"I suppose change is inevitable, whether we're ready for it or not," Faye replied sagely.

"That seems a little callous for someone who just lost their husband," Jen said defensively. I gave her a sideways glance. Jen was the one spreading rumors that Tansy and Bob had a romantic connection, but what if she was just trying to throw suspicion off herself? She was much closer to Mayor Bob's age. She was single. She seemed at home inside the Bobbert's house. If anyone was having an affair, Jen would be at the top of my suspects list.

"Oh for Pete's sake, Jen, how would you know?" Faye snapped. "I've been married to that man since the seventies. Am I gonna miss him? Of course! Was our marriage perfect? Not even close. You of all people should understand that." She glared at Jen Rachet, confirming my suspicions that Jen and Mayor Bob might have had secrets of their own.

"Why, I never!" Jen exclaimed.

"Save it," Faye said, cutting her off. "Have I even

thought about killing Bob myself once or twice? Guilty as charged. Good thing that unlike Tansy Jessup, I was on the other side of the country when he kicked the bucket."

Jen let out an exaggerated gasp. "My word," she said. "Have some respect."

"Respect?" Faye asked angrily. "Do you have any idea what I put up with, being married to that man? First, he drags me to Texas, of all places. Texas! Then he quits practicing law, cutting his salary in half so he could run for mayor. I pinch pennies. I make it work. Even when I find out he's been stepping out on me, I forgive him, for the sake of our family. But then I find out he'd drained our savings buying those puerile trinkets of his. Worthless old maps. Useless ledgers from the fifties. Silly bluebonnet paperweights."

"Hey, those weren't worthless," Marcus said. "They were priceless."

"You know what's priceless?" the widow replied. "Freedom. Retirement. The prize at the end of the day. But what am I left with? Nothing. When he declared he was running for *another* term as mayor, I made up my mind. Fifty years was enough. I was cashing in and retiring, with or without him. Then I found out he'd mortgaged our home. Our home! The only thing we had left worth a nickel was Bob's life insurance, and good golly if he didn't do me a huge favor when he dropped dead."

"Faye, you didn't, um, do anything to Bob, did you?" my mother asked in the tone of voice she used on me when I'd misbehaved as a kid. I'd heard that tone an awful lot, come to think of it.

"Don't be silly, Bea," the widow replied. "Bob was never in the best of health. After he got diagnosed with diabetes, I tried to get him to cut back on sugar, but he never could stick to a diet. He was one candy bar away from an early grave. Besides, I was on a cruise ship in Alaska when he died, remember?"

"Yes, you certainly were," I said. Everything fit. The suspect with the most to gain from Mayor Bob's death was the only one with a rock-solid alibi. But that didn't mean she didn't have plenty of opportunity. "You were four thousand miles away. You couldn't have possibly killed your husband." I paused for dramatic effect. "Except, you doctored his amaretto creamer with cyanide before you left on your cruise." There were more gasps this time, but none of them fake like Jen's earlier reaction.

"Why, I never," Faye Bobbert said, drawing herself up to full height. Any pretense of being a grieving widow was gone as her face twisted with anger. "Juniper Jessup, you will leave my house right now." She turned to my mother and shook her head. "Bea, I thought you would have raised your daughters better."

"Oh, I raised my daughters just fine," Mom replied, looking horror-struck as she realized the lengths Faye had gone to. "Juni turned out a whole lot better than you did."

I don't think I've ever been so proud to be my mother's daughter. I felt a hand on my shoulder, as Beau joined us. He cleared his throat to get everyone's attention and said, "Mrs. Bobbert, I need a word with you down at the station."

"Not you too! I have half a mind to press charges against the lot of you. Juni, her meddling sisters, her mom—yes, you too, Bea—and the Cedar River Police Department. You'll be hearing from my lawyer!"

"About that," Beau said. He held up a gallon jug attached to a spray nozzle. "If I test this homemade weed killer I found out back, and it comes up as a match to the poison we found in the mayor's coffee, you're gonna need that lawyer, ma'am." He turned to Jayden, who had followed him. "Why don't you escort Mrs. Bobbert out to your car?" he asked.

CHAPTER 30

A week later, sweat rolled down my face as I sorted through boxes in Tansy's attic. She hadn't lived in this house for long, but when Mom had sold her house, all of the junk that the family had accumulated for generations ended up here.

For the record, an attic in Texas wasn't the ideal place to store anything. I'd already found several unidentifiable lumps of plastic that had probably started out life as a piggy bank or a child's beloved toy. Cardboard boxes were brittle with age, plastic totes had warped after continued exposure to the heat, and even wooden chests were riddled with holes from burrowing insects.

After what felt like an eternity, I found what I was looking for—an old metal trunk. I dragged it until it was directly under one of the lights. If I'd asked for help, my sisters would've helped me get the heavy trunk out of the attic, but I didn't want to get anyone's hopes up until I was certain. I pried open the lid and stared at its contents.

My father's entire life fit in this trunk. All the bits and pieces he'd collected throughout his fifty-seven years on this planet, the doohickeys and whatnots that he'd never thrown away were here, in all their unorganized glory. I hadn't realized it until this moment, but that was something else I'd inherited from him. Without Mom constantly cleaning up after him, Dad would have ended up like me, with clothes strewn across every surface and books haphazardly piled on the shelf.

The thought made me smile. When my life got too chaotic, I would try to remember this moment. I wasn't messy. I was just my dad's daughter.

I dug into the trunk with gusto. Here was a wallet Maggie had made for him at summer camp, neatly hand stitched together. I found handfuls of crumpled paper bands, the kind they handed out at concerts and clubs. There were no names on them, no dates, just the logos of sponsors and memories long forgotten.

There were loose, unlabeled photos. I recognized the people in the pictures as my mother as a young woman, my father and his brother as kids, and my grandparents posing beside their old Buick. I found ticket stubs galore for bands that no longer existed and singers who had died before I was born. Scattered throughout were guitar picks and 45 adapters. I even found Dad's original plastic name tag from when he worked at my grandparent's record shop. The letters were barely visible anymore.

Finally, at the bottom of the trunk, I found the clue I was looking for. Over the course of the next week, after everyone else was asleep, I went out for long walks by myself until I was certain that I knew what it meant.

While I was enjoying my late-night strolls, Faye Bobbert was awaiting trial for first degree murder. The lab confirmed that her homemade pesticide was nothing fancier than a mix of two brand-name weed killers, but the blend was an exact match for the poison in Mayor Bob's coffee. Another search of her house had found a box of syringes that matched the holes punched in the lids of the creamers in Mayor Bob's trash can.

Beau had already noticed the puncture holes before I pointed them out, and deliberately kept that clue to himself. I didn't blame him. Much.

Faye protested her innocence, but changed her tune when all the evidence was laid out before her. She admitted spiking each cup of creamer with a small dose of pesticide, knowing that the amaretto flavor would overpower the bitter taste of the poison. She tried to hire my brother-in-law to represent her in court, but J.T. wouldn't take the case. She ended up with a big-shot lawyer from Houston instead.

In an ironic twist, it turned out that Mayor Bob's incompetence was practically the only thing Faye hadn't accounted for. When the coffee machine at Town Tall broke, instead of signing off on getting it fixed, he developed a new habit of buying coffee at Sip & Spin Records. If he'd stuck with his old routine of fixing his coffee at the office, he probably would have consumed the fatal dose on a normal business day instead of on the Saturday of the Bluebonnet Festival. Then all evidence of her crime would have been taken out with the trash.

Main Street was quiet as I pedaled my tricycle to the shop the next Sunday, soon after sunset. The shops in Cedar River closed early. Sip & Spin was the only storefront on the block that still had its lights on. I pulled up in front, gathered the duffle bag I'd crammed into the basket behind my seat, and rattled the front door. It was locked. Tansy let me in.

As soon as the door opened, Daffy ran up to greet me, purring as he brushed up against my legs. The customers were gone for the day. James Brown was playing on the turntable.

"What's that?" Tansy asked, pointing to the oversize duffle over my shoulder.

"Juni's got a brand-new bag," I said, in beat to the music.

Maggie groaned. "You and your puns."

"Speaking of which, how did What About Robust do today?" I asked. It was a simple dark roast drip coffee that even Teddy would appreciate, sweetened with a dash of pink sugar that reminded me of the cotton candy at the Bluebonnet Festival.

"We had plenty of sales, but most of the customers didn't get the reference," Tansy said.

"That's a shame. I'd hoped there were more P!nk fans in this town." Even though there was already music playing over the speakers, I started humming "What About Us" to myself. "I should have called it Brew + UR Hand instead."

"But enough about that, what are we doing here so late?" Tansy asked.

"Simple." I smiled and unzipped the duffle bag. I gingerly placed the framed brochure I'd dug out of our dad's trunk on the counter and tossed black sweatsuits to each of my sisters. "We needed to wait for nightfall for my plan to work."

"You can't expect me to wear these," Maggie said, holding up the baggy pants.

"If I can survive a day in one of your dresses, wearing sweatpants for an hour won't kill you," I told her.

"Enough already," Tansy said, folding her sweats over her arm. "Out with it."

"Fine," I agreed. I fished a map of Cedar River out of the bag and spread it out on one of the café tables. It wasn't an antique like the one Jimmy took from Mayor Bob's office, but that didn't matter now that I knew what I was looking for. I took a marker out of the pen cup next to the register. I drew an X over the First Bank of Cedar

River. Then I circled Rawlings Hollow, far from the center of town.

I put a finger on the bank. "It's April 14, 1956. Four armed robbers just emptied out the bank."

"We should have invited Uncle Calvin along to explain this to us," Tansy said to Maggie in a stage whisper.

"Shush," I told her. "An hour later, they're killed in a gun battle with police as they're leaving town, here." I drew a thick line over where Main Street splits.

"What other event was happening that day?" I asked. Maggie stuck her tongue out at me. "Real mature, sis." I tapped Rawlings Hollow. "The Bluebonnet Festival. Practically everyone in Travis County was here, at the old fairgrounds on the edge of town near the Garza Farm."

"We already know this," Tansy said.

"Yeah, but do you know how long it takes to drive from the First Bank of Cedar River to Rawlings Hollow?"

Maggie shrugged. "I don't know, half an hour maybe?"

"Thirty-five minutes. I timed it."

"So?" Maggie asked.

"So," Tansy said, leaning in to look closer at the map, as if it held previously undisclosed secrets, "the robbers hold up the bank. Then they drive thirty-five minutes to Rawlings Hollow, on one of the few days of the year that people would be out that way. They manage to bury their loot without anyone noticing them, despite the crowd. That takes, what, ten minutes? Twenty? Then they drive thirty-five minutes back, in time to run into the police exactly one hour after the teller reported the robbery. It's impossible."

"The employees were freaked out," Maggie suggested. "The tellers took some time to compose themselves before they reported the robbery."

"Nope," I said. "There was a phone behind the teller

stations, and one of the tellers managed to get through to police dispatch while the robbers were still in the bank."

"In that case, Tansy's right. The timing doesn't line up. Besides, if you're sneaking around trying to bury all that money, why would you go all the way out to Rawlings Hollow when the rest of Cedar River is practically deserted?"

I put my finger on the tip of my nose like we used to do when we were kids and one of us made a good guess during game night. "Bingo."

"All that tells us is that the treasure isn't buried in Rawlings Hollow," Tansy said. "Could be literally anywhere else."

"Not anywhere," I pointed out. "When the robbers were killed, one of them had bluebonnets crushed in his boots." Beau wouldn't let me borrow the bluebonnet paperweight that Jimmy had stolen from Mayor Bob, something about it being material evidence against Jimmy, Butch, and their two friends. But, I found a cached copy of the auction online and printed a screenshot of it.

"Yeah, and in April, in Texas, bluebonnets are everywhere," Maggie said.

"This was 1956," I reminded them. "Remember when Uncle Calvin was giving that speech at Mayor Bob's funeral service about the Wildflower Protection Act? It was enacted because the bluebonnets needed protection. In 1956, they were still endangered. It wasn't until twenty-ish years later that they were plentiful enough to not need a law against disturbing them."

"Which is why back then it was such a big deal that Rawlings Hollow was covered in bluebonnets," Tansy said, bobbing her head in agreement.

"But it wasn't the only place in town where the bluebonnets grew." I walked over to the counter and picked up the framed brochure from 1957, the year *after* the heist. "The next year, the Bluebonnet Festival was moved closer to town, to Cedar River Memorial Park, where—and I quote—'an unexpected bumper crop of bluebonnets sprang up.' Almost as if someone had dug up the park right as the bluebonnets were going to seed, causing them to multiply exponentially."

"Let me guess," Tansy said. She pulled out her phone. "Lookie here. According to the *Farmers' Almanac*, it should have been an unusually hot spring, almost ten degrees warmer than average. We hold the Bluebonnet Festival on the second week in April precisely because it's near the end of the season, for maximum blooms. But if it was that hot, the bluebonnets would have gone to seed earlier than normal." Then she looked up at me, comprehension dawning in her eyes. "You know where the money is buried."

I grinned. "I do."

My sisters changed into their black sweatsuits with no more complaints. I passed around heavy-duty flashlights and gardening gloves. "We should take your car, Tansy," I suggested.

"The park's just a couple of blocks away. Why don't we walk?" she asked.

"Because I've already put the shovels in your trunk," I told her.

Tansy drove to the park. It was late. Cedar River Memorial Park technically closed at sunset, so we were the only car in the lot. I knew from my recent excursions that at this time of night we might bump into teenagers or people taking their dogs out for one last walk for the night, but I didn't think my sisters would agree to meet me out here at three in the morning.

We carried the shovels over our shoulders as we headed down the paved trail. During the Bluebonnet Festival, this was where all the food trucks had lined up. Just thinking about them made my mouth water. "I should have brought snacks," I said.

"That's our Juni, always thinking with her stomach," Maggie teased.

Frankly, I didn't see why that was such a bad thing. Thinking with my heart never got me anywhere. I still had no idea what I was going to do about Teddy or Beau. It wasn't fair to string them both along forever, but every time I thought I made up my mind, something happened to make me swing the other way. My stomach was much more reliable. It knew what it wanted.

"This is it," I said, stopping to survey the area. "This is where the treasure is buried."

CHAPTER 31

My sisters and I were near the center of the park, where the bluebonnets had grown thick and lush. It was late enough in the season that almost all the wildflowers had withered and died for the year. The seeds would scatter, go dormant, and rise once again next spring.

"Are you sure this is the place?" Tansy asked.

"Yup. When Teddy and I caught those men tearing up Rawlings Hollow, they had a metal detector with them. That got me to thinking."

"You know the robbers took cash money, right?" Maggie reminded me. "No gold. No coins. Nothing that a metal detector could pick up."

"Yuppers," I agreed, "but they didn't walk out of the bank with a wad of bills in their hands." I scrolled through the saved photos on my phone and showed her a drawing. "They put the money in suitcases the bank tellers later described to a sketch artist. Look at all those hinges and clasps."

Maggie leaned in to get a better look. "There's metal on the handles, too. And that one looks like it might have a zipper."

"It does. I found a listing for one just like it on eBay," I told her. "I borrowed Esméralda's drone to fly over the park so I could map it, and then used Samuel Davis's metal detector to scan every inch of it. This is it. I can feel it." I switched to the map app on my phone. I hadn't trusted myself to find this exact spot again. I'd considered marking the location with sticks, but if it had gotten run over with a lawnmower, we'd be back to square one. In the end, I'd gone with dropping a GPS pin. It was accurate to within a few feet and, unlike with a stick, a dog wasn't going to run away with the global positioning satellite network.

"Good enough for me," Maggie said, as she started to dig.

"That's what you've been doing late at night," Tansy said. I must have looked as surprised as I felt, because she elaborated. "I'm a light sleeper. You've been sneaking out of the house in the middle of the night all week."

"And you didn't say anything to me?" I asked, moving a shovelful of dirt.

"Or to me?" Maggie asked.

"I assumed you were going out to meet someone."

"You thought she was sneaking out to meet a boy," Maggie said. She turned to me. "Who is it, sis? Spill the beans. Beau or Teddy?"

I shook my head. "Neither," I insisted. "I was here, in the park. Alone." I turned on my flashlight and focused it on the hole. We'd only been digging for a few minutes, but with three of us working together, we were making good progress. Then again, we always worked better when we were on the same groove. "But if I was meeting someone, it wouldn't be any of either of your business."

"Really?" Maggie asked. "None of our business? We're your sisters."

"Cut her some slack, Maggie. If it doesn't affect the family or Sip & Spin, what Juni does on her own time is her own business," Tansy said.

"Thanks," I told her, surprised she was backing me up.

"As long as she's not sneaking around with Beau Russell," she added hastily.

"Geez," I said.

"Less bickering, more shoveling," Maggie chided the two of us.

"Tansy has a point," I said. Maggie snorted. "And you do, too, Maggie. If it affects all of us, we should all be involved, but who I date or don't date isn't up for debate. I mean, take Mom and Marcus." I jumped as Maggie's shovelful of dirt landed on my feet. "Watch what you're doing! Maggie, you were so determined to prove that Marcus murdered Mayor Bob that we almost didn't figure out who the real killer was."

"She's got a point," Tansy said.

"And you, Tansy, were so convinced that Leanna was the killer, we missed what was really going on with her," I said. "She needed a friend, not someone suspecting her of murder."

"Speaking of Leanna," Tansy said, "we have plans to go for a run tomorrow morning."

"You *what*?" Maggie asked. "Your nemesis since childhood and you're voluntarily hanging out together? You're not planning on killing her and dumping her body in the river, are you?"

"Of course not," Tansy said. "I'd be too afraid Juni would figure out what I did and go blabbing to the cops."

"Would not," I said. The longer we dug, the more difficult it got. I had no idea how Teddy and the other hole-digging contestants managed to move as much dirt as they had, and in the heat of the day at that.

"Would too," Tansy countered.

"See? This is what I'm talking about." I took a brief rest against my shovel. "We make a great team when we work together, but when we're all going in different directions, nothing ever gets done."

"Like how this hole isn't going to dig itself," Maggie said.

"Yeah, yeah, yeah." I scooped out another shovelful of dirt. "Just look at Faye and Mayor Bob. Everyone thought they were the perfect couple, but it turns out they weren't. Promise me that will never happen to us."

"I could never kill you," Maggie told me. "At least not with poison."

"Speak for yourself. You don't have to clean up the kitchen after her," Tansy said.

"El oh el," I replied, sarcastically. "I'll try to do better. Or, with my share of the money, I'll hire a maid."

Maggie wiped sweat off her forehead. "How deep do you think they hid the money?"

"No one knows," I said. "It can't be too deep. They were in a hurry, and they planned to come back and pick it up soon." My mind wandered to Calvin's theory. All the evidence pointed to the robbers having a fifth person, but if that were the case, they would have retrieved the loot decades ago and my sisters and I were doing all this digging for nothing.

And then I hit something.

"Um, guys?"

My sisters looked at me.

"What?" Maggie asked.

"You found something, didn't you?" Tansy said. She shone her flashlight at my feet. Something glittered.

"Keep the light steady," I said, tossing the shovel away as I dropped to my knees and began digging in the dirt with my bare hands. A minute later, I came up with a piece of metal.

"What is it?" Maggie asked. I handed it to her. She

rubbed the dirt off it. Tansy passed her a bottle of water. Maggie poured the water over the metal piece and then held it under the flashlight's beam. "Samsonite," she said in a hushed tone of voice usually reserved for museums and libraries.

"You think that came off one of their suitcases?" I asked. I was so excited I wanted to do a little dance. People have been searching for this treasure since before my parents were born, and I found it. No, scratch that. *We* found it.

"Uh, not quite." Tansy rooted around in the dirt and came up with something that might have been half a clasp. She handed it to me. She poked around a little longer, coming up with a handle and a zipper. "I think these *are* their suitcases."

"Huh?" Maggie asked. I was glad I wasn't the only one confused.

"The robbers intended to come back as soon as the heat died down so they could retrieve the money, but they were killed trying to get out of town."

"And?" Maggie asked.

"And they never came back." Tansy nudged the disturbed dirt of the hole with the toe of her shoe. "These suitcases have been buried for almost seventy years. This is all that's left of them."

I felt like someone had knocked the wind out of me. "You can't mean . . ." I said, in a daze.

"Yeah." She picked up a handful of dirt and let it sift through her fingers. "Maybe if they'd buried the money in a modern suitcase instead of one made of cloth and wood, or wrapped it in a waterproof tarp, it might have survived, but without any protection from the elements, I think this is the treasure everyone's been looking for."

"Paper money's nothing but a blend of cotton and linen. It breaks down like anything else. No wonder the bluebonnets grow so well here," Maggie said with a heavy sigh. "They're literally growing in a million dollars' worth of fertilizer."

"Let me see that sketch of the luggage again," Tansy asked, holding out her hand. I pulled it up on my phone and we compared it to the hardware we found. It was a match, or close enough. "So, what do y'all want to do?" Tansy asked.

"What do you mean? We might not have gotten rich, but we finally figured out what happened that day," Maggie said.

"Not completely," I said. "Uncle Calvin's got a theory that the robbers had an inside person. Finding this proves that they never managed to retrieve the money. So what happened to the fifth bank robber?"

"There were only four men killed leaving town, right?" Maggie asked. "Four known robbers. No locals died."

"That's not exactly accurate," I said. "A local cop was also killed in the shoot-out."

"You have got to be kidding," Tansy said.

Then it hit me. "Who better than a crooked cop to tell the bad guys when the bank vaults are full, or act as the lookout so they can rob the bank while everyone else was on the other side of town at the Bluebonnet Festival?" I asked.

"The cops blocked their way out of town, right? If I'd just robbed a bank, and during the getaway, I found myself on the wrong side of a standoff with a person I thought was my partner in crime, I'd probably be pretty upset," Maggie suggested. "Come to think of it, that might be what set everyone off to begin with. The robbers had to assume they'd been double-crossed. One of them took a shot at their lookout, and the next thing you know, they're in the middle of a fire fight."

"We could do a little digging and see if that's true," I

said. "With a little research, it shouldn't be hard to prove the cop who died was crooked." Then I looked around at us. We were covered in dirt and standing in a hole that came up to our knees. And all we had to show for it was some vintage suitcase hardware. "But the only digging I want to do tonight is filling in this hole."

"We can't do that," Tansy said. "The people of Cedar River deserve to know what really happened back in 'fifty-six."

"Do they?" Maggie asked. "Or do they deserve to hold onto the fantasy for a little while longer?"

I raised a weary hand. "I vote for the fantasy."

"Are you sure?" Tansy asked.

"Some mysteries are better left unsolved," I said.

"Well, that's a first." She shrugged. "I guess it's decided."

It should have taken less time to fill in the hole than it had to dig it, but we were all sore. Plus, when we were digging, we were full of hope and excitement. Now we were just dirty and tired. When we were done, we shone our lights over the ground.

"It looks like we buried a body here," Maggie said.

"She's right," Tansy agreed. "There's no way this is going to go unnoticed."

"I guess we're going to have to go public with this after all," Maggie said.

"Not necessarily." I brushed off my hands as well as I could and pulled out my phone. It was a little past midnight, much later than I thought. To my astonishment, I had service. I sent a text. "U up?" Instead of getting a response, my phone rang. I showed the caller ID to my sisters.

"Might as well," Tansy said.

I answered the phone and put it on speaker. "Hey Beau. Wanna hear a long story?"

As my sisters and I trudged back to Tansy's car, filthy and exhausted, we told him everything. I promised to turn over the metal bits we'd dug up in exchange for him helping us keep the whole thing quiet. Since we hadn't technically done anything illegal, he agreed, with one caveat.

"Junebug, next time you decide to start digging holes on public property in the middle of the night, call me first," Beau said. I'm not sure what it said about me that we both knew that I was likely to find myself in a similar situation again in the future.

"I'll try, but no promises. 'Night," I said, disconnecting the call.

"You know, it's probably for the best anyway," Tansy said.

"How so?" Maggie asked. "A million dollars would have solved all of our money problems, and then some."

"Yeah, but it was never our money," Tansy pointed out. "We would have had to turn it in. Even if we got a finder's fee, a big chunk of that would go to taxes."

"It's so not fair," Maggie said.

"You're telling me," Tansy said. We loaded the shovels into the trunk, and then took turns ducking into the bushes to change out of our dirty sweat suits so we didn't track half of the park into Tansy's car. As I was removing my shoes, I noticed a crushed bluebonnet stuck in the treads. I hoped that we had managed to spread some of the seeds as we walked.

Who knew? Because of us, bluebonnets might grow in places of Cedar River Memorial Park where they'd never grown before. Maybe we'd even seeded an entire new field. Because bluebonnets, like my sisters and me, were better when they weren't on their own.

ACKNOWLEDGMENTS

When I was growing up in Texas, I was taught that it was illegal to pick bluebonnets. I didn't realize until I was researching for this book that it wasn't, at least not in my lifetime. Legal or not, no self-respecting Texan (or recovering ex-Texan as the case may be) would ever intentionally pick a bluebonnet, and I assure you that no bluebonnets were harmed in the writing of this book. The lovely flower on the gorgeous cover of this book is a plastic bluebonnet that fell off a souvenir Cedar River Bluebonnet Festival hat. That's my story, and I'm sticking to it.

I am constantly inspired by my readers, and I want to give credit to those of y'all who participated in the "Name That Brew" contest for helping name Sip & Spin drinks in this book, including Rebecca Worley for "I Will Always Love Brew," and Adrian Andover and Elisa Shoenberger for "Sweet Chai O'Mine."

I'd also like to give thanks to the immensely talented authors who took precious time out of their busy schedules to blurb the Record Store Mysteries, including Elle Cosimano, Mia P. Manansala, Gigi Pandian, Diane Kelly, and S.C. Perkins/Celeste Connally. I'm such a huge fan of y'all, and your kind words mean everything to me. And of course, all my love goes out to the magnificent writer community, booksellers, reviewers, and especially, the readers!

I'm so very lucky to have Nettie Finn and my fantastic team at St. Martin's Press, including Sara Beth Haring, Sara LaCotti, John Rounds, Janna Dokos, Jen Edwards, Olya Kirilyuk, Mary Ann Lasher, and John Simko: I literally couldn't do this without y'all.

For my agent, James McGowan, and the team at Book-Ends, I'll have you know that not only is James a fantastic agent, but he's always there in a pinch when I need a pun. He gets the credit for suggesting the incredibly effective earworm "I'll Bean There for Brew" as a coffee special. Talk about the GOAT!

Another special shoutout goes to the amazing Jessica Joyce for inspiring (and naming!) Buttercup, the accidental cow, and to all the zany Berkletes and Killer Caseloaders for providing constant support, encouragement, and entertainment.

As always, I want to thank my friends and family for their support. To my fellow hockey stans Michelle, Ellen, and Danica—keep those pictures of hockey players with puppies coming! And to the Little Screaming Eels (Ris, La, Liz, and Dare), who have known me the best and the longest and are somehow still around. What's wrong with y'all??? And, finally, to Potassium: Who loves ya, babe?

I also want to take a minute to acknowledge the copious amounts of caffeine and music that inspired and fueled this book. On that note (for once, pun *not* intended), I want to thank all the artists who fill this weird little planet with music. Keep up the good work!

And please, y'all, don't pick the bluebonnets!